A PUFFIN BOOK
PROPERTY OF

EVE GARNETT was born in 1900 in Worcestershire. She was educated in Devon, and then studied art at Chelsea Polytechnic and the Royal Academy School of Art. While a student in London, she used to wander through the slums of London, appalled at the conditions, yet surprised by the cheerfulness of the children who lived there. She sketched what she saw, and was commissioned to illustrate Evelyn Sharp's *The London Child*. Eve Garnett wrote and illustrated many books for children. She died in 1991.

EVE GARNETT

HOLIDAY AT THE DEW DROP INN

A ONE END STREET STORY

PUFFIN BOOKS

UK | USA | Canada | Ireland | Australia
India | New Zealand | South Africa

Puffin Books is part of the Penguin Random House group of companies
whose addresses can be found at global.penguinrandomhouse.com.

www.penguin.co.uk
www.puffin.co.uk
www.ladybird.co.uk

First published by William Heinemann Ltd 1962
Published in Puffin Books 1966
This edition published 2019
001

Set in 10.5/15.5 pt Sabon LT Std
Typeset by Jouve (UK), Milton Keynes
Printed and bound in Great Britain by Clays Ltd, Elcograf S.p.A.

A CIP catalogue record for this book is available from the British Library

ISBN: 978-0-241-35587-9

All correspondence to:
Puffin Books
Penguin Random House Children's
80 Strand, London WC2R 0RL

To my sister

K.R.O.M.

who also loves the country

Contents

1. The Holiday Begins

ON THE morning Kate Ruggles set forth to spend her summer holidays with Mr and Mrs Wildgoose at The Dew Drop Inn at Upper Cassington a mizzly rain was falling.

'It's damping!' called her mother, holding a hand out of her bedroom window to make sure it was truly rain and not mist. 'You'd best put on Mrs Beasley's present.'

Mrs Beasley's present – or rather part of it – was a shiny black macintosh which had belonged to her niece who, though only a year older than Kate, was several sizes larger, and given to growing out of her garments with such rapidity that many of them made their way to the Ruggles children at No. 1 One End Street; 'almost' as Mrs Ruggles, harassed with trying to clothe her family of seven warmly and neatly, would gratefully remark, 'as good as new'.

Kate had never had a macintosh of any kind before – old or new, nor a pair of gum-boots – the other half of Mrs Beasley's present, that had not been 'passed on' to her by her elder sister, Lily Rose, usually in a condition as far as possible removed from 'as good as new'.

The new gum-boots were black and shiny like the macintosh and at the moment were packed, the legs stuffed with her scanty underclothes, in the battered-looking suitcase that stood ready in the kitchen.

'If Kate is going to be two months in the country,' Mrs Beasley had said one morning when Mrs Ruggles, who washed for her, had gone to return some laundry, 'she'll need a pair of strong gum-boots; country mud's not like town mud, her ordinary shoes will only be ruined or damp all the time – or both – and she really ought to be careful of colds so soon after measles.'

And Kate, who had gone too, to help carry the laundry basket, remembering the squishiness of the fields by the river after a good downpour, and the apparently permanent mud in the lane leading to Mr Digweed's farm at Upper Cassington, knew Mrs Beasley spoke truly.

She stood now at her bedroom window at No. 1 One End Street gazing out at the mist-like rain and the little redbrick, grey-slated houses opposite, each with its brown-painted front door and downstairs window filled with pots of geraniums or an aspidistra. Could it be possible that in only four – no – she counted on her fingers – *less* – in not much more than three and three-quarter hours – she'd be looking out of The Dew Drop Inn and seeing orangy-coloured cottages with thatched roofs, and gates opening into gay little gardens? Perhaps – and she did hope so – from the same dear little room she'd had before – though of course any room at The Dew Drop Inn was lovely . . . Was it really only six weeks since she and her little brother and sister had returned from staying there? In some ways it seemed *months*! Perhaps it was the three weeks she had spent in the isolation hospital with measles, on her return, that made it seem so long. How lovely it would be to see Mr and Mrs Wildgoose again, and Elsie who helped them at the Inn . . . and, of course, Miss Alison, and Mr Shakespeare . . . and all the other friends she had made . . . If only she hadn't got to leave Cuckoo-Coo, the white kitten they had brought home with them! Already he had grown so much she had hardly known him when she returned from the hospital; by the time she came home again he'd be no longer a kitten but an almost grown-up cat. She gave a little sigh.

'Sakes alive!' exclaimed Mrs Ruggles, coming into the room, her hat and coat on, and clutching an umbrella. 'Sakes alive! Do you want to miss the train! Standing there gazing at nothing – and Mrs Beasley's present not even *on*! Really I never did see such a dreamer as you're getting to be! I'd have thought today at least you'd have been ready and waiting all right! There! I thought so – there's the town clock struck the quarter! You'll have to put your best foot forward if we're to catch that train! Look sharp now!' And she hurried down the stairs.

How you looked sharp – a favourite expression of her mother's – Kate could never decide, but she struggled into Mrs Beasley's present, put on her school hat with its striped ribbon and imposing badge, and seizing her little cardboard attaché case, containing her autograph book, two other books, a pencil-box, and a present she had made for Mrs Wildgoose while at the hospital, from the dressing-table, she clattered downstairs after her mother. Miss the train! Especially after what had happened last time* – the very idea was unthinkable! But time or not, she *must* say good-bye to Cuckoo-Coo. Farewells to her five brothers and sisters before they went off to school – all trying not to look too envious – to William, the baby, temporarily 'parked' with Mrs Hook next-door, had all been said. Also to her father, who had given her a surprise present of a whole shilling, remarking as he went off to work, the next holiday was *his*.

Where *was* Cuckoo-Coo! Not in the kitchen where Mrs Ruggles, picking up the suitcase, was preparing to set forth. In the back kitchen? No, not there either . . . In the yard . . . Kate peeped out of the window. Yes, there he was, caring nothing whatever for the elements, sitting curled up outside the door of the toolshed, his greeny-yellow eyes fixed and unblinking on a small pile of wood heaped up in a corner, watching for a mouse – real or imaginary. Leaving her attaché case on the draining-board by the sink, Kate dashed into the yard, caught him up, kissed his small pink triangular nose passionately, and whispered endearments in his ear.

'Drat the child – where's she got to now!' exclaimed Mrs Ruggles poised, suitcase in hand, between the kitchen door and the street, 'we'll miss that train for sure!'

* *Further Adventures of the Family from One End Street.*

But the next minute Kate came rushing in – suddenly remembered the attaché case, doubled back, retrieved it, and Mrs Ruggles fairly clucking with impatience, at last they set forth.

'Do you think Mrs Hook will have William at the window, Mum, so's we can wave to him?' asked Kate, still a little breathless as they approached the house next-door.

'I should hope not,' replied Mrs Ruggles tartly, 'seeing as I told her "no" particular. Why, pore l'il mite, what 'ud he think seeing us go past and waving – have a bit of sense *do*!'

After that there was silence until they had almost reached the station. There were just three minutes to get

Kate's ticket, bundle down the steep stairs of the bridge, and to push her and her suitcase into the train, which was standing steaming impatiently at the platform. A hurried but affectionate kiss, breathless last-minute instructions in regard to sense and behaviour generally were given by Mrs Ruggles, then a whistle shrilled, the guard waved his flag, and the train moved off.

Kate stood waving and blowing kisses until it curved round a bend and her mother was lost to view, then, feeling quite like an old and experienced traveller, she sat back sedately in her seat and took stock of her fellow passengers. These consisted of an elderly gentleman completely immersed in *The Times* newspaper, a youth concentrating earnestly on a crossword puzzle, and a young lady absorbed in a fashion journal and, very audibly, sucking sweets. Beyond glancing up from their several occupations when Kate and her suitcase were thrust into the carriage, none of them took any further notice of her, and remembering the hazards of her previous journey to Upper Cassington, she sat thankfully in her corner and presently began to enjoy watching the landscape flying past.

It seemed no time at all before they were at the station where she had to change trains. The young man with the crossword puzzle having kindly handed out her suitcase, she dragged it to a near-by bench where, remembering all too clearly her previous unhappy adventures at this spot, she sat patiently waiting until the train for Upper Cassington arrived. A jovial porter picked up her suitcase – almost with one finger, or so it seemed, banged it down on the seat of an empty carriage, slammed to the door, and the next minute she was off again.

The misty rain was clearing now; patches of blue sky began to appear, and before long the sun was shining. How lovely the country looked – and what a difference a few short weeks had made! Then hay-cutting had been in full swing; where it was still uncut the long, sweet-smelling grass had swayed silkily, showing patches of red-brown sorrel and white dog-daisies, or lain in long flat swathes where the mower had been at work, while the corn was still short and a bluish-green. Now nothing remained of the hay-fields' glory! They lay pale and bare, with here and there a blade of vivid green spearing through the shorn grass; but the corn had not only almost doubled its height but ripened!

Some of the tawny gold wheat was already cut and stooked, but the cream-coloured oats and the bearded barley were not yet – what was it the Bible called it – 'white unto harvest'. She used to wonder, thought Kate to herself as she gazed out at the cornfields, why it said 'white'. One always thought of corn as yellow – there was a hymn about 'fair waved the "golden" corn' . . . Perhaps they only grew oats and barley in the Holy Land . . . or the writer of the hymn had not known – as she herself had not known, until Mr Digweed the farmer at Upper Cassington had explained, that there were several kinds of corn . . . perhaps . . . Phew! Kate shook herself . . . It *was* getting hot – or was it Mrs Beasley's present – in which she had sat wrapped throughout the journey, wanting Mrs Wildgoose, who was to meet her, to see it in action so to speak. Now the rain had all cleared away it surely looked silly to be wearing it? She stood up to take it off, and as she did so the train began slowing down, and looking out she recognized a landmark or two – the willow-fringed, twisting river, and the bare hills and little wood she used to see from her bedroom window at The Dew Drop Inn. She had just time to wriggle out of the macintosh and push it into the suitcase when the train gave a cheerful little whistle and chug-chugged into the station.

Kate could hardly open the door quickly enough! There stood Mrs Wildgoose, waving and smiling, and farther up the platform George, the porter, grinning a welcome from ear to ear!

'Well, you're good and punctual *this* time!' exclaimed Mrs Wildgoose, helping her out with the suitcase. 'Come, give me a kiss and let me look at you! Why, I do declare, you've grown just the tiniest bit – though no one could say as there was much flesh on your bones! How dared you go and get measles the very minute my back was turned! Really, I nearly cried! But come along,' she continued, 'or Mr Washer'll be grumbling he's been kept waiting. All right, George,' as he came forward, 'I'll manage the suitcase – it's light enough.'

'You give 'un to me, Mrs Wildgoose,' replied George, taking it from her, 'I'm porter here,' and he winked an eye at Kate and said how pleased he was to see her again.

Outside in the station yard, and apparently neither pleased to see her nor the reverse, sat Mr Washer in his dilapidated old taxi – looking older and more dilapidated than ever, one of the front mudguards being now tied up with rope.

'One day,' whispered Mrs Wildgoose, the self-starter having refused to work and Mr Washer puffing and blowing and muttering to himself as he wrestled with the starting handle, 'one day the whole thing will just fall to pieces – then he'll *have* to get a new one!' But at last the engine started, and except for an occasional mild explosion or two the taxi rattled happily along, and Kate had barely finished giving news of Peg and Jo and Cuckoo-Coo, and all the rest of her family, before the first orangy-coloured cottages of Upper Cassington came in sight, and a few minutes later The Dew Drop Inn itself, 'almost smothered', as Mrs Wildgoose remarked, in roses and honeysuckle, and with its green signboard with 'The Dew Drop Inn' and the inviting 'Do Drop In' on the reverse side, swaying gently to and fro.

They were hardly out of the taxi before Mr Wildgoose, in his shirt-sleeves, green baize apron, and one of his gayest pullovers, appeared in the porch and came towards them throwing up his arms in greeting.

Kate, who had prepared to shake hands, was a little disconcerted – no hand being available to shake. She had never kissed Mr Wildgoose. Was she expected to? She rather hoped not, though she could not have said why, for she liked him very much! But Mr Wildgoose solved the problem himself by clapping both hands on her shoulders and lightly kissing the top of her hat!

'Well! Here we are again!' he exclaimed, 'but no less welcome – if anything rather more; and I'm only sorry you haven't brought my friends Peg and Jo with you!'

How very kind that was, thought Kate – and she knew Mr Wildgoose meant what he said – he wasn't the sort who talked just for something to say. It wasn't everyone, she reflected, who wanted small children about – especially ones who behaved as her little brother and sister had done once or twice during their stay at The Dew Drop Inn. And then, almost before these thoughts had flashed through her mind, out came Elsie – 'Elsie as helps me' as Jo had persisted in calling her – helping still, and apparently so

pleased to see Kate that she kissed her heartily on both cheeks! It was certainly a very warming welcome all round!

'We've put you up at the top again,' said Mrs Wildgoose as they all went into the house, 'and you can have the big room, or the little one leading out of it that you had before – just as you like; both beds is made up so it won't make no difference which you choose.'

'Oh, Mrs Wildgoose, the little one! I'd like the *little* one, *please*!' said Kate.

So the little one it was – the dear little white-walled room with its deep-set window framed in thick thatch and through which the sprays of roses and honeysuckle were now almost climbing into the room itself. And outside the row of orangy-coloured cottages, and behind them the fields, the little wood, and the bare faraway hills. Everything – just as she had remembered it!

Kate stood gazing out, entranced, and it was some time before she became aware that insistent voices were calling from below.

'Tea! *Tea!* Come along down!'

'I'm coming! I'm coming – *just* coming!' she called and she hastily tidied her wispy hair, dashed into the bathroom across the little landing for an even hastier wash, and rushed as quickly as she dared, for the stairs at The Dew Drop Inn were mostly polished oak and slippery as ice, to where tea was laid in the sitting-room leading out of the kitchen.

Behind the teapot Mrs Wildgoose sat smiling, and at the other side of the table – much to Kate's surprise for he seldom came in to tea except on Sundays, and on *very* special occasions – his green baize apron removed, and a coat over his gay pullover, was Mr Wildgoose, while through the doorway from the kitchen came Elsie. In one hand she carried a large toast-rack full of crisp, newly made toast, and in the other a saucer with an egg-cup in which sat the biggest pinky-brown hen's egg Kate had ever seen.

'Double – I'm not sure it's not a treble-yolker, that is,' said Mr Wildgoose to Kate. 'We've been keeping it special for you, haven't we, missus?' he asked, smiling at his wife. Mrs Wildgoose nodded, and though Kate was not feeling particularly hungry, and rather appalled at the idea of possibly having to consume the equivalent of three eggs at a blow, so to speak, she attacked the monster egg valiantly. It turned out to be a two- not a three-yolker after all, and the toast (and the butter that went with it) was so good that her appetite came, as the French say, 'with eating', and very soon little remained of the egg but its shell, and almost all the toast had disappeared. Mr Wildgoose then said how about finishing the remains of a dish of stewed apples on the table – and some honey with them – so much nicer than sugar – remarking it wasn't every day he came in to tea and he liked to see people make a good one.

'Yes,' put in Mrs Wildgoose. 'You're honoured, Kate – you are indeed! But there's great doings afoot here' – she turned to Mr Wildgoose – 'you tell her yourself, Charlie.'

'Great doings is right,' said Mr Wildgoose, observing with satisfaction the apples and the honey were going the way of the toast and the egg, 'and there's a lot to be told. It's close on five now,' he went on, glancing at the grandfather clock in the corner, 'in less than an hour I'll have to be getting ready in the bar – Fridays and Saturdays are always specially busy, you know – and when I pop in for supper it'll be in a hurry; by closing time you'll be in bed and – I hope – asleep; and tomorrow I've to go to Ailesford to see the brewers and that always takes the best part of a morning and more, so now's the time for talk. There's a lot to tell and more to do. You've guessed now, surely, what it's all about?'

'Is it THE FLOWER SHOW, Mr Wildgoose?' asked Kate, clasping her hands in excitement, and speaking in solemn capital letters. 'Oh do say it's The Flower Show – I was *so* afraid it might be over before I got here!'

In Upper Cassington – not to mention Lower Cassington, the village which joined it – The Flower Show was one of the chief events of the year, ranking, as Mr Wildgoose had once told Kate, 'about equal' with Christmas, Bank Holidays, and, of course, *The* Fair – held every September on the green by the cross-roads. Even before Kate and Peg and Jo had left, people were beginning to talk of *The* Flower Show, 'sometime end of July' – the date had not then been decided. What they were going to show – or not show; their chances – and their neighbours' chances. Prowess in shows of the past was recalled with pride, often going back to their parents', and even in some cases, their grandparents' days – the further removed in time it seemed to Kate, the greater the glory. There were some dark references to the fairness – or otherwise – of last year's awards and much speculation as to who the judges would be this time. Special 'entries' were included for children.

'*Lovely* prizes they get too,' Miss Midgley at the post office had told Kate almost enviously, 'very different from when *I* used to compete.' What sort of 'entries' Kate had asked, only wishing she might be there when this great event took place though never, for an instant, imagining such a thing might really come to pass.

'Oh, collections of wildflowers, or things they've grown in their gardens – if they have them; radishes and mustard-and-cress is about all I've ever seen,' Miss Midgley had replied. 'Then there's cake- and jam-making for the girls – or boys too for all I know; and carpentry or hobbies of something like it – it's not all flowers you see. And in the evening there's generally games and bowling for a pig and dancing. And then in August there's The Concert.' What did they do at that? Well, there was some singing, and some played the piano or violin, and last year some of the children had recited. All rather old-fashioned perhaps but then Cassington folks *liked* that sort of thing even in spite of the wireless and cinemas. 'And a good thing too!' she had ended, smiling at Kate, and Kate remembered smiling back and feeling somewhat consoled, for even had she been in Upper Cassington she felt far from qualified to take part in any of these activities. Her knowledge of wildflowers, though certainly increased during her stay here, was very limited; she had no garden so could produce neither radishes nor mustard-and-cress; while as for jam- and cake-making though she was sure she knew exactly how these were done, having often watched her mother, she had never actually tried her hand at either, Mrs Ruggles being adamant about what she called 'Experiments' and 'waste of good ingredients'. Carpentry was definitely 'out', and she was very doubtful whether any of her interests could be classed as 'hobbies'. As for reciting at The Concert! She liked poetry it was true; was, in fact, beginning, secretly, to enjoy it very much – but, well, she'd just die if she had to stand up and recite before the critical inhabitants of Upper and Lower Cassington, however 'old-fashioned' in their choice of entertainment.

And now, back there, here was Mr Wildgoose suggesting – nay taking for granted almost, she should do every one of these very things! He was fairly *pouring* forth suggestions! Entries for The Flower Show from the Inn, he announced, had never been exactly in what you might call the back row for prizes, but *this* year, and he tapped the table impressively, *this* year, The Dew Drop was going to what he called 'sweep the board!' There were to be entries in almost every class. Mrs Wildgoose was showing roses and carnations in the flower section; sittings of hens' and ducks' eggs; Elsie, cakes and jam; and himself, vegetables of every variety – barring marrows. Anyone, he maintained, could grow marrows – and did – if only to cover up their rubbish heaps. He was leaving the marrows to others. As for Kate, since there were no children at the Inn, they were relying on her to compete in every single one of the children's classes! And after that . . . 'Why, bless me,' he exclaimed, 'if I hadn't almost forgotten the other item! *The Concert*. They're close together this year,' he went on, 'because The Flower Show's late – too late for most people's liking – summer flowers and soft fruit are past their best by August. It's on Bank Holiday too – I like my pleasures spread out myself – but there, it's a case of who pays the piper calls the tune! Mrs Ayredale-Eskdale has lent her grounds as usual but she's gone away visiting so the show has to wait for her to come home. And that,' taking off his glasses and fairly beaming at Kate, 'that seems to me all to the good – give you plenty of time to learn a nice poem to recite – if you don't know one already, which I'm pretty sure you do! But to return to The Flower Show. Now listen carefully!' and drawing a pink printed notice from his pocket, he replaced his glasses, and apparently quite oblivious of Kate's expression of bewilderment or the despairing glances she was casting at Mrs Wildgoose, proceeded to read aloud as follows:

'"Upper and Lower Cassington Flower, Fruit, and Vegetable Show. Entries for Children.

'"There are two classes in each entry and two prizes in each class. Competitors in Class I must be over nine years of age and under sixteen. In Class II over six years of age and under nine. (Age will be taken into account in judging exhibits.)

'"The first prizes in each class have been presented by residents of the parish; the second prizes by The Flower Show Committee."

'Now listen with all your ears!

'"Entry No. 1. Best collection of wildflowers, picked, correctly named, and arranged in jam-jar or jars (limit two jars). First prize presented by Miss Ayredale-Eskdale!" And a very nice prize it is,' added Mr Wildgoose, and he wagged an impressive forefinger. 'I know because I've seen it; I wouldn't mind it myself!

'"Entry No. 2. Best exhibit of flowers, fruit, or vegetables entirely grown by candidate. First prize presented by Mr Edward Smallpiece." That's Mrs Ayredale-Eskdale's head gardener – I seem to remember as you and his daughter Angela didn't get on together too well?' And he glanced at Kate for a moment over the top of his spectacles.

'"Entry No. 3",' he went on. '"Best plate of six home-made rock cakes. First prize presented by Mrs Ayredale-Eskdale" (and it won't surprise me, not at all, if her cook isn't one of the judges!)

'"Entry No. 4. Best pot of jam or jelly (not to exceed one pound in weight). First prize presented by Mrs Midgley." You'll remember her – the nice, lame old lady at the post office? Yes,' as Kate nodded, too overcome to speak, 'of course.

'"Entry No. 5. Best piece of handwork. This may include carpentry, needlework, knitting, painting, or model-making. Must be candidate's entirely unaided work. First prize presented by" – Ah! who do you think? And I wonder she doesn't insist on judging it herself – especially the knitting! Well, I can see by your face you don't need three guesses – or even one. Of course! Your friend at the stores – Mrs Megson! Now the last:

'"Entry No. 6. Best essay, not to exceed 1,000 words on 'My Hobby and Why'. First prize presented by" – another of your friends – "The Vicar" – Mr Wilson. And – oh yes – I nearly forgot – there's a table decoration in the adult section in which children can compete. There!' concluded Mr Wildgoose, handing the paper to Kate, 'that's the lot. You can do all those – easy – and more!'

'One thousand words!' exclaimed Mrs Wildgoose, referring to the essay, 'that's a lot of writing surely?'

'Oh no, Mrs Wildgoose,' said Kate, 'it's not – not really; it's – it's only about five pages of an exercise book – I could write *that* – easy!'

'There you are!' said Mr Wildgoose triumphantly – 'and you can do the others easy too; and bring fame and glory on The Dew Drop Inn!'

'But, Mr Wildgoose,' objected Kate glancing down the list in her hand, 'I – I don't know the names of hardly *any* wildflowers; and I haven't got a garden, and, and anyway I couldn't grow anything by . . . by Bank Holiday . . . that's – that's only eleven – no *ten* days away! . . . And I've never made any sort of cakes – or jam; only watched . . . and, and I can't do carpentry, and only frightfully messy painting, and my knitting and sewing is just *awful*! . . . and I'm not quite sure what a table decoration *is*! The essay's the only thing I could do, truly! And, oh, *Mr Wildgoose*, The Concert! Recite! in front of all those people – I simply *couldn't*!'

But Mr Wildgoose only laughed. 'When I were young,' he said, 'I used to be told – very irritating it was too, "there's no such word as 'can't' ". At the risk of being irritating to *you*, Kate, I'll say you won't find "couldn't" in the dictionary either! But don't look so worried – and never mind The Concert at the moment, we can talk about that another time. Just consider, quite calmly now, about The Flower Show. Take the first thing – the wildflowers. There's ten days before the Show. Every day you can go out and see what you can find. I've got a book that gives a picture and the name of pretty nearly every wildflower in the country. You'll soon learn to find plenty; then, day before the Show, you pick all you can, name them from the book, and there you are! No, there's nothing against using the book, there's a copy in the village library – anyone can see it. But I'll let you into a secret – they're too lazy – most of them – or too uninterested! What next? Oh, something you've grown. Well, I admit you can't grow much in ten days but you can grow a fine crop of mustard-and-cress if you start right away. Chief thing is – you must grow it *imaginatively*. We'll talk about that tomorrow,' he added seeing Kate looked puzzled.

'Cakes and jam: Mrs Wildgoose will put you wise about those, won't you, missis? And between you and me,' he lowered his voice and leant confidentially towards Kate, 'I don't believe it's all *that* difficult . . . Table Decoration – just some flowers in a vase or bowl. You say you can do the essay so that's all right; and if you can't use a hammer, or sew, or knit, what about a model? Elsie here's first rate on models, you should see what she made for her little niece out of old matchboxes! She'll show you . . . Now I must be off. You talk it all over quietly with Mrs Wildgoose, but I know you won't let The Dew Drop down, sure as my name's Charlie Wildgoose!' And pushing back his chair, he stood up, patted her shoulder, blew a kiss to his wife, and went whistling out of the room.

Kate and Mrs Wildgoose looked at each other in silence for a moment. Then, suddenly they both laughed.

'Oh well,' said Mrs Wildgoose, 'you know what he is, once he's made up his mind to do a thing! But I don't want you worried, my dear,' she went on. 'You've come here for a rest and holiday – some of this' – she tapped the leaflet, 'that essay for one, looks to me too much like school work. I'm not having you do *none* of it unless you *want* – and I told Mr Wildgoose so from the start, so don't you let it worry you for one minute!'

Kate sat silent for a moment, thinking. Now that everything had been more or less explained, it didn't sound quite so difficult, especially if someone would show her how to do the things first. And if *not* doing them meant letting down The Dew Drop well, she just couldn't, as Mr Wildgoose knew very well . . . so in a way he was making her say yes . . .

'If you'll help, I'll try, Mrs Wildgoose,' she said at last, 'but it's awfully near – only nine days after tomorrow. Don't you think I'd better look at Mr Wildgoose's book of flowers straight away now? And perhaps I could walk round by Mr Shakespeare's path to his house. It's only raining a bit,' she went on glancing out of the window, 'and that doesn't matter because, oh, Mrs Wildgoose!

I'd almost forgotten to tell you! I've got the most *marvellous* macintosh, and a pair of absolutely *new* gum-boots in my suitcase, so I can go out in a thunderstorm, or floods, or *anything*!'

'Well, that's something I won't agree to – going out now I mean,' replied Mrs Wildgoose decidedly. 'You've come a journey; you're tired – now don't tell me not because I *know.* It's raining quite hard and coming on worse in a minute or two; you've come here to get well and strong and there's no sense rushing out in the damp catching cold the minute you come. There's more than time to find all the flowers you'll want. Far better come upstairs now and we'll unpack your things and you can show me the lovely new mac and gum-boots you've got, but first we'll just help Elsie to clear away,' she added, 'because it's time she was off home.'

Kate, blissfully happy, lay in bed in the little white-wall room. Through the open window drifted the sweet smell of roses and honeysuckle – all the sweeter for the recent rain. From under the thick thatch came subdued rustlings and twitterings, and from far away a pair of owls called plaintively to each other. What a perfect day it had been! Nothing, for once, had gone wrong! No bothers on the journey, everyone pleased to see her again, and Mrs Wildgoose's admiration of Mrs Beasley's present only surpassed by her pleasure at Kate's own present to her.

'You naughty girl – saying you can't sew!' she had exclaimed when after unwrapping several rather crumpled pieces of paper a patch-work pincushion was revealed. 'It's made beautiful! It shall go straight on my dressing-table. Not able to sew indeed!' And in spite of Kate's insistence that a nurse at the hospital had done 'quite *half*' Mrs Wildgoose's enthusiasm was so warming that it helped to dispel some of the lingering doubts about The Flower Show entries. Anyway, as she had told Mrs Wildgoose, she could *try*. And when he 'popped in' at supper-time as he had said she rather shyly announced this to Mr Wildgoose.

'I knew it!' he exclaimed, beaming with pleasure. 'I knew it – in my very *bones*; I knew you'd never let The Dew Drop down!'

'And that's enough about it for tonight,' interrupted Mrs Wildgoose firmly. 'Not another word or Kate'll be lying awake worrying, or dreaming of flower shows all night.'

'Not she!' replied Mr Wildgoose, 'she's half asleep now – in another hour or so she won't know where she is!'

She was not the least bit sleepy – *really*, Kate had protested; and now, quite two hours later, she knew exactly where she was. How absurd Mr Wildgoose could be! She gave a big yawn and stretched her toes luxuriously, then rolled over on her side. An owl began hooting vociferously in a near-by tree, and a minute or two later a motor-bicycle went roaring furiously past the Inn. But Kate heard nothing; time and place had ceased to exist for her; she was fast and dreamlessly asleep.

2. Old Friends and New

THE NEXT day was what Mrs Wildgoose called 'real summer'. There was a shimmery haze on the fields in front of the Inn, and from the orchard behind came the cluck-cluck of contented hens. Bees roved happily from plant to plant or crept unhurried into flower-bells, emerging pollen-coated, satisfied; and from beyond the church sounded the pleasant whirr of a reaping machine.

Kate stood on the little lawn outside the kitchen looking up into the twisted branches of the two old apple trees that grew there. Mrs Wildgoose was dishing up the breakfast and through the open window wafted appetizing smells of sizzling bacon, and newly made toast and tea.

'Slept like a top I hear!' said Mr Wildgoose as, dressed in his best suit ready for his visit to the brewers, he joined her for a moment or two on the little lawn.

Kate nodded. 'And I didn't dream of flower shows, Mr Wildgoose!' she said, 'I didn't dream of *anything*. But I've been thinking – a lot – ever since I woke up, and directly after breakfast I'm going down by Mr Shakespeare's to look for flowers!'

'That's the spirit!' cried Mr Wildgoose, 'and before I forget, I'll write it down – "mustard-and-cress seed".' And he took a little notebook from his pocket and wrote in it, very carefully. 'We'll sow it – or rather *you*'ll sow it, when I've showed you how, when I get back this afternoon,' he added as he put the little book back in his pocket. 'Come on now, there's the missus calling; breakfast's ready and I mustn't miss my bus.'

Kate did full justice to the meal; and how lovely it was not to have to rush off to school the very minute it was over, or help with a laundry basket, or 'mind' William, or any other of the numerous little jobs that came her way at home. Mrs Wildgoose didn't seem to want her even to help with the beds or clear away the breakfast things.

'You skip out in the sunshine – while it's there, and get all the fresh air you can,' she said when Mr Wildgoose having hurried off to catch his bus Kate lingered beside the breakfast-table. 'Elsie'll see to your bed, and the clearing and washing up. There's just one thing you *can* do though,' she added, 'leave this list at Mrs Megson's shop – I'll call for the things later on, tell her. Oh – and some stamped postcards from the post office – I'm right out. Here's the money. They'll be pleased to see you there, anyway, and Mrs Megson – well, you never know!'

No, thought Kate, as she ran upstairs to fetch her hat, you never did – especially with grown-ups. And not only grown-ups, she decided some minutes later, for as she came out of the door of the Inn a small figure standing on the gravelled sweep outside approached her. A thin little boy, a size or so larger than her eight-year-old brother Jo, wearing a pair of large, steel-rimmed spectacles.

'Hullo!' he said, and then after a pause, as Kate stared at him with apparently no sign of recognition, '*Hullo!*'

Johnny Sears! Jo's enemy! The boy who had 'dared' him to ride a cow, and who had succumbed with measles just before they left so that she had never had a chance to tell him what she had thought about him! How Jo was hurt, and lucky not to have been killed, and he, Johnny Sears, in – in Borstal – and – and, she wasn't really sure she hadn't got her measles from him too – though perhaps he *couldn't* help that . . . But how different he looked! Much taller – almost as tall as she was though he must be quite three years younger (very small for her age herself, Kate was always particularly conscious of other children's size) – and wearing glasses! He appeared also to have lost some of his swaggering and unpleasant ways.

'I heard as you'd come!' he announced sidling nearer to her. And then as Kate still stood regarding him, so surprised at his changed looks and demeanour that for a moment she was at a loss for words, 'How's Jo? I were sorry he got hurt,' he added handsomely; then looking at Kate rather sheepishly, 'Mr Wildgoose, he told my Dad to give me a good hidin', but,' he giggled, 'I got the measles – so he couldn't! I had 'em real bad,' he went on proudly, 'and my eyes gone funny. My Mum said it were a punishment for Jo – me getting him hurt, I mean, but the doctor said it were the measles as done it and I oughted to have had glasses long afore anyway. Coo! She wasn't half mad at him, she wasn't!' and he grinned broadly. 'I've growed a lot too,' he continued, 'I'm nearly as tall as you!'

'Well, perhaps it was the measles,' said Kate hurriedly changing the subject of size, 'and,' she considered a moment, 'and the *measles* was because of Jo! You might have killed him – then you'd have been in prison or – or Borstal! He missed Mrs Ayredale-Eskdale's party, anyway,' she went on, 'and I'm not sure it wasn't you who gave *me* measles. I've had them quite badly too,' she continued, not to be outdone. 'Is it because of measles you aren't at school or because it's Saturday?'

'Measles,' replied Johnny Sears, 'but it's holidays now anyway; broke up yesterday they did. I'm glad Jo's all right,' he continued after a pause, '*I* missed the party too! Where you going? Can I come along?'

It seemed rather unkind, especially after such a whole-hearted apology, to say 'no' but Kate was not at all anxious to have Johnny Sears what she called 'tagging on'.

'I'm going to Mrs Megson's,' she announced, hoping this might deter him, 'and then to the post office, and then – oh, several places. I'm doing messages for Mrs Wildgoose,' she added impressively. But Johnny Sears was neither deterred nor impressed. 'All right,' he said. 'Then I'll come along of you.' And 'along of her' he came.

I'll go to Mrs Megson's first, thought Kate as they walked past the orangy cottages on the main road and turned into Post Office Lane and the village itself, and get it over.

There stood the funny little shop with its tiny three-sided window, and green half-door like a stable, and at the foot of the steps leading up to it the laburnum tree, a graceful green sentinel. Its May-time splendour was over, and its sprays of yellow-gold petals – the petals Mrs Megson had so disdainfully swept from her floor – all gone.

'I'm not coming in,' announced Johnny Sears. 'I don't like Mrs Megson – I'll wait here.' And although Kate felt that for once she and Johnny Sears were in agreement over something, she wished very much he would go home.

'What! *you* here again!' exclaimed Mrs Megson as Kate rather timidly approached the counter and held out Mrs Wildgoose's list. 'Well I never! No,' waving away the list, 'Estelle – Mrs Edwards that is, she'll attend to you – I'm not doin' much in the shop these days. I've been in the hospital I have; real bad I've been. Estelle!' she called, and receiving no reply she disappeared through a door at the back of the shop.

It was better than anything Kate could have hoped for! Like Johnny Sears, the once so-alarming Mrs Megson seemed subdued by illness. She was just beginning to wonder how long Mrs Megson had been at the hospital when Mrs Estelle Edwards made her appearance. Mrs Edwards, Kate was to learn later, was one of Mrs Megson's nieces, though in looks, no one she was sure could ever, possibly, have imagined they were any relation. Mrs Edwards had golden hair piled high on her head; long golden ear-rings swung from her ears; her cheeks were a beautiful rose pink, and her nails even pinker – and highly polished. Kate looked at her with awe and some admiration.

'Not seen you before, have I?' asked Mrs Edwards casting a sweeping glance over her, that took in everything from school hat to newly soled but very worn brown sandals. 'You're not from these parts, are you? I've been here three weeks and I flatter myself I just about know every child in Upper – and Lower – Cassington by now! High School girl by your hat, aren't you?' she went on. 'Those hats! My word how they take me back! Maybe you

won't believe it – but I wore one of those horrors once!' And she smiled, showing dazzling white teeth, and her gold ear-rings shook and glittered in the rather dim light of the little shop. But Kate was struck dumb. Her school hat – almost, if not quite, her most treasured possession – a *horror*! Even the implied compliment of 'High School girl' passed for the moment unheeded. Speechless, she held out Mrs Wildgoose's list.

'Oh, The Dew Drop,' said Mrs Edwards taking it in her pink-tipped fingers and scrutinizing it carefully. 'Stayin' there, are you? *Nice*, isn't it?' ('Nice' Kate was to learn was Mrs Edward's favourite word.) 'Stayin' long?'

Kate managed a nod, then 'all the holidays', she said. 'Mr and Mrs Wildgoose wrote and *asked* me,' she added as impressively as she could. Her invitation was as treasured in its way as her school hat. It was better received by Mrs Edwards. 'That's nice,' she said. 'You'll be here for The Concert then? Play the piano do you – or any other instrument? We're short of Talent,' and she spoke the words as if they were written in capital letters, 'very short.'

'Oh *no*,' said Kate, 'and . . . and,' she stammered as she sometimes did in moments of confusion, 'I – I'm not High School – at least I *am* – only – well, it's the same – I mean we *do* the same things but it's called different. I – I,' and she almost muttered this because of course one oughtn't to boast – and yet how could one explain things otherwise? 'I've got a scholarship.'

'Well, that's nice – and more than I ever done – did I should say,' remarked Mrs Edwards, 'not but what I passed all my musical exams – Associated Board – right up to Intermediate – with Distinction in some too, though I say it as shouldn't! Mustn't boast, must we?'

Kate felt rather uncomfortable. Was this a rebuke she wondered? She said nothing. But Mrs Edwards was asking her a question.

'Can you Recite?' she inquired. 'We're short there too; the kids around here don't seem to have much Enterprise' – she spoke again in capital letters – 'I must say! The youngest Smallpiece girl – the one they call Angela – she's the only one that's volunteered so far – she and the Digweeds – the farmer's girls; They Play!' she concluded – almost reverently.

Kate suddenly found her tongue. If Angela Smallpiece could recite, so could she, Kate Ruggles; and anyway she had half-promised Mr Wildgoose she would. With the Digweed girls she would not compete; they were her friends, and anyway, she could not Play.

Pushing back her offending hat, she took a deep breath, and looked bravely at Mrs Edwards. 'I *can* recite,' she said. 'Would it have to be a long or a short piece, please? What's Angela chosen for hers?'

'Let me see – what was it?' said Mrs Edwards tapping her shiny pink nails on the counter. 'Oh yes – I can't remember the title but something about a little Quaker maiden. Nice little piece, I thought – very nice.'

'That!' exclaimed Kate in scorn. 'Why I learnt that years ago! It's – it's a *baby* thing!'

'Seemed nice to me,' said Mrs Edwards again, and she stifled a yawn. 'And Angela – she's not High School – or whatever you say you are. I wouldn't choose anything Too Highbrow – if you know what I mean, if I were you – not for Upper Cassington I wouldn't. I'm giving them something simple myself. Oh yes –' as Kate looked questioning, 'I'm Playing. Just some nice Chopin – and a little Grieg for those as like Modern Music – and perhaps a Jolly Military March to start them all off cheerful! Not but what it all needs *practice*,' she continued, 'but then an artist never minds that! Of course I've always been an artist to my finger-tips' – and she played an imaginary scale on the counter as if to confirm this, 'though it's difficult I must say – the practising I mean – assisting in the shop as I am; hardly what I'm used to, but there! *Someone* had to help poor old Auntie out. Really bad she's been. Well,' as Kate still lingered, 'you'd best skip along and introduce yourself to Miss Ayredale-Eskdale at The Priory and see about your recitation. She's managing The Concert – manages everything here for that matter so far as I can see, and . . .'

'Oh I *know* Miss Alison – Miss Ayredale-Eskdale!' interrupted Kate joyfully.

'Oh you do, do you!' replied Mrs Edwards, and, thought Kate surprised, it might have been Mrs Megson herself speaking! '*That's* all right then. Ah!' as the little half-door was pushed back and some shoppers made their appearance, 'here we go round the mulberry bush! You run away now. I'll have Mrs Wildgoose's list ready for her; off you go! Good-bye.'

'I thought you was never coming,' grumbled Johnny Sears as Kate came down the steps and crossed the road to where he stood leaning against the post office gate and scuffing at the grass by the flint wall beside it with his toes. 'And you've bought nothing! I thought you might have some biscuits to give away!'

'Well you thought wrong,' said Kate sharply. 'I only went to leave Mrs Wildgoose's list. And if I *had* got biscuits I wouldn't have given them to you. They'd be Mrs Wildgoose's, not mine.'

'Go *on*!' said Johnny Sears derisively.

'I *am* going on – into the post office,' said Kate crossly – 'if you'd move and let me open the gate; are you coming too?'

'No,' said Johnny Sears briefly, 'I'm not. Old Mrs Midgley don't like me – nor Miss Midgley neither.'

And I don't much wonder, thought Kate to herself. She was beginning to suspect measles had not improved Johnny Sears as much as she had first thought.

But she quickly forgot him in her pleasure at seeing Mrs Midgely and her daughter again, not to mention their beautiful white cat Thomas, who sat as usual, placid and purring on the counter and looking, as his owner had once said of him, 'everything a cat ought to be.'

The old postmistress and her daughter were pleased to see Kate too, and to hear the latest news of her small brother and sister; Peg and Jo it seemed had particularly endeared themselves to the ladies at the post office. But it was of Cuckoo-Coo, the white kitten, Kate was far more anxious to speak for, as she reminded them, was he not a cousin or stepbrother to their Thomas? 'Of course he's simply *sweet*, but oh, Miss Midgley, he's not a bit like you say about Thomas, "everything a cat ought to be" – he's everything it *oughtn't*! He's always in the coal; Lily Rose says he's the colour they call "off-white" – but I call it just pale grey – with streaks. And he simply *won't* wash – not like all the cats I'*ve* ever seen, so that doesn't help. And I'm afraid he *steals*! We can't leave him alone near food for a single minute. One day he ate a whole kipper that was put ready for Dad's tea! Mum *was* angry!'

'And what about Dad?' asked Mrs Midgley. 'It was his tea!'

'Oh he just laughed and said, "Well what do you expect if you bring a cat into a place this size." And Mum said, "He's not a cat yet, and *I* didn't bring him"; and then we *all* laughed and he, Cuckoo-Coo, just sat there licking his whiskers and looking so pleased with himself – almost as if he was laughing too! He's got the *wickedest* greeny-yellow eyes!'

'Well now,' said Miss Midgley, 'how old's your kitten – just about six weeks when you took him home, wasn't he? And you've been away what – four, five weeks?'

'Nearly five,' said Kate. 'I was three weeks in the hospital with my measles – I went the very day after we got back; then ten – no,' counting on her fingers, '*twelve* days at home – that's four weeks and five days, and of course, yesterday and today. That's *just* five weeks. He was *exactly* six weeks when he was given to us – that's eleven. He's,' she hesitated a moment, for arithmetic was never her strong point, 'he's two and three-quarters – *almost* three months!'

'Well that's not so very old,' said Miss Midgley. 'You mustn't expect too much yet. He'll learn. Thomas was a little trouble at first – and look at him now!' Yes indeed, but Kate found it hard, almost impossible, to visualize Cuckoo-Coo ever attaining to such elegance and dignity.

'I heard,' said Mrs Midgley, 'that Mrs Ayredale-Eskdale was giving a white kitten – that'ud be a brother or sister of your Cuckoo-Coo – to be raffled in aid of some charity at The Flower Show. Funny, wouldn't it, if you won it and went home with another!'

'I don't think Mum would think it funny,' replied Kate – so seriously that both ladies laughed.

'I'm pleased,' said Mrs Midgley after a pause, 'you'll be here for the Show. Fancy, when we talked so much about it before we never thought you would – at least not this year. We'll soon be getting busy here,' she went on. 'Minnie's showing some knitting, I'm making a cake – yes,' as Kate looked surprised, 'I can do quite a lot from my old wheel-chair – and I can still walk a little, you know! Then we've some fruit – currants and gooseberries – beauties they are too though I say it; but really,' she sighed, 'we hardly like to show them – just in case we beat old Mr Milton and Mr Shakespeare. The poor old chaps – they've won time and time again, almost as long as I can remember, but they're getting on in years now and they can't do what they did – specially Mr Milton. Still, there's others showing too so they'll have to take their chance – and after all if we all held back there'd be no prize at all – must be six entries in each class. They'll be busy up at The Dew Drop, I'll be bound,' she went on. 'Always take a lot of prizes there! And The Concert – you'll be here for that too!' Mrs Midgley, it seemed, was looking forward particularly to The Concert. 'When you can't get about much, like me,' she explained, 'you welcome something like that. I like a bit of real good music. Mrs Edwards she plays beautiful – almost a real professional she is. We hear her practising away, hours on end, don't we, Minnie?' Miss Midgley agreed, but with no great enthusiasm, Kate thought. The talk reverted to The Flower Show again. Kate would be entering for some of the children's classes, they supposed? Kate nodded. 'Actually – it's rather secret but I know you won't tell,' she replied, 'but I'm on my way *now* to see Mr Shakespeare – and Mr Milton too, I suppose, if he's about – and to *practise* looking for wildflowers! I've got Johnny Sears with me – he's waiting outside. I didn't want him – I'd much rather look for flowers alone, but he would come, and I dare say he'll tell me some of their names if I ask him.'

The post office ladies looked at each other. 'I'm afraid,' said Miss Midgley, 'Johnny Sears won't give you much help *there*! He's out to win the wildflower prize himself! He won first prize in the younger children's class last year,' she went on, 'and the year before. He's old enough for the top class now – and he means to be first – not even second! He's announced it to everyone! Mrs Smallpiece was in here yesterday and she told me' – she turned to her mother – 'very indignant she was. I think that she considers that prize to be Angela's almost by right, Mr Smallpiece being a gardener!'

'*Head* gardener,' corrected Mrs Midgley with a smile.

'I beg his pardon, *Head* gardener; I wouldn't mind,' she said turning to Kate once more, 'Johnny Sears winning the prize – *any* prize – if he wasn't so horribly *boastful*!'

'But he's only quite a little boy!' exclaimed Kate, 'not much older than Jo, though he's bigger; and I'd *never* have thought he liked wildflowers or knew anything much about them.'

'Whether he really likes them or not I don't know,' said Miss Midgley, 'but he likes getting prizes, and he certainly knows where to find flowers – and he *does* know their names. His collection was out and away the best last year. After all, he's a country boy and he's been born and brought up here; I should think he knows every hedge and field for miles around. You'll have to get up early,' she laughed, 'to beat Johnny Sears!'

'I don't mind *how* early I get up,' said Kate vehemently.

'I didn't mean it that way,' explained Miss Midgley, 'I meant you'd have to be extra sharp!'

But, had they only known it, when the time did come, it was that way, and Kate had to get up very early indeed!

Meanwhile she had stayed longer at the post office than she had intended. Stroking the immaculate white coat of the sedate and purring Thomas, she reluctantly said good-bye, received an invitation to 'come again when you feel like it', and came out into Post Office Lane once more. Of Johnny Sears, there was no sign at all. Perhaps, she thought hopefully, he had got tired of waiting and gone home, and she walked on, gazing into each cottage garden as she passed. Like the cottages themselves, no two were alike, and how neat and tidy they all were – and, above all, how *well stocked*! Gardens, for Kate, had suddenly taken on a new significance; every flower and every vegetable became a possible candidate for The Flower Show! She walked slowly, peeping through gates and palings, and over the tops of little hedges. Mature late-summer flowers bordered trim little paths. Flaming scarlet poppies; big blowsy hollyhocks; sweet-Williams patterned like old-fashioned print dresses; velvety red, orange, and yellow snapdragons; deep blue cornflowers; canterbury bells, pink, hyacinth-coloured, and bright, garish purple; and many, many more whose names she did not know. Most of the vegetables were hidden away behind the cottages, but there were little plats – small squares and oblongs – filled with rotund and firm-hearted cabbages; dark, wine-red, shiny-leaved beetroots; and crisp-looking lettuces, with here and there a row of perky shallots. In some gardens pinks and catmint bordered these plats, or an old apple or plum tree stood benevolently among the vegetables; and in many – far too many, thought Kate – were rows of currant and gooseberry bushes, showing shining clusters and globes of fruit, each bush carefully and most efficiently netted. All, she felt sure, potential 'exhibits'. And her heart feared for old Mr Milton and Mr Shakespeare who had won 'time and time again', but particularly for Mr Shakespeare who was her very special friend. She had misgivings on her own account too. Of all The Flower Show competitions, with the exception of the essay, the wildflower collection had seemed to her to present the least difficulties. Moreover, Mr Wildgoose had implied that competition was not keen. And now here was Johnny Sears of all people – a mere *kid*, apparently a more than determined competitor, and, almost certainly, the superior Miss Smallpiece another!

'Oh *come* on! *you!*' called a voice, and there, lurking between a high brick wall which bordered some property at this part of the village, and a trio of old chestnut trees growing, for no apparent rhyme or reason, in the very roadway itself, was Johnny Sears.

Kate glanced towards him, and squared her shoulders. In that moment she had determined, whatever else happened, he was not going to win the wildflower prize – nor, for that matter, if she, Kate Ruggles, could help it, was Angela Smallpiece.

'What do you mean, "you"?' she demanded, as he came sauntering slowly towards her. 'You know what my name is quite well.' Johnny Sears took no notice of this rebuke. 'Where you going now?' he inquired.

'I'm going down Pond Passage – to see old Mr Shakespeare', said Kate rather reluctantly. 'Why don't you go home if you don't like waiting about?'

'Pond Passage!' echoed Johnny Sears. 'Coo! that a' minds me of . . .' and he broke off and giggled.

'Reminds you of *what*?' asked Kate. But Johnny Sears made no reply. He seemed to have a special talent for not answering direct questions.

They walked on together in silence, and a moment or two later turned the corner where Post Office Lane led into Church Street.

Leaning against the wall of the now deserted school, a large shopping basket at her feet, was a big sturdy girl with long yellow curls. She was busily engaged in blowing off the seeds from a dandelion clock.

'He *loves* me; he loves me *not*; he *loves* me; he loves me *not*!' they heard her say as they came nearer. A moment later, throwing away the dandelion, she picked up her basket, and came towards them. It was Angela Smallpiece.

'What! It's never you come here *again*!' she exclaimed scornfully by way of a greeting to Kate. 'And you, Johnny Sears – what do you think *you're* doing – taking her for a walk? . . . or looking for *flowers* perhaps? Think you can find 'em better now you've got those big glasses of yours? I hear,' she went on, 'I hear you've told my Mum you're going to win the wildflower prize in the top class at the Show this year! Well shall I tell *you* something, Johnny Sears,' and she giggled a little, 'it's this: I've a fancy I'd rather like to win it myself! There! And shall I tell you something else? Do you know what my dandelion clock's just said? It's said "he loves me *not*". And dandelion clocks – you know – well as I do – *always* tell true!' and she giggled again.

Neither Kate nor Johnny Sears said anything. They stood staring silently at the owner of the yellow curls and pretty but mocking face.

'And what about Miss Kate Ruggles there?' went on the scornful voice. 'The Town girl who thinks she knows All-About-the-Country! Perhaps she'll be having a try too? Coo!' as the church clock struck ten. 'I must run! Bye-bye!' And her long yellow curls streaming behind her, she rushed past them and disappeared round the corner into Post Office Lane.

Still silent, Kate and her companion walked on again. Suddenly, nearly tripping her up, Johnny Sears stopped dead in his tracks.

'*Are* you?' he demanded.

'Are I *what*!' cried Kate, nearly thrown off her balance physically – and certainly grammatically.

'You knows what I mean all right!' said Johnny Sears standing in front of her, his hands on his hips and looking thoroughly aggressive. 'Ah!' triumphantly, as Kate, greatly to her annoyance, felt herself blushing to the roots of her very red hair. 'You *are*! Look at you! Look at you blushing! You *are* having a try! But you won't win, you won't; no, nor Angela neither!'

'And how do *you* know!' cried Kate angrily, and blushing an even brighter pink in her annoyance at this laying bare of her plans.

'I know,' said Johnny Sears simply, 'because I *know*; I'm going to win it myself!'

They stood for a moment glaring at each other, like two dogs about to fight; then by a kind of mutual consent they walked on again. Neither spoke. But war was definitely declared.

*

'Well if it ain't my young friend from foreign parts!' exclaimed old Mr Shakespeare putting down a large garden fork and shading his eyes with his hand as he looked across to where Kate stood at the far end of the small plank bridge which led across the stream near the bottom of his garden. Standing sulkily behind her was Johnny Sears, neither of them having spoken a word to each other the whole way down the little pathway known as Pond Passage.

'You come along over, my dear,' called Mr Shakespeare, 'you come along over!' Then sighting her companion, 'Is that young Johnny Sears I sees there? Ah, 'tis. You come along too, young man. We've got a job for you, Mr Milton and I have. A little bird told me as you were a-coming,' he continued, addressing Kate when she and Johnny Sears, walking in single file over the plank bridge which shook and bounced in a delightfully springy way under their combined weights, arrived on the strip of velvety green grass between the stream and his garden gate, 'yes, a little bird told me all right but I didn't cotton to it t'was so soon. Mr Milton'll be as surprised as me – not forgotten Mr Milton have you, my dear?' No indeed, thought Kate, who had found poor old Mr Milton's deafness and her own inability ever to make him hear one syllable she said, something of a trial.

'Ah, here he comes! Hi! John, see who's here!' shouted Mr Shakespeare across the fence – composed chiefly of old iron bedheads – which divided his garden from that of his neighbour.

Old Mr Milton seemed older than ever, thought Kate. His long beard was, if possible, whiter; his arms even more stick-like and scrawny, and all his clothes looked capable of going quite twice round his thin old body. Under his battered straw hat, however, his faded blue eyes were bright, and his face had a soft, pink look like a baby's. He still wore his gardening apron with its kangaroo pocket in front from which dangled wisps and taggles of raffia and string.

'What's that you say?' he inquired, not seeing the visitors at once, 'nettin' not enough? Isn't that what we've been sayin' these ten days or more? Nothing near enough!'

'Nettin' – you've got nettin' on the brain!' cried Mr Shakespeare, 'it's *visitors* – look!' And he pointed towards them.

'Well there now!' exclaimed Mr Milton focusing at last in the right direction. 'Well now, if t'aint her as never heard tell o' the Mr Poet Milton! Come to see us again, have you? I hopes as you're well? But you must speak up when you speaks to me, my dear, for I'm just a trifle deaf I am. And who's that,' he went on, 'along of you – that there boy? William,' addressing Mr Shakespeare, 'a *boy* – what you've suggested. Well you talk to 'un, but *mind*, tuppence is all I can spare, and rightly I can't spare that!'

Kate and Johnny Sears stood listening and wondering, as well they might, what these strange remarks might mean. They were not left long in doubt.

''Tis our exhibits for The Flower Show as we're worrit about,' explained Mr Shakespeare. 'Both of us.' He jerked his head towards Mr Milton, 'he's a-got the gooseberries and I've a-got the currants, and better of both we've never had, no never. You shall see 'em in a moment. But whether we'll have a berry of either left by time of the Show – well I don't know! 'Tis birds, birds, birds, all day long, and sometimes all night too! As I says to John there,' he went on,''tis the thanks you get for feedin' 'em in winter. Come summer, and they eats *you* – in a manner of speaking – out of house and home! Yes, we've gone without to buy nettin' and that's the truth; and we can't afford to buy no more.' And Mr Shakespeare paused for breath.

'But Mr Shakespeare!' cried Kate, 'wouldn't someone *lend* you some netting – just till the Show's over?' Mr Shakespeare shook his head. 'We're never ones to borrow to start with,' he replied slowly,'and anyways there's not an inch of nettin' but's as you might say *employed*. And for why? Because this year everyone's showin'; man, woman, and child. I'm fair wore out,' he went on, 'jerkin' strings a-scarin' birds. Up four o'clock *mornings* I've been. Mr Milton, well, he's gettin' on, you know, and he can't do it.' The birds, it seemed, were becoming used to his 'contraption' as he called it, and he pointed to an assortment of tin cans dangling from strings attached to the fruit trees, which Kate remembered in action on her previous visit. What was needed, he went on, was a boy about the place; a boy who could *jerk*, and, when occasion required, shout. In short, a bird-scarer such as the big cherry orchards away across the valley still employed – a calling Mr Shakespeare himself had frequently followed, some sixty odd years ago.

'Aye, and glad to do it – and t'weren't pocket-money neither – like it'll be to this little varmint,' and he nodded his head at Johnny Sears. Yes, a boy about the premises was the thing, and he and Mr Milton were willing to pay twopence an hour every morning – fourpence a day till Flower Show day – nine days in all. In fact there was three shillings ready and waiting for any boy willing to get up early and use his arms – and, if necessary, his lungs. *Three shillings!* If Johnny Sears would like the job . . .

''Tis good money!' Here interrupted Mr Milton who stood watching his friend's gestures and explanations and for once coming in at the right moment. 'Good money,' he repeated, 'and easy come by!'

Johnny Sears evidently thought so too for in less time than it had taken to tell, the bargain was struck and he was being instructed in his duties by both old men simultaneously.

Kate stood looking about her, marvelling at the size of the gooseberries and currants but wondering a little about the wisdom of employing Johnny Sears as a bird-scarer. Would he ever get there as early as four o'clock – the hour agreed upon; and every day – wet or fine? And – would his parents *let* him? Almost in answer to her thoughts she heard Mr Milton putting the very same questions, and Johnny Sears *bawling* replies. What a noise he could make – he'd certainly scare any bird! All the Sears family it seemed were astir early 'along' of the milking, and neither his Dad nor Mum knew, or apparently cared, where their son spent his time.

'Four o'clock, sharp, tomorrow then,' said Mr Shakespeare. ''Tis sunrise not long a-fore, and 'tis then the little beggars gets starting. And mind,' he went on, 'you don't go a-picking or a-touching nothing – understand, *nothing*. And,' following the direction of Johnny Sears's eyes which kept straying to the bottom corner of the garden, 'you keep right away from the pond. We've some water-lilies there,' he went on turning to Kate, 'not many hereabouts there aren't, and last year, just round about Flower Show time – they all disappeared – yes, disappeared! Not one left there wasn't! They're a bit late this year but they'll be out any day now.'

Kate stole a look at Johnny Sears. He was standing with his back towards her; she could not be sure, and it might have been the light, but she thought the backs of his ears looked a *very* bright pink.

'I'll be gettin' along now,' he remarked to Mr Shakespeare. 'Be here four sharp tomorrer.' And without so much as a look at Kate, he rushed down the path, over the bridge, and disappeared up Pond Passage.

It was nearly half an hour before Kate herself walked up Pond Passage again, and emerging from its narrow leafy entrance collided with a lady and gentleman walking briskly along Church Street, followed at a short distance by a fawn-coloured bull-terrier.

'*Miss Alison!*' exclaimed Kate. 'Oo! I *am* sorry, nearly knocking into you like that – I'm afraid I was thinking of so many things all at the same time I just didn't look where I was going! Oh, it *is* nice to see you again!'

'And it's nice to see you, too, though I should have minded – very much – if you'd upset these!' and Miss Ayredale-Eskdale held up a large basket of ducks' eggs. 'I've just fetched them from The Dew Drop,' she went on. 'I saw Mrs Wildgoose for a minute and she told me you'd arrived safely – and *no* adventures this time! Colin,' turning to the gentleman with her, 'this child comes from near where you've been staying. Her name is Kate Ruggles, she's recovering from measles and spending her holidays at The Dew Drop with Mrs Wildgoose.'

The gentleman smiled. 'How do you do?' he said, and he took off a very battered-looking felt hat. Then he looked rather earnestly at Kate. 'Did you say "Miss Ruggles"?' he asked, turning to his companion. 'Yes? – then I have a very strong suspicion I've met some of this young lady's family; I seem to remember being told some of the members were away recovering from measles. Her father,' he went on, 'got landed by mistake with a sow I bought instead of his own pig, so I went and saw him about it. Number – I think *one* One End Street, Otwell-on-the-Ouse was the address.'

'Are you Lord Glenheather!' gasped Kate. 'Oh, you *must* be – you're just like Lily Rose (that's my sister) said you were; and not a bit like –' and she broke off in some confusion for she was going to say, what Lily Rose had also said, 'not a bit her idea of a lord'.*

'Well this is a surprise!' exclaimed Miss Alison. 'You're quite right – he is Lord Glenheather – but what were you

* *Further Adventures of the Family from One End Street.*

going to say – what is he "not a bit like"?' But Kate was saved from replying for suddenly the air was rent with the sound of shrill squawkings and the flutterings of startled hens.

'Oh, Colin! Quick, Jaeger!' cried Miss Alison.

Lord Glenheather turned sharply. 'Jaeger!' he shouted, '*Jaeger!* Come here, will you! Come *here*, you disobedient brute! *Jaeger!*' And he strode angrily in the direction of the squawkings where through a cloud of dust, a flutter of wings, a dog's tail, and an old lady emerging from a cottage door wildly waving a stick, could be dimly discerned.

'Oh, dear – Mrs Blossom's bantams!' exclaimed Miss Alison. 'Oh, Jaeger, you *haven't* killed one!' as a moment later, cunningly evading its master, the dog Kate had noticed earlier came lolloping up. In its mouth was a bunch of feathers; its tail wagged fitfully with a guilty uncertainty of reception, and after the manner of bull-terriers, its three-cornered-looking eyes gleamed humorously.

'It's only feathers, Colin!' called Miss Alison bending down to investigate. 'Tell Mrs Blossom. I'll hold him. Drop it, Jaeger!' she went on, putting her hand through the dog's collar, '*drop it!*' and she gave him a sharp smack on the nose. Jaeger dropped the feathers; skilfully swallowed one inconveniently near his throat, then looked up at her, wagged his tail furiously, lowered his ears, and wrinkled up the sides of his mouth showing a fine set of shiny white teeth.

'He *laughs*!' exclaimed Kate in astonishment, 'he really does! I never knew dogs laughed!'

'This one does,' replied Miss Alison, laughing herself, 'and of course he just melts my heart, but oh, he's so naughty! He killed a cockerel the day he arrived, and yesterday he stole a whole leg of mutton out of the larder! No, Jaeger,' she said sternly, 'it's no good looking at me like that. You're a naughty, *very* naughty dog!'

But Jaeger only wagged his tail more vigorously, licked her hand ingratiatingly, and looked up at Kate out of the corners of his eyes as if to say 'what an unnecessary fuss about nothing!'

'Oh, he *is* lovely!' cried Kate. 'But is his name really Jaeger, Miss Alison? I thought it was a sort of stuff? Mrs Beasley's niece's mother once sent us a dressing-gown with "Jaeger" written inside on a label. It was just his colour' – she nodded towards the dog – 'the dressing-gown I mean.'

'Yes, it is his name – *and* it's a kind of dressing-gown,' replied Miss Alison, 'and that is why . . .' but she was interrupted by Lord Glenheather who came striding up.

'Now my lad, you're for it!' he said, grabbing the dog by the scruff of the neck and unbuckling its collar.

'Oh please!' began Kate, 'please, *must* he be beaten?'

'I'm afraid he must,' said Lord Glenheather, 'or before long there won't be a hen or a cockerel or a bantam left in Upper or Lower Cassington.'

Jaeger took his beating well. He gave only one short little squeak. When it was over, and his collar buckled on once more, he shook himself, then lay down in the road in abject apology. But Lord Glenheather had not finished yet. Carefully collecting the feathers, he tied them together in a bunch and fastened them to the collar. 'And you keep that on you – for the rest of the day,' he said. 'Get up now – and behave yourself! I'm sorry for the interruption' – he turned to Kate – '*One* One End Street – I was right, wasn't I?'

'Yes, quite right, Lord . . . Sir . . . please, what do I call you?' answered Kate, rather shyly.

'You just call him Lord Glenheather,' said Miss Alison, 'but please don't stop to call him anything now if you don't mind because we must go. My mother is catching the two o'clock train to London and we're already late for lunch. Perhaps you'd like to come to tea one day – would you? We'll arrange something another time.'

'Oh, I'd *love* to,' cried Kate, 'and please, will . . . will Lord Glenheather be there, and if he is *could* I bring my autograph book along – for his signature?'

Miss Alison laughed. 'He's not going yet – yes, of course you can – can't she, Colin? Though no one will ever read the signature because his writing is quite *un*readable. Now good-bye, we really must go!'

'Perfectly correct,' said Lord Glenheather looking up from knotting a large silk handkerchief through Jaeger's collar by way of a lead. 'I often can't read my writing myself, but bring the book by all means; and I want to hear about the piglets – and, of course, what it is I'm "not a bit like"! Come on you,' to Jaeger. 'Good-bye,' and raising his battered-looking hat he hurried after Miss Alison, Jaeger, his tail drooping with the humiliation of the bunch of feathers and the handkerchief-lead, subdued at his side.

Kate stood looking after them. The dust had settled, and old Mrs Blossom had retreated indoors again, but on top of the wall which adjoined her cottage and bordered the road, sat four bantam hens and a cock, all of them – especially the cock, looking very much the worse for wear about the tail feathers.

As Jaeger was led by he glanced up at the wall, then he looked round. His tail wagged very slightly, and though it was too far off to see properly, Kate felt sure he was laughing again.

3. Preparations and an Invitation

KATE ARRIVED back at The Dew Drop Inn somewhat bewildered with her morning's experiences. Her pleasure at seeing old friends again; the meeting with Mrs Megson's niece; Johnny Sears and his ambitions; what she described to herself as Angela Smallpiece's 'horridness'; and certainly not least, the surprise of finding Lord Glenheather in Church Street, Upper Cassington!

When had he come? Was it the first time? Would he stay long – and all the time at The Priory? And the dog, Jaeger, had he come before too?

Mrs Wildgoose, in the throes of cooking the dinner, was fairly bombarded with questions. 'Stop! stop! One at a time, *please*!' she cried, laughing. Yes, Lord Glenheather often stayed at The Priory . . . a cousin of Miss Alison's she thought – some relation anyway . . . A *very* nice gentleman . . . But fancy his having been to Kate's home! 'Yes,' as Kate reminded her, 'yes, I do remember you wrote and told me about the pigs and all, and a grand gentleman calling, and how you'd missed everything being in hospital; but I'm sure you never said his name or I'd have remembered.

And what's this,' she went on, 'you being asked to tea at The Priory! Why, all the years I've lived here that's more than I've ever been! Not of course but what I've been there to meetings – and to jumble sales and church bazaars and such like . . . As for "Jaeger" – an outlandish name for a dog if ever there was one that is – no, I've certainly never seen *him* before!'

'When Lord Glenheather came to see us,'* said Kate, 'he told Lily Rose he'd only got shooting dogs. Labradors he said – all black, though I suppose he's got sheep-dogs for his farm? Perhaps he's just bought Jaeger? Oh, I *do* think he's lovely, Mrs Wildgoose – Jaeger I mean – though Lord Glenheather seems very nice too,' she added.

'Well you'll be able to find out all about everything when you go to your tea-party,' said Mrs Wildgoose smiling. 'And I don't know about lovely – a curious-looking dog I must say *I* thought it, but there, I'm not all that partial to bull-terriers – though I'd hardly dare say it in front of Mr Wildgoose, he's so fond of them. And now, no more questions because in two minutes I'm going to dish up the dinner. Off you go and tidy yourself up, and if you haven't got a good appetite after such a morning – well – I just don't know *what* I'll say!'

But Kate did full justice to the meal and Mrs Wildgoose noted with approval the disappearance of a large helping of Irish stew followed by two of stewed fruit and custard.

* *Further Adventures of the Family from One End Street.*

Kate wanted to be loyal to Mrs Ruggles's cooking, but there was no denying Mrs Wildgoose's custard tasted ever so much nicer than what they had at home.

'I know Mum buys the best,' she told Mrs Wildgoose, 'and it says "extra creamy" on the tin, but it's not creamy like yours. Would you please tell me the kind you use when I go home so's I can ask Mum to get it?' But when Mrs Wildgoose explained that it was not out of a tin at all, but made with fresh eggs and milk, Kate looked not only disappointed, but faintly shocked. 'Real eggs – *in custard*, Mrs Wildgoose!' she exclaimed. (What *would* Mum say to such extravagance!)

'Well it's different with hens at your back door so to speak,' replied Mrs Wildgoose. 'I've often more eggs than I can do with. I sell some it's true, but most people hereabouts have got their own hens and don't need to buy. But I can see you're beginning to be interested in cooking! And that's just as well,' she continued, 'for don't forget – you've to learn to make cakes and jam for the Show!'

Coo! So she had! Thinking about the wildflower competition, and the other events of the morning had temporarily driven all other activities from Kate's mind.

'Let me see,' said Mrs Wildgoose. 'Tomorrow's Sunday; Monday morning we'll be busy with the wash; Monday afternoon, though, I'll be doing a bit of cake-making – I'll give you a lesson then – how'll that be?'

Kate thought it would 'be' very well, but remembering Mrs Ruggles's objection to such activities added she was afraid she might waste a lot of 'ingredients'.

'We won't worry if you do,' said Mrs Wildgoose consolingly; 'though that doesn't mean I approve of waste – for I *don't.* "Waste not, want not" I were brought up to – and there's not much wasted at The Dew Drop I can assure you. If what you make *should* turn out heavy, or burned, the hens'll enjoy it so you needn't worry on that score. And now we'll give Elsie a hand with the clearing for she goes early today, and then – you know my little rule – up you go for a rest on your bed for an hour.'

'I did think,' said Kate a little shyly, 'I did *think*, Mrs Wildgoose, of going to look for flowers this afternoon – it's such a *lovely* day!' she added persuasively.

'So it is,' agreed Mrs Wildgoose, 'and what's more, it's going to stay lovely – right up to sunset. And it's going to be real hot this afternoon – I'm putting my feet up for half an hour or so myself. And, another thing, have you forgotten – you've to sow that mustard-and-cress seed with Mr Wildgoose when he gets back. He'll be here soon after three, if not before, but he'll be busy after tea – you can go flower-hunting then.'

Of course! The mustard-and-cress! How could she have forgotten! 'It's that Jaeger-dog,' said Mrs Wildgoose laughing, 'sent everything out of your head, he has! Off you go now – and don't you stir still you hear the clock strike three.'

And though odd indeed as a rest on one's bed in the afternoon had seemed to Kate, Peg, and Jo when they first came to The Dew Drop Inn, it was queer, reflected Kate as she remembered Mrs Wildgoose's instructions to fold back the quilt, and remove her dusty shoes, how soon you got used to it. And anyway Mrs Wildgoose didn't 'boss' you into doing it. She never said you've *got* to, or you *must*; she just made it seem a sensible sort of thing to do. And really it was rather lovely up here all alone with a nice book! Although close under the thatch, the little room was not hot or stuffy. Outside, the sun blazed down but a soft breeze blew in through the deep-set window, stirring the tiny, spotted muslin curtain, and the room itself was filled with a strange, greenish light reflected from the rose and honeysuckle sprays that trailed and hung thickly about the thatch. It was very quiet. Not a sound but the droning of bees among the honeysuckle flowers, and now and then a car or a lorry rattling by on the road. Kate lay down and opened her book. She certainly meant to read but instead she lay watching the shadow-patterns of the leaves dancing and flickering over the whitewashed wall, listening to the droning bees, and every now and then sniffing delightedly at the sweet honeysuckle smell wafting in and out with the breeze. A warm, sweet, intoxicating smell . . . an overpoweringly drowsy smell . . . When the church clock struck three she sat up with a jerk, uncertain whether she had been to sleep or not, but quite certain she had not read one word of her book!

Kate found Mrs Wildgoose, her feet still 'up', yawning sleepily. 'Gracious me!' she exclaimed. 'This won't do! Forty winks and more I've had! Must be the heat for, if there's one thing I never do it's sleep in the afternoon! And dreaming too; some nonsense about that Jaeger-dog if you'll believe me! My goodness me, after three o'clock, the dinner not washed up and me dreaming about a bull-terrier!'

'Who's been dreaming about a bull-terrier?' asked Mr Wildgoose, opening the door at that moment, and he took off his hat, mopped his forehead with a gaily-patterned handkerchief and deposited several bulging paper bags and parcels on the table. 'Phew! it's turned warm! I was fair stifled in the bus. You looks half-asleep still, my girl!' he laughed, bending down to kiss his wife. 'Dreaming about a bull-terrier – *you*! Well I never! Now that's a breed of dog I *like*!' he exclaimed, turning to Kate. 'A young bull-terrier is what I'd like to . . .'

'Now, Charlie!' interrupted Mrs Wildgoose, getting to her feet and beginning to bustle about, 'if you're thinking of bringing a young bull-terrier here please think again. Old Snuffy was a different matter; quiet, and gentle as a lamb. No trouble at all. You get a young dog and you'll have trouble all round. With the poultry; the garden; the traffic – and like as not with the customers themselves – not to mention dog-fights and all *that* leads to!'

'Gracious me!' exclaimed Mr Wildgoose. 'How you do jump ahead! I haven't said I was even *thinking* of getting a dog – bull-terrier or any other – young or old. Now *have* I?'

'I'm warning you in time,' replied Mrs Wildgoose. '*Don't* think of it!' Mr Wildgoose laughed. 'What we've to think of at the moment,' he said, 'is sowing mustard-and-cress, and here it is,' and he produced two small packets from his coat pocket. 'There,' laying them down, first one and then the other on the table, 'mustard; cress.'

Kate stood fingering the packets gently. The mustard felt hard and Knobbly, the cress soft and yielding.

'You said, Mr Wildgoose, I must sow them "imaginatively" – how – what – did you mean exactly?' she asked.

'I meant – but bring the seed along to the toolshed and I'll explain there. We'll have to sift some soil for it – but first I must change my clothes – you skip along – I won't be five minutes.'

The toolshed was a little, black-painted hut at the bottom of the vegetable garden. It had a sloping roof, a narrow rickety door, and one small and rather cobwebby window. Various gardening tools and trailing bunches of raffia hung from hooks and nails. The floor was heaped with flower pots of every size. There were cans, long- and short-spouted, coils of hose, and mysterious sacks and bins. On a dilapidated table and the remains of a kitchen chair stood innumerable ancient tobacco tins, chipped cups and jugs, and many old jam-jars housing an assortment of pest-destroyers, paint-brushes, garden labels, candle ends, screws, nails, and other oddments. A delightful smell – earthy, mealy, with a hint of tar, pervaded everything.

'I feel,' said Mr Wildgoose when he presently appeared, clad once more in his working clothes, including his green baize apron, 'I feel when I come in here, rather like the Youghy Bonghy Bò. You've not read about the Yonghy Bonghy Bò?' as Kate looked rather blankly at him. 'Never read Lear's *Nonsense Rhymes*? Well,' as she shook her head, 'you've got a treat ahead, you have! Ah!' he paused a moment, 'that's an idea; why shouldn't you recite one of *those* for The Concert now! I'll give you the book to read tonight. In the meantime, the Yonghy Bonghy Bò had:

> "Two old chairs, and half a candle –
> One old jug without a handle." . . .

'Very like,' and he waved his hand towards the dilapidated chair and the array of cups and tins and jam-pots, 'Charles Henry Wildgoose. But never mind that for now. What we've got to think of is mustard-and-cress.' And he began to explain to Kate what he meant by sowing it 'imaginatively'.

Different from anyone else's it had got to be. *Not* on a piece of flannel; *not* on a tin tray; not even in a nice garden saucer. And, above all, *not* one's name or initials. 'Quite half of 'em do that,' said Mr Wildgoose scornfully. 'Now what's it to be? Remember it's got to be your idea, not mine.' And he took the two seed packets from the table where Kate had put them and began opening them very carefully.

What indeed! Kate stood thinking deeply, ideas crowding into her head only to be discarded as soon as they occurred.

'How about "Welcome to Upper Cassington Flower Show", Mr Wildgoose?' she said at last. Mr Wildgoose shook his head. 'Too long – even if you left out *Lower* Cassington which you well couldn't – seein' it's their Show too.'

'Then how about just "Welcome" – by itself?' suggested Kate after a pause, 'with a big exclamation mark after it?'

she added hopefully. But Mr Wildgoose only 'um-umed' without enthusiasm. Kate tried again, '"God Save the King", Mr Wildgoose – surely *everybody* would like that, and it's not very long?'

'Been done before,' said Mr Wildgoose, 'though that's no reason you couldn't do it better . . . still . . .'

Several minutes went by. Kate stood frowning with thought, staring at the cobwebby window but seeing neither the cobwebs nor the garden outside.

'I know!' she exclaimed suddenly, turning round and facing Mr Wildgoose. '*I* know! Your *sign* – The Dew Drop Inn – and – and Do Drop In on the other side! Oo! I can just see it! You – you . . .' and she began to stammer slightly as she sometimes did when excited, and to forget her grammar badly, 'you – c-could plant it in boxes, sort I've seen Dad use for – for cabbage seedlings afore he puts 'em out on the allotment . . . They – they could lay flat till the day of the Show and then they could be stood up back to back like! Oh Mr Wildgoose it would be *just* like the sign! The letters in the mustard, and all the rest in cress!'

'There!' exclaimed Mr Wildgoose delightedly. 'I knew you'd think of something bright! That's a fine idea that is! I couldn't have thought of a better myself! The good old Dew Drop in mustard-and-cress! And won't the missis be pleased! Tell you what, we'll keep it a surprise, shall we?' And Kate agreeing enthusiastically, 'to work then!' said Mr Wildgoose and for the next ten minutes or so she carefully sifted soil and filled two large seed boxes under his directions. 'I can *show* you,' he insisted, 'but you must *do* it all yourself, otherwise I can't certify it's your "own unaided work" as it says in The Flower Show rules. Now for the letters. You know, don't you, the cress has to be sown first – four to five days afore the mustard? We'll make it five to be on the safe side.'

'I know you don't sow them *exactly* the same day,' said Kate, 'because the twins had some once. They sowed it on their *face-flannel*, Mr Wildgoose – wasn't that awful! Coo, Mum wasn't half angry when she found out! and they watered it too much or something – anyway the mustard never grew properly and went all mouldy – and it smelt – just *terrible*!'

'Well we mustn't over-water ours,' said Mr Wildgoose, 'but first let's get it sown.'

It was not at all easy to get the letters neatly spaced. Kate had wanted them exactly as they were on the sign but Mr Wildgoose pointed out that, although it might not look so hanging up, it was really twice the size of the boxes, and this was impossible. It was a long time before she could get them to her satisfaction, but Mr Wildgoose was very patient, and at last, with the assistance of a wooden plant label, the task was completed, and neat grooves representing the words Dew Drop Inn in one box, and Do Drop In in the other, were all ready to receive the mustard seed in five days' time. Then, tense with excitement, and almost holding her breath, Kate sowed the cress seed very neatly around and between the grooves, and covered it with a light sprinkling of the sifted soil. Finally she filled a can, to which Mr Wildgoose attached a fine-sprinkling rose, from a tap in the corner of the shed, and carefully watered both boxes.

'Oh I do hope it'll come up!' she said as they walked back to the house; Mr Wildgoose, like a true gardener, stopping every few steps to look at various nurslings as if he had not seen them several times already that day!

'Don't you worry about that!' he replied, 'it's the very best seed – *and* there's a waxing moon. Some country folk, you know, think things grow better then. I don't know myself if there's anything in it though there's times I've thought so. One thing's certain – it can't do no harm. Bless me!' as the church clock began to strike, 'it's four o'clock! *Four o'clock!* It'll be opening-time before I know where I am, and my proper day's work not begun!'

Immediately after tea Kate set off on her flower-hunting expedition.

'Don't go near the river, please, will you?' called Mrs Wildgoose just as she was about to start. 'I'll come along with you one day – or Elsie will if you want flowers from there, but I'd rather you'd not alone. Promise now.'

How ridiculous! muttered Kate crossly to herself, the river being one of the places she had specially in mind. Just as if I was a baby! And just like Mum, too. For the river at home was strictly forbidden to all of them though Kate knew well enough the twins went there and, she sometimes suspected, Jo. She did not, however, reveal any of this information to Mrs Wildgoose, and gave her a very reluctant promise.

She went across the road and through the gate opposite, the scene of Jo's unhappy exploits with Mr Plodder's cow.* There was no sign of the cow today and of the millions of shiny yellow buttercups that had carpeted the field, and the big dog-daisies just coming into full flower when they left to go home, there was only a stray one here and there. Even so, Kate noted with approval, they were still flowering and would be two specimens, anyway, towards her collection. She walked across the field and along the hedge at one side, picking whatever showed a vestige of flower, until she came to a gate. She was leaning over this undecided whether to go through it or continue to the end of the field where there was a stile and a footpath leading to the water meadows near the river, when there was the sound of a gate on the farther side of the field being unlatched. The next minute, a couple of cart horses, released from their day's labour, manes flying, and neighing loudly, careered wildly towards her. The sun glittered on the metal of their heavy shoes as they kicked their hooves high in the air, and the ground shook as they came thundering over to where she stood.

'They won't hurt 'ee, lass! They won't hurt 'ee!' called a voice reassuringly across the field.

That might be true but Kate was very glad to be on the far side of the gate, and she retreated several paces as they came galloping up to it, stopped abruptly, then thrusting their heads over snorted and whinnied in what was evidently

* *Further Adventures of the Family from One End Street.*

intended as a friendly greeting. Her acquaintance with horses of any kind was of the slightest, and these were so very large! Still, if one was going to farm, one must certainly not be afraid of farm animals. She took a couple of timid steps towards them, murmuring endearments, but now they turned away and immediately began to graze, totally absorbed and apparently as indifferent to her as they had previously been interested. She stood watching them for a little while then continued along the hedge, over the stile and down the path to the first of the water meadows. It was a perfect evening, not so much as a wisp of cloud in the sky. It looked as if it might stay fine for ever and ever and though of course one knew it would not, it seemed somehow impossible to imagine it rainy, or blowing, much less foggy, or cold with snow and frost.

She wandered on through several fields, her bunch of flowers changing rapidly to an armful. It was heavy too and suddenly she felt tired. She sat down under a hedge, resting her back against an ash sapling. How quiet it was! Not a sound; not a single sound! Just the faintest little rustling made by the wind in some fallen hedge leaves. She sat listening idly for a moment or two. The little rustling noise became louder. *Was* it all the wind? She listened intently; then peered about among the leaves. There was a sudden movement under them; a little head poked through, and two beady eyes looked up at her. She put out her hand, and her fingers closed over a tiny, furry body. Oh! . . . she gave a gasp of delight, as slowly uncurling her fingers but sheltering one hand with the other lest her treasure should escape, she gazed down at it. In her palm lay a baby vole. Its body of soft reddish-grey fur was barely an inch in length; its little tail half as long. Its eyes were bright like a robin's, its little rounded ears translucent in the sunlight, and although its tiny nose and whiskers twitched and quivered nervously, it made no effort to escape.

'Oh, you little *angel*!' breathed Kate ecstatically, and keeping the fingers of one hand closed over it to prevent its escape, she stroked it gently with the forefinger of the

other. How tiny, yet perfect it was! And suddenly a picture of the huge cart horses came into her mind . . . This little creature was no larger than the tips of their ears . . . oh, it was a faery thing . . . yet it, too, had its own mysterious way of life.

'You little angel!' she repeated. Should she take it home? It would be so lovely to have it . . . to feed it . . . But how *would* she feed it? . . . perhaps Mr or Mrs Wildgoose would know what it ate? . . . but, perhaps not, and then it would die . . . she couldn't bear that . . . But the vole settled the question itself. With a sudden, twisting movement it squirmed from her hand and leapt to the ground. There was a sharp rustling in the leaves and then – silence; utter stillness . . .

Kate walked slowly home, her burden of limp and half-dead wildflowers growing heavier and heavier.

'Good girl!' said Mrs Wildgoose approvingly as she came in, 'you're well in time for supper; but what have you got there – half the wildflowers in Upper Cassington I should think! Mr Wildgoose has left the book for you – there on the chair – and Mr Lear's poems he's so fond of. You amuse yourself with those till supper-time.'

But neither Mr Wildgoose's flower book, nor Edward Lear's poems could compete with the enchantment of the baby vole to Kate and at supper she could talk of nothing else.

'I'm glad you didn't bring it back,' said Mr Wildgoose coming in for a few minutes from the bar. ''Twouldn't have lived. Wild animals is best left wild. They're beautiful little things, though, those voles . . . There was a poet once who said a mouse was "miracle enough to stagger sextillions of infidels" – perhaps he'd one of them in mind. They certainly stagger me, and this one seems to have fairly bewitched you, Kate!' smiling at the rapt expression on her face.

'What are sextillions, Mr Wildgoose?' she asked wonderingly.

'Of that I'm not rightly sure,' he replied, 'but I guess it's more than you or I have ever counted – and knowing neither of us is all that fond of arithmetic, would want to!'

'And what's more,' said Mrs Wildgoose getting up and beginning to clear the table, 'I hope neither of you is going to try. Kate looks half-asleep now. Up you go to bed, my dear,' she continued, 'and don't you lie reading long or I'll be up to turn out the light!'

But Kate was too sleepy to read at all. She lay, surfeited with fresh air, thinking over all the events of the day. Presently she began murmuring over to herself the names of some of the flowers she had brought back, and identified from Mr Wildgoose's book. They were strangely satisfying; even the queer ones like toadflax and fleabane; others you wanted to say over and over again – like a poem! She began arranging them in her mind in alphabetical order to remember them better. Agrimony, archangel . . . bed-straw, betony . . . comfrey, centuary, chicory . . . dead nettle . . . Before she was less than half-way through the alphabet she was asleep; and so soundly asleep that even the rather noisy shouts and talking that sometimes accompanied a Saturday night's closing-time at The Dew Drop Inn failed to wake her.

When she next opened her eyes it was a new day – and pouring with rain!

4. Tea with Jaeger

'BUT LAST night it looked as if it would be fine for ever and ever – anyway for simply *ages*!' said Kate as she and Mr and Mrs Wildgoose sat lingering over a late and very succulent breakfast of sausages and bacon, hot rolls, honey and tea.

'It began to blow up sudden round about closing-time,' said Mr Wildgoose, 'and by eleven or so when I'd tidied everything and locked up, the wind had gone right round to the east. It's there now, and when there's heavy rain like this with an east wind it generally means twenty-four hours of it, like as not.'

'Cheerful, my dear, aren't you!' laughed Mrs Wildgoose, 'but I'm afraid you're right all the same; there's not a hen put so much as a claw out of doors – t' wasn't for the ducks splashing about out there like as if they were in Heaven, I'd think a fox had got in during the night and had the lot! Well, there's plenty wants doing indoors,' she went on, 'and there's a service here this morning; you remember' – she turned to Kate – 'how we "share" our clergyman, Mr Wilson, turn and turn about with the next parish? Yes – of course – so if you like to come along with me we'll go. Fine chance to christen that lovely new mac and gum-boots of yours!'

'But, Mrs Wildgoose!' protested Kate. 'I can't go to *church* in *gum-boots*!'

'Whyever not!' exclaimed Mrs Wildgoose. 'It's fair teeming down, and it's not much short of ten minutes' walk to the church. You can get very wet in that time, and you don't want to sit with damp feet and catch a cold either. I'm wearing my galoshes if that's any comfort to you!'

It was, and thus reassured Kate presently wriggled into 'Mrs Beasley's present' on top of her school blazer; put on her precious school hat, and finally the shiny new gum-boots, and descended to the sitting-room. A few minutes later, she and Mrs Wildgoose – each under a large umbrella – leaving Mr Wildgoose to mind the Inn, said 'good-bye', and set forth.

'Teeming' was certainly the word for the rain. It came down very much, as Mrs Wildgoose said, 'as if it meant it'. And almost as much splashed up from the ground. Little rivulets of water ran in every direction over the road and outside Mrs Megson's shop the laburnum tree dripped in a very melancholy manner. Only the three tall chestnuts stood looking aloof as usual and as if proud that their foliage was so thick that small dry patches still showed beneath them. The cottage gardens that only yesterday had appeared so gay and sprightly, looked sad and dispirited, and the doors and windows of the cottages themselves were firmly shut. There was not a soul in sight. And when Kate and Mrs Wildgoose finally arrived at the church, folded their dripping umbrellas, and divested themselves of their streaming macintoshes, there was not a soul there either.

'I've never mistook the day, surely?' whispered Mrs Wildgoose when they were presently settled in a pew halfway up the aisle. 'No, I can't have . . . I *know* there was no morning service last Sunday . . .'

'P'raps it's the rain?' Kate whispered back. And she felt rather apprehensive. If nobody else came would there *be* a service, and if so would Mrs Wildgoose and herself sing hymns and everything just alone with the vicar?

''Twouldn't surprise me,' said Mrs Wildgoose in reply to her question. 'Though there'll be some who always come. It's a shame when people who can turn out don't, I always think – not fair on the vicar. After all, he's got to – even if it snows ink. Why, *whatever's* the matter?' For Kate was suddenly overcome with a fit of the giggles at this seemingly harmless expression.

'What! Never heard that before!' said Mrs Wildgoose. 'Hush! there *is* Mr Wilson,' as the vicar, still in his cassock, emerged from a side door. 'We're early, that's what it is – it's that clock of ours . . . For goodness' sake!' And she looked apprehensively at Kate. 'Stop, *do*!'

But of course, as everyone knows, who has ever tried to stop in similar circumstances, stopping is the last thing one can achieve. Kate's efforts ended in such a fit of coughing and choking that Mrs Wildgoose began to be

quite alarmed, while the vicar, who had been arranging some books in the choir-stalls, came down the aisle and stopped beside their pew.

'Good of you to turn out,' he said in what was intended for a low voice but audible over the whole church. 'That child's got a very nasty cough. Give her some of these,' and he handed a small tin to Mrs Wildgoose, 'they're rather nice. I keep a different brand for the choir-boys,' he added smiling, 'otherwise they would all be coughing,' and he went on into the vestry.

'Take one,' said Mrs Wildgoose opening the tin and handing it to Kate. But Kate, still choking, shook her head. '*Take* one,' repeated Mrs Wildgoose firmly, 'or you'll have to go out!' That was impossible. Reluctantly Kate obeyed. The lozenge was blackcurrant, sugary on top, and delicious-tasting. She swallowed it and took another, and another. 'Don't *swallow* them, *suck* them!' commanded Mrs Wildgoose, fearful lest the whole tinful might vanish, and Kate obediently sucked, thankful that both giggles and choking seemed abating, but feeling faintly guilty. Had Mr Wilson known the real cause of her affection might he not have produced the brand specially reserved for choir-boys? . . .

The church was filling up a little now, and Kate recognized several friends, Mr Shakespeare, very solemn and clasping the offertory bag; Miss Midgley from the post office, wet and somewhat flustered; Mr Digweed the farmer but no Mrs Digweed, or Kate's special friends, the two Miss Digweeds; Mrs Smallpiece with a most elegant grown-up daughter but minus the objectionable Angela; Mrs Megson's niece in a hat like a flower garden and a very imposing macintosh which, on being removed, revealed an even more imposing silk dress; and finally Miss Alison in a very *un*imposing macintosh that looked as if it had experienced many a downpour, and a plain felt hat. With her was an elderly lady, similarly attired who, Kate thought, bore a slight resemblance to the redoubtable Mrs Ayredale-Eskdale. Of Lord Glenheather there was no sign at all. Kate was disappointed; she had taken for granted he would be there and, secretly, she had even hoped might be wearing a kilt. But her disappointment was short-lived, for – there he was – not in a kilt, however, but a grey flannel suit, walking up the aisle with the vicar. They stopped at the reading desk. The visitor was evidently going to read the lessons and the vicar in his loud low voice was giving some instructions.

'No – you leave out verses *six* to *ten*,' Kate heard him say, 'and stop at verse *twenty-three* with "here endeth", etc. How do you pronounce that?' – in answer to some query. 'Optional, my dear fellow – optional. I'm immensely obliged to you,' he continued, 'it'll rest my voice. I had a parish meeting last night, and I've two more services after this – excluding a christening and a Sunday-school class, and tomorrow is the Ruridecanal Conference . . .'

Lord Glenheather read awfully well, Kate decided, and it was somehow consoling to know even he was uncertain how to pronounce a word. And although she regretted the absence of a kilt, she thought he looked very nice standing up there in his grey suit and stripy silk tie. She wondered how old he was . . . it was always difficult to tell with grown-ups . . . about forty, she decided . . . And . . . and he wasn't a bit like Miss Alison – even if he *was* a cousin – as Mrs Wildgoose had said . . . It was hard to keep her mind on the service, but she made efforts, particularly in singing the hymns – very nicely, too, thought Mrs Wildgoose. And she listened intently to Mr Wilson's very short sermon. He rarely exceeded five minutes, and spoke briefly and to the point. Today he was even briefer than usual. 'Envy, hatred, and malice, and all uncharitableness', was the subject, 'shortcomings', as he expressed it, common to all – young and old, child or adult, and alas, all too frequently encountered. During the next ten days – as he need hardly remind his parishioners – they would be preparing for two of the chief social events of the year in the village. Before, during – and after these, he would ask them, one and all, to think very earnestly about these lamentable – yes, lamentable failings . . . And before Kate, busy visualizing a truly seraphic scene in which she, Angela Smallpiece, and Johnny Sears were judged equal in every competition at The Flower Show, but allowed Johnny Sears all the prizes because he was the youngest, realized it, the sermon was over and the last hymn being announced. Old Mr Shakespeare emerged from his pew with the offertory bag, and everyone fumbled for their collection money.

The rain was coming down as heavily as ever when, the service over, most of the congregation stood crowded together in the porch looking hopefully for a break in the grey, water-laden sky. Mr Digweed, appealed to as a weather expert, quickly dispelled any optimism, however, by asserting cheerfully it would 'keep on steady for some time now', and turning the brim of his hat down, and his coat collar up, departed, splashing happily homewards between the tombstones.

'All very well for him,' complained Mrs Edwards, 'with his leather leggings and all! My word! It certainly knows how to rain in these parts!'

This remark was received in silence. However much you might deplore the local climate yourself, it was unseemly criticism if its shortcomings should be voiced by a stranger.

'It's raining over most of England, according to the wireless this morning,' said Miss Midgley rather tartly after a moment or two, 'and what's a drop of rain anyway?' And she prepared to open her umbrella and follow Mr Digweed's example.

'Oh, Miss Midgley!' called Miss Alison, now appearing with the lady Kate had remarked resembled Mrs Ayredale-Eskdale, 'I was just going to offer you a lift – the car will be here in a minute – and you, Mrs Wildgoose, and Kate, and the lady who's helping Mrs Megson – I'm afraid I don't know her name? That's all from the upper part of the village, isn't it?' she added looking round. 'And if you don't mind waiting, Mrs Smallpiece, we can come back for you and your daughter – and you too, Mr Shakespeare – though I'm afraid we *can't* take you down Pond Passage!'

'Thank you kindly, miss,' replied Mr Shakespeare, 'but I'll walk it. The wet don't worry an old tough like me. And I've Mr Milton's umber-ella as I've borrowed.' And he produced the largest specimen of its kind Kate had ever seen, with a knobbly, yellow-varnished handle as thick as a broomstick, and stepping out of the porch, he opened it and went stumping down the streaming cobbled path beneath its voluminous shelter, just as Lord Glenheather arrived with the car.

It was a tight squash inside. The lady whom Miss Alison addressed as 'Aunt Mary' sat in front with Lord Glenheather, and Miss Alison herself, with Kate on her knees, Mrs Wildgoose, Miss Midgley, and Mrs Edwards all tightly wedged together in the back. But in less than three minutes they were at the post office; Miss Midgley levered herself out and with a hasty 'thank you very much

indeed', bolted inside. But the departure of Mrs Edwards was both dignified and prolonged. As the car drew up outside Mrs Megson's shop, without so much as a word to Miss Alison, she slowly emerged, and opening her umbrella, stood offering not only profuse thanks to Lord Glenheather but insisting on shaking his hand through the half-opened window of the driving seat.

'What a day!' exclaimed Miss Alison as the farewells finally over, they drove on again and she and Mrs Wildgoose and Kate settled themselves more comfortably. 'That's a lovely mac you've got, Kate – and what looks to me like *brand*-new gum-boots! Really, we should have let you walk – you look prepared for anything in the way of weather! How about coming to tea this afternoon – it's just the day for a nice long talk! You'd like to? Very well then, about three o'clock. No,' in reply to Mrs Wildgoose as the car drew up at the Inn door, 'no, thank you very much, we won't come in – we've to go back for Mrs Smallpiece and her daughter for one thing, and – what's that, Kate? Will Jaeger be there this afternoon? Oh very *much* there, I'm sure! Most probably sitting in the best chair if he can get it!'

Long before ten minutes to three – the hour decreed by Mrs Wildgoose as time enough to start for The Priory – Kate was ready, and punctually to the minute, carrying a large umbrella to protect her precious hat, she set forth. The pocket of Mrs Beasley's present bulged with a school-book of poems – about which she wished to consult Miss Alison, and her autograph book; the other with her sandals, for, as Mrs Wildgoose had rightly said, she could not sit dripping on to the grand Priory carpets in gum-boots all the afternoon.

The rain was coming down as steadily as ever. The gravel sweep outside the Inn was a miniature lake, and the Ayredale-Eskdale's long, elm-bordered drive – the drive whose use as a short cut between Upper and Lower Cassington, granted to the inhabitants by her late husband, seemed to cause so much annoyance to Mrs Ayredale-Eskdale – a sea of puddles. Mrs Beasley, thought Kate, would be pleased to know the good use to which her present – the gum-boots in particular – was being put. It was lovely to slosh right through the puddles and know your feet were dry as a bone, something which had most certainly never been the case when wearing Lily Rose's 'cast-offs'! As she approached the bridge near the turning to the house she was reminded of her first and somewhat alarming encounter with its owner, and although in the end all had turned out well – and included above all things the gift of Cuckoo-Coo – she couldn't help feeling glad the formidable Mrs Ayredale-Eskdale was away from home.

As she neared the house itself, Kate saw that the big front door was standing open. Shutting up her dripping umbrella and shaking rivulets of water from her macintosh, she stood for a moment in the high, pillared porch, gazing in at the big hall; the wide staircase leading away out of sight on one side; at the huge pictures in heavily carved and gilded frames; and at the big glass chandelier which hung from the ceiling, its myriad crystal drops shining and twinkling as they caught the light from the open door. And all at once she felt very small – and horribly shy! She was just trying to summon up courage to pull the curious-looking bell handle when there was the sound of barking, a door opened, and out came Miss Alison preceded, not, to Kate's disappointment, by Jaeger, but by two other dogs. A fat black spaniel, rather grey about the muzzle, and a sprightly wire-haired terrier. 'Sheila and Twiggy,' said Miss Alison introducing them; Jaeger, she explained as she led Kate to a small cloakroom off the hall to take off her macintosh and gum-boots, was in the kitchen 'drying', Lord Glenheather having taken him for a walk on their return from church. 'He'd been shut up in the stables while we were out,' she went on, 'because we never know what he may do; and he gets *so* rampageous if he doesn't get exercise! I expect he'll be dry soon – we'll fetch him in after tea. But first you and I will have a nice talk in peace. My aunt is having a rest on her bed, and Lord Glenheather is writing letters so we'll have the drawing-room all to ourselves. How sensible of you to bring your sandals,' she continued, as Kate produced these from her pocket, 'and is that *the* autograph book! What is the other one? Poems! I didn't know you liked poetry – though I'm very glad if you do!'

'I'm only *beginning* to,' said Kate truthfully, as she followed Miss Alison across the hall to the drawing-room. Coo! what a huge room! She stood in the doorway almost afraid to venture farther. It was as big as the biggest classroom at school! It . . . it was like a museum – except that there were no notices, and . . . and ropes round things . . . It . . . it was rather like the sort of the room you sometimes saw in a film . . . Mrs Ayredale-Eskdale must be a *millionaire*! . . . On one side, windows framed in soft green velvet curtains opened to the garden, between them glass-fronted cabinets filled with china. From the ceiling hung another chandelier – even bigger and more twinkling than the one in the hall. On the floor was a grey carpet, thick, and soft as fur; and there were more huge pictures! One, over the big fireplace at the end of the room, of Mrs Ayredale-Eskdale, holding a fan and looking her very haughtiest; and on the wall opposite the windows, another, a little girl with big grey eyes and very yellow hair sitting in a swing, holding a doll.

'That,' said Miss Alison, following Kate's gaze, 'if you can believe it, is *me*! But come and sit down, I want to hear all about Peg and Jo, and Mum and Dad and the others – and of course about Cuckoo-Coo! And what you meant by getting measles almost the *minute* you got back from a country holiday!' And she drew up two big arm-chairs covered in cool-looking pale green linen. For a few minutes Kate was so awed by her surroundings that she found it hard to say more than plain 'yes' and 'no' to all Miss Alison's kind inquiries, and it was only when she came to telling about the progress of Cuckoo-Coo – his growth, his wickedness, and his endearing ways, that she lost her shyness. Very soon she was chattering away as happily as if she was in the crowded little kitchen at One End Street.

The all-important question of what she should recite at The Concert was carefully discussed.

'I can't recite a bit well, Miss Alison,' she insisted, 'honest I can't. And I know I'll be simply *terrified* in front of all those people! But I've promised Mr Wildgoose I would so I'll have to. I know heaps of poems by heart,' she went on, 'but they're nearly all rather long. Mr Wildgoose gave me a book called Edward Lear's *Nonsense Rhymes*. I like them, and they're funny, but I think they're rather *babyish*. I'd rather recite a proper grown-up poem – like these.' And she jumped up and handed Miss Alison the book she had brought with her. 'That one,' she knelt down beside her hostess and pointed to the page, '"The Scholar Gypsy" – I think it's lovely! Bits of it make me go all goosey down my spine! Does poetry ever do that to you, Miss Alison?'

'Yes, it does – sometimes,' replied Miss Alison smiling, 'and I love that poem, too. But – do you really know it all by heart? Anyway,' as Kate nodded vigorously, 'I'm afraid it would be much, much too long for The Concert. What are the others you've thought of?'

'There were seven altogether,' said Kate, and she began ticking them off on her fingers, '"The Scholar Gypsy", "The Lady of Shalott" – that's awfully long too. "The Roman Centurion's Song". Oh, Miss Alison, I *almost* cry when I read that – I feel so sorry for him! And I love that bit about "the clanging arch of steel grey March". I don't know a bit what it means but it makes me think of hail and snow, and simply *frightful* storms . . . Then there's "Nod" by Walter de la Mare. I *love* that, and it's short, but it's rather sad too, though it's a different sort of sad somehow from the "Centurion" . . . Then the one about "What is this life if full of care we have no time to stand and stare". I like that ever so, but they were just awful at home when I was learning it, 'cos you see Mum's always saying I'm standing and staring – so I'm sort of shy about it now – the poem, I mean. How many is that – five? Oh yes, two more – and they *are* short; but one's about the war – dying and all that, and I don't feel that would do for a concert?

It's queer, isn't it,' and she sat back on her heels and looked up at Miss Alison, 'how most poems seem to be about sad things? The last is sad too, and,' Kate slightly lowered her voice and spoke very slowly, 'I'm afraid, Miss Alison, I've never been able to say it without going all weepy, so I don't feel I could recite it at The Concert because it would be just too awful if I was weepy there! It's a pity though,' she added, 'because it's a country sort of poem – at least it's about sheep – and I should think Cassington people would like that? It's called "A Child's Pet" and it's by Mr W. H. Davies – shall I find it for you?'

'I think I've read it a long time ago,' replied Miss Alison, 'but I've forgotten it. Suppose you recite it – or rather *say* it – sit there on the floor where you are.'

Kate obeyed. She looked up shyly at Miss Alison for a moment, hesitated a little, then she began. Before the end of the second verse she had forgotten she was sitting on Mrs Ayredale-Eskdale's beautiful grey carpet in a strange and very unfamiliar room; forgotten everything but the pet lamb crossing the stormy Atlantic with its poor seasick companions.

When she had finished, she sniffed hard – determined not to be 'weepy' as she called it, but it was not entirely successful. And – oh where was her handkerchief! . . . A frantic search ensued . . . Not in her knicker-legs . . . not in either sleeve . . . She went over to the chair in which she had been sitting . . . No . . .

'Perhaps,' said Miss Alison, 'it's down the side of the chair? Scoop round with your hand!'

Sniffing still, Kate obediently scooped. Her fingers encountered no handkerchief, however, but a cold, round object. She drew it up. *A shilling!* In her astonishment she almost stopped sniffing, she also remembered the whereabouts of her handkerchief . . . Left in her blazer pocket in the cloakroom! . . .

When she returned from retrieving it, Lord Glenheather was in the drawing-room. 'Hullo!' he said. 'I hear you've just found a shilling down the side of a chair! As a thrifty Scot of course that appeals enormously to me! How about a treasure-hunt, Alison – scooping down all the arm-chairs in the house?' he suggested, and he smiled at Kate, lifting one eyebrow to see how she felt about it. Kate was ready to begin that moment, but Miss Alison said she was afraid 'no', not today anyway. It was just tea-time and Emily's evening out and they must not to be late. And almost before she had finished speaking, the door opened quietly and there *was* Emily – whom Kate recognized at once as the parlourmaid who had been so kind when Peg had disgraced herself at Mrs Ayredale-Eskdale's hay-party.

'Tea is ready, miss,' she said, and she smiled at Kate before closing the door as quietly as she had opened it.

'We're having tea in the little library,' said Miss Alison to Lord Glenheather. 'Aunt Mary is not coming down and I thought we three would prefer a good solid table to balancing cups and saucers on our knees here.' To Kate the little library seemed anything but little, and she could only suppose it was in comparison with some other apartment or perhaps with the vast room through which they entered it where there was a long dining-table, so polished that it shone like a mirror, with a big bowl of flowers in the middle, and still more large pictures on the walls.

'Your mother,' said Lord Glenheather to Kate when they were presently settled round the 'good solid table' enjoying tea and hot buttered scones with what Miss Alison called 'extra special apricot jam', 'your mother gave me the best cup of tea I'd had since I left home. Though cup,' he added on reflection, 'is not quite true, for I had three – which shows just how good it was!' Kate blushed with pleasure at this tribute to Mrs Ruggles, and the progress of the piglets left with Mr Ruggles duly reported on, and her interest in farming explained by Miss Alison, she thrilled with delight when Lord Glenheather spoke of his own pigs and gravely discussed the feeding, habits, and the general upbringing of little pigs, 'just', as she told Mrs Wildgoose that evening, 'as if I was *properly* grown up.'

The scones and the apricot jam having been followed by a Dundee cake, '*covered* with almonds' as Kate reported later, 'and chocolate biscuits – specially for me – *wasn't* that kind, Mrs Wildgoose?' Miss Alison suggested Kate might like to see the white cats?

'Oh yes, Miss Alison – and oh, *please* – Jaeger too!'

'Poor old Jaeger! I'd almost forgotten him!' said Lord Glenheather. 'He must be bone-dry by now. I'll go and get him. By the way,' he added, turning to Kate as he got up, 'Jaeger comes from near your home. He was given to me by Mrs Mellish – the wife of your Member of

Parliment – I was staying at their house when I came over to see your father about the pigs. Mrs Mellish breeds bull-terriers for showing, and Jaeger for some reason turned out too pale. "Just the colour of my old jaeger dressing-gown," I said, and because of that and because he seemed to take a violent fancy to me, she insisted, alas, on giving him to me. I say "alas" because I'm afraid Jaeger and I will have to part company if his behaviour doesn't improve. Mind he doesn't knock you over when he comes in,' he added as he opened a door on the far side of the room. 'He's as strong as a young lion – and about as obedient!'

'I'm afraid,' said Kate sorrowfully when the door had closed, 'Lord Glenheather doesn't like Jaeger very much?'

'He does really,' replied Miss Alison, 'it's just that the poor dog has never been properly trained – he simply doesn't know what obedience *is*! And he's not a pup – he's nearly eighteen months old! Mind now! Here he comes!' . . .

Jaeger came in with a rush and a bound; flung himself first at Miss Alison, licking her hands in wild exuberance and uttering little cries of delight, and then at Kate, nearly knocking her over as Lord Glenheather had foreseen. Then suddenly he wheeled about, leapt on to a chair, grabbed a scone from a plate which happened to be near the edge of the table and leapt down again, catching a foot in the tablecloth and nearly dragging a large silver teapot and hot-water jug after him. He then gulped down the scone, and stood wagging his tail wildly, wrinkling up his mouth, and looking up at them each in turn, so obviously laughing that they all had to laugh too!

'Oh, Colin! – he's never done that before!' exclaimed Miss Alison, who had just managed to save the teapot and hot-water jug. 'I mean take food off the table!'

'I'm afraid he's showing off for the visitor,' said Lord Glenheather a little grimly. 'How *is* he to be controlled! He's not coming near the cats anyway – that's certain! Now where can I leave him . . . not in the drawing-room – he'll knock something over or chew up a cushion . . . I know. I'll tether him to that oak settle in the hall – it must weigh half a ton if it weighs an ounce. He can't pull it over, and there's absolutely nothing he can eat!'

'Oh *poor* Jaeger. It does seem a shame!' exclaimed Kate when some minutes later Lord Glenheather having suited the action to the word, they set off with the other two dogs leaving Jaeger securely tethered with a stout length of rope to the settle, whimpering miserably.

'Don't mind him,' said Lord Glenheather as they went through the big front door into the still pouring rain. 'He's had a walk today – of a sort – the others haven't had even that – and it's only for a little while. I'll take these two a short run-round, Alison,' he went on, 'and meet you in the stables in ten minutes – you'll have had enough of the cats by then, won't you?' Miss Alison thought they would, but when Lord Glenheather returned, dripping in every direction, with Twiggy and Sheila looking like half-drowned dogs but apparently perfectly happy, Kate could hardly tear herself away. She stood lost in wonder and admiration at the perfection of Cuckoo-Coo's parents, larger, white, more beautiful even than

Thomas at the post office – which was saying a good deal! The possibility of Cuckoo-Coo – though considerably larger than his remaining brother and sisters – which it was gratifying to see – ever attaining to such elegance, seemed very remote! But at last fond farewells were said and they splashed their way back across the sodden, rain-swept lawns to the house. In the hall, Jaeger, still attached by his rope to the settle, was lying quietly beside it. He thumped a welcome on the floor with his tail as they came in but he did not get up. He held something between his paws and was chewing happily, uttering occasional little growling noises, rather like a lion at the Zoo at feeding-time.

'Jaeger!' said Lord Glenheather sharply and, going to investigate, 'What have you got there?' Jaeger looked up. His three-cornered eyes had a very guilty expression; something dangled from his mouth – something that looked suspiciously like part of a shoe – and *was*! The remains of one of Kate's sandals!

Much as she loved and admired Jaeger, Kate was really upset! Her sandals – the only shoes she possessed except her very best Sunday ones – and her gum-boots! Newly soled too before she came away! Even with the shilling she had just found (and which Miss Alison had insisted on her keeping), and the money Dad had given her, she wouldn't have nearly enough to buy another pair! . . . And however had Jaeger got hold of them – or rather one – for the other was still intact?

'The cloakroom door must have been ajar,' said Lord Glenheather when he presently returned from shutting Jaeger in the stables as 'the only safe place', 'and the rope was *just* long enough for him to nose it open and grab something.' He was most dreadfully sorry, he went on – he, himself he meant – Jaeger of course was never sorry about anything! She was not to worry another minute. Tomorrow he had to go into Aliesford; he would call for her at The Dew Drop Inn at nine-thirty sharp – if that was not too early – and they would go straight to a shoe shop and find another pair of sandals.

That was very kind, but did Lord Glenheather mean to pay for them, Kate wondered when at last she splashed her way homewards through the still driving rain? They cost five and elevenpence halfpenny – she remembered the amount only too well because she had had to wait so long for Mum to save it up . . . Supposing he didn't . . . What should she do? . . . Perhaps Mrs Wildgoose would lend her the money and she could somehow earn enough to pay her back . . . These worrying thoughts accompanied her almost the whole way home and it was only when she was nearing The Dew Drop Inn she remembered she had left both her books behind, and that the question of what to recite was still undecided.

'And all that Jaeger dog's fault!' exclaimed Mrs Wildgoose when she had been told the sad tale. 'Yes, of course I'll lend you the money, my dear, though I'm sure you'll find his lordship will want to pay for them himself seeing as how it was his dog as did the damage! What's that! You can't help loving it all the same! Well that's more than I'd feel like doing if it had eaten my shoes, I can tell you!'

Long before nine-thirty next morning Kate was ready. She wore her Sunday frock and shoes, school blazer and hat, Mrs Wildgoose for once being in agreement that the occasion warranted such attire. Lord Glenheather arrived on the stroke of nine-thirty. The sun was shining as if it had never stopped, the glistening wet on the roadside grass, the still dripping hedges and trees, and the large puddles in the road the only reminder of yesterday's downpour. His car, as he had told Lily Rose,* could not truthfully be described as 'posh', but to Kate who had hardly ever been in a private one, it seemed the essence of comfort and luxury, and although at first she felt a little shy all alone with him, she was soon leaning back in her seat in great contentment enjoying the way they sped past pedestrians, plodding country carts, cyclists, and even the local bus and some other cars. The eight long miles to Aliesford seemed no distance at all. Very soon they were driving through its narrow crooked streets and had drawn up outside a shoe shop in the little market square. Here she had quickly found her five and elevenpence halfpenny sandals, and though Lord Glenheather protested that they couldn't possibly be leather at that price – and even when the salesman assured him that they were – 'a special line, sir – very hard-wearing – we sell hundreds of pairs' – still

* *Further Adventures of the Family from One End Street.*

looked unconvinced, she had resolutely declined any others. 'Then let us have *two* pairs!' said Lord Glenheather. And before Kate could do more than open her mouth with astonishment, he had given the order and handed a one-pound note to the salesman. 'And the change is yours,' he said, handing it to her as they presently emerged from the shop each carrying a very neat brown-paper parcel, 'with my apologies for Jaeger's disgraceful behaviour!'

'I always said he was a very kind gentleman,' said Mrs Wildgoose when half an hour or so later Kate walked into the kitchen and proudly displayed her two parcels.

'It looks to me,' said Mr Wildgoose who happened to be passing, 'as if what the missis calls "that Jaeger dog" had done you a good turn – two pairs of new sandals for one pair of old ones! Three cheers for all bull-terriers!'

'Go along with you!' said Mrs Wildgoose, but Kate felt rather inclined to agree!

5. The Flower Show

Part One

Never, surely, did days go by so quickly as they did at The Dew Drop Inn! Waking rather earlier than usual one morning, Kate realized with a shock she had been there a whole week. In four days – no less, *three*, because you couldn't really count the day itself, it would be The Flower Show! Only three more days, and though she had hardly wasted a minute, still so much to be done! The mustard-and-cress was what Mr Wildgoose called 'coming along nicely'; the cress beautifully thick, green and even; the dark mustard well away to a good start. She had made, with a little assistance from Mrs Wildgoose, some curious flat-looking objects politely called rock cakes, and some rather watery jam; and she was going to have another try at both – more or less on her own – before making the final 'unaided' attempt. Infected with Elsie's enthusiasm for the art, she had also made some dolls' furniture – from match-boxes; a chest of drawers, a writing-table, and a bed, and herself had the brilliant idea of using toothpaste tops for 'legs' – with most effective results! More than three-quarters of her essay was written (although so untidily she was afraid she would have to copy it all out again), and between them, she and Mrs Wildgoose had thought out a lovely idea for a table decoration. As for wildflowers, she had learnt the names of dozens – *and* found the places where they grew, but, and it was a very big 'but', they all had to be picked, named, and 'arranged'; wildflowers did not last like garden ones; some drooped – even died – before one could get them home. The actual picking could not be earlier than the day before the Show – some the very morning itself, and this applied particularly to the water-lilies Mr Shakespeare had promised her and which were to be such a very special feature in both her collection and her table decoration. There were no others in the district, he had told her – not even at The Priory; Johnny Sears, or

anybody else, would be 'hard put to it' to find any; and that mindful of last year's disaster, he was keeping a sharp eye on his little pond . . . But should it rain or as seemed more likely at present, become terrifically hot – what then? Ever since the downpour on Sunday the weather had been gloriously fine and sunny, each day warmer than the one before. 'Too good to last' seemed the general opinion; and there was concern about fruit becoming over-ripe or flowers past their best. Jumping out of bed and leaning her elbows on the narrow little window-sill, Kate looked out anxiously at the new day. In a sky the faint, pale blue of early morning, the sun was shining brightly; the creamy-pink roses and the honeysuckle sprays round the window glistened with dew, and swallows were already on the wing busily fly-hunting for their young. Everything seemed to promise another fine, hot day. She stood for a little breathing in the intoxicating sweetness of the air. A roving bumble bee hummed by, and a rather-worse-for-wear tabby cat belonging to the orangy-coloured cottages opposite came softly pad-padding up the road on its return from some mysterious nocturnal expedition. Presently a door in one of the cottages opened and a farm labourer came out, whistling cheerfully, to be joined a few seconds later by Willie Sims, one of Mr Digweed's men and a great favourite with Kate, being not only a mine of information on all country matters, but an apparently tireless answerer of questions thereon. Casting a sweeping glance skywards after the manner of all countrymen, he jerked his thumb over his shoulder as he and his companion moved off together. What was he saying? . . . Kate strained her ears to hear . . . Willie Sims was saying that he didn't 'much care for the look of they clouds a-comin' over the 'ill,' and looking in the direction he indicated – the direction always referred to by Mr Wildgoose as 'the rainy quarter' – she was concerned to see the tips of large billowing white shapes rearing up like giant icebergs on the horizon. She stood watching them apprehensively for some time but they moved very slowly – almost imperceptibly, and after a little while there seemed no movement at all. By breakfast time, some two hours later, they had grown no longer, and there they remained, almost stationary, throughout the day. Mr Wildgoose, asked for his opinion, was non-committal, while Mr Digweed, encountered later in the morning and appealed to as a farmer and therefore an expert on all weather conditions, only smiled, shrugged his shoulders, and said the next few days were likely to be what he called 'anybody's guess'. Only at Pond Cottages, visited later in the day, definite views seemed to prevail and these could hardly be called comforting, Mr Shakespeare apparently liking 'they clouds away over the hill' even less than Willie Sims; while Mr Milton, when Kate eventually succeeded in making him hear, pointed jerkily skywards, and looking like some ancient seer with his long white beard, announced prophetically, 'There's Tempest about, that's what there is – Tempest; and Tempest's what 'twill end in. You mark my words.' And as if the better to emphasize these, retreated abruptly into his cottage, shutting the door firmly beind him. 'Tempest', being interpreted, apparently meant thunder, and it was not encouraging on returning to The Dew Drop Inn, to learn that heavy storms in other parts of the country had just been reported on the wireless. There was nothing for it, said Mrs Wildgoose, who was busily polishing spoons and forks, except to hope for the best. But she sighed a little, and Kate saw her glance through the window at two little standard rose trees where slender pale pink and deep red buds were promising to open in unblemished beauty exactly in time for the Show. The little trees had been a wedding anniversary present from Mr Wildgoose; Mrs Wildgoose cherished them greatly and had watched over them with love and tenderness for several years now. Never had they done so well; two more fine, sunny days and they'd be just perfect . . . glossy-leaved, long-stemmed, lovely . . . not a breath of blight or suspicion of greenfly . . . Arranged in the big silver bowl won many years ago by Mr Wildgoose's father at the old 'Cat and Cavey' show at Ailesford, they'd be a picture – good as anything Mr Smallpiece grew for The Priory – almost, she dared to think, as good as anything he grew for himself . . . Heavy rain, though, or a blustery wind . . . Well, no use to worry. There were worse things in life than Show flowers spoilt . . . But she sighed again as she turned away from the window for she had set her heart on 'Charlie's roses', as she called them, winning a prize – even if it were only a third.

'And where else have you been since tea?' she continued, returning to her polishing. 'You've never been all the time at Pond Cottages surely!'

'Yes,' said Kate, 'I have. Making Mr Milton hear takes up a lot of time. Then I simply *had* to look at the lilies, and find out when Mr Shakespeare wanted me to come for them. I'm to go there after breakfast on Monday and take a bucket so as they needn't be out of water a minute! Oh I do think they're lovely, Mrs Wildgoose,' she went on. 'They're not like any other flowers, somehow. They seem almost not real . . . like something out of a fairy tale, or, or –' she hesitated a moment – 'or even Heaven,' she added softly.

'You love flowers, don't you, Kate?' said Mrs Wildgoose pausing for a moment in her polishing and looking fondly up at her.

'Yes, I do, Mrs Wildgoose – but I love *thousands* of other things too! Oh, coming back I met Miss Alison. She said Lord Glenheather had gone away and taken Jaeger with him but she hopes he'll be back in time for the Show. She was with Mrs Edwards. I don't think somehow they like each other very much, at least I don't think Mrs Edwards likes Miss Alison. They were talking about The Concert and Mrs Edwards said had I learnt my poem yet? *Learnt it*, Mrs Wildgoose! Why I haven't even decided *which* yet, but Miss Alison has promised to help. Anyway I simply must finish the Show things first; there's not much time – even if it doesn't rain a drop! There's the cakes and jam to do tomorrow. I finished my essay when I was resting this afternoon, but it's dreadfully untidy; I'll have to copy it all out again and that will take *ages*! Sunday morning I've promised to help Mr Wildgoose with some of the fruit and vegetables; then there's the "surprise" in the toolshed to show you; and Sunday afternoon I'll be frightfully busy getting my flowers – at least most of them. I'm getting up specially early on Monday morning to pick the ones that don't last well.'

'You'll tire yourself out before the Show starts,' said Mrs Wildgoose, 'that's what you'll do. And what do you mean by "specially early"? – seven o'clock is quite time enough.'

But at that moment there was a knock at the back door and Mrs Wildgoose hurried away. Kate was saved from replying – and fortunately. For what she meant by 'specially early' was as soon as it was light. She had said nothing to anyone but she was sure – as sure as if he had told her, that Johnny Sears meant to steal Mr Shakespeare's lilies. She had a plan all worked out and nothing – rain, hail – not even 'tempest' was going to prevent her from carrying it through.

Saturday and Sunday were busy days, but they remained fine. Stormy weather kept being reported from other parts of the country, the big clouds came and went on the horizon – Willie Sims liking them less and less – but in Upper and Lower Cassington the sun still shone. From every little garden could be heard the rustle of leaves and the occasional crack of a twig as precious fruit was stripped from jealously guarded trees and bushes, and the snip of scissors as cherished flowers were cut. Kate's cakes and jam were made and though the former were slightly burnt, and the latter still a little watery, a decided improvement on her earlier efforts. The new copy of her essay not even the kindest of critics could have commended for tidiness but it was, as she said, tidi*er* than the first. On Sunday morning she helped Mr Wildgoose to wash and trim some of his vegetables, only wishing Mr Ruggles was there to see and admire them. The big, perfectly shaped carrots, the fine beetroots and turnips; the bulging pea pods; the enormous silky-skinned onions! Surely they would all have first prizes – there couldn't be bigger or better ones?

'There'll be many as big – of that I'm sure,' replied Mr Wildgoose, '"better" – ah! that's what I *don't* know! But you remember this – just *size* in vegetables – as in lots of other things for that matter – isn't everything – not by any means – though there'll always be plenty will think so.'

Later in the day Mrs Wildgoose was invited to the tool-shed, and her astonishment and delighted admiration of 'The Dew Drop Inn' in mustard-and-cress left nothing to be desired! The seed had indeed come up beautifully – the cress as even as a newly mown lawn; only here and there the mustard was a little patchy and uncertain. For Kate nothing now remained to be done but the picking and naming of her wildflowers, and as soon as tea was over, she set forth, taking, on Mr Wildgoose's advice, a bucket half filled with water, and hoping fervently she might encounter neither Johnny Sears nor Angela Smallpiece on the expedition. But there was not a sign of them – nor indeed of any other child; only a pair of lovers wandering hand in hand, oblivious of anyone but themselves. She returned an hour or so later with such a variety of flowers, and such fine specimens, that both Mr and Mrs Wildgoose were genuinely impressed, Mr Wildgoose hurrying her to the cellar where he had filled various buckets and tins with water in readiness, in order that the flowers might, as he expressed it, 'breathe easy', and so keep fresh and fragrant till tomorrow. And in the cool dimness, the only light supplied by a rather dusty grating, sitting on an upturned box and surrounded by crate upon crate of beer-bottles, the flower book for reference beside her on the stone floor, Kate wrote out her list. Forty-eight different flowers! Forty-*eight*! Forty-*nine* with Mr Shakespeare's lily! And tomorrow she would add another half dozen at least . . . There would be well over fifty anyway . . . Last year Johnny Sears had had forty-seven.

'Now don't you go getting up at some silly hour,' said Mrs Wildgoose when Kate said goodnight. No answer seemed expected and she made none, thankful no special time had been named. The silliness of the hour, surely, depended on what one thought silly? She hurried happily along the oak-panelled passages where the creeping shadows she disliked so much were beginning to gather, and up the steep stairs to her little room. As to waking in time – that would present no difficulties. She would do as she had done on another early rising occasion;* put her hairbrush in the bed. Every time you turned over, the bristles stuck into you and woke you. It was uncomfortable – but very effective.

* *The Family from One End Street.*

Either the hairbrush was particularly prickly or Kate was unusually restless, but she woke several times during the night. Towards dawn, however, she slept very soundly and then, waking suddenly with a start, and finding the darkness gone, she jumped out of bed, fearful she had overslept after all, and looked anxiously out of the window. It was not really properly light yet; the sky was still tinged with the pink and grey of early dawn, the trees and cottages opposite barely more than vague shapes, but every moment brightness was growing and spreading in the sky. There was no time to waste. Washing could be left till later in the day, she decided as she hurried into her clothes . . . She would need her gum-boots . . . everything would be very wet with dew . . . In less than five minutes she was ready. On the dressing-table lay various lengths of wool and string for tying her flowers together. Collecting these and stowing them safely in her knicker-legs, she gently opened the door, tip-toed across the big room leading from her own to the top landing and then crept cautiously down the first steep flight of stairs. Goodness how they creaked! They *never* did this in the real day-time! But the creaks were nothing to the creaks – almost groanings – in the long passage on the floor below – the passage that led past the room where Mr and Mrs Wildgoose slept. It was darker again down here and everywhere the eeriest of shadows were lurking, only Mrs Wildgoose's little sheep-skin mats showing clearly, like white stepping stones on the dark polished oak floor. Now she was nearing the bedroom door. Creak! Groan! went the boards and Kate paused for a moment, holding her breath, almost afraid to put a foot forward for fear of even louder noise. Suppose Mrs Wildgoose woke? She had often said how lightly she slept! It would be 'back to bed till seven' for a certainty and then the whole plan would be spoilt! . . . Oh! – Kate almost jumped – *whatever* was that! 'That' proved to be snoring – loud and very whole-hearted snoring, not usually the most soothing of sounds, but at the moment nothing could have been more helpful – more welcome. She waited a second, then tip-toed rapidly past the door. The next moment she was at the end of the passage, down a short flight of stairs, down another, longer one, and finally in the passage outside the kitchen where her old straw hat and gum-boots were kept. The hat she decided could be done without, and pulling on the gum-boots and taking a half-filled bucket of water left ready overnight for her flowers, she made for the back door, silently slid back the bolts, and turned the big key; as silently shut the door behind her, and with many a glance over her shoulder at Mr and Mrs Wildgoose's bedroom window, crept as quietly as the crunchy gravel of the sweep outside the Inn permitted, away round the corner and out on to the main road.

The sun was well up now, very low on the horizon but beginning to break through the hedges and the lower boughs of the trees to the roadside grass still grey and wet with dew. The orangy-coloured cottages looked sunk in sleep; not a soul was astir, and only a young rooster, far away, trying out its powers against a more mature rival, broke the stillness. Post Office Lane, when she turned into it, presented much the same picture but the sun was rising higher every moment and the little gardens, most of them denuded now of their best in readiness for the Show, gleamed and glistened in the new day. The air was still and sweet-scented. Over everything an enchantment seemed to linger; as if some magic, some wonder, had been abroad, some happening one was just too late to see – to hear . . . Sniffing delightedly at the scents wafting from the different gardens, Kate walked quickly along. Past the sleeping post office; past Mrs Megson's; past the three chestnut trees, green and aloof, their leaves still cold and damp with dew. As she drew near the church she looked eagerly towards the clock on the tower. Twenty minutes past four! She could not have timed things better, and feeling well satisfied with herself for once, Kate turned happily into Pond Passage.

Towards its end Pond Passage curved sharply; the hedges on either side were thick, reinforced by the brushwood of the elms that grew at intervals throughout its length and which, by mingling their upper branches overhead gave it its tunnel-like character. But the hedge on the left-hand side was not only thick but, towards its end, like another, smaller tunnel. There was a hole in one place if you looked very carefully, and through which if you were thin and agile enough you could wriggle and, once through it, crawl comfortably along to arrive, unseen, but all-seeing, exactly in front of Pond Cottages. All this Kate had discovered when flower-hunting through catching a glimpse of what she took to be a new flower – new at least to her. It had turned out to be a particularly brightly coloured and extra large specimen of Herb Robert – due no doubt to its shady and sheltered position. Any disappointment she had felt about it at the time, however, had been more than compensated for by the discovery of the little leafy tunnel. Not only was it delightful in itself but it was something she felt certain was unknown to Johnny Sears, and something she determined should remain so. Glancing quickly to either side to make certain no one was coming, she wriggled her way through the opening; hid her bucket behind a high tuft of grass and began crawling on her hands and knees, trying hard to subdue the occasional snap of a twig or rustle of last year's leaves. She soon reached the end and knelt peering out at Pond Cottages.

The sun was shining brightly now but complete silence reigned and in both cottages the upstairs window-curtains were still closely drawn – green in Mr Milton's, blue in Mr Shakespeare's. Even from where she knelt, Kate could see most of the fruit had been picked, as arranged, the evening before; otherwise all seemed as usual in the two little gardens, except that over Mr Milton's biggest gooseberry bush – already netted to defy the ravages of any possible bird, was poised what Mr Shakespeare called the 'Umberella'.

But interested as she was in her old friends' fruit bushes, at the moment it was Mr Shakespeare's pond and his lilies that mattered most to Kate. She bent forward to see better . . . *Oh!* . . . Her heart seemed to miss a beat . . . Of all the lovely lilies she had seen three days ago not one remained – not *one*! Only right out in the very middle of the pond were what looked like some small, unopened buds. What had happened last year, had happened again; they had been stolen! Early as she was, she had not been early enough! She was sitting back on her heels, tears smarting in her eyes, with the shock of the discovery, when she heard a slight noise. A blackbird disturbed at its breakfast flew off with a shrill clatter, and looking in the direction of the sound Kate saw a figure climb over the stile at the side of Mr Milton's cottage, and with many backward glances at the curtained windows come stealthily down his shell-bordered path, then turn and walk quickly along the bottom of Mr Shakespeare's garden towards the

pond. It was Johnny Sears. As soon as he came nearer the pond, he suddenly stopped dead; then he walked close up to it and remained for a moment or two stock still. Though she could not see his face, Kate began to think he was as surprised as herself. But – what was he doing now? For Johnny Sears was walking slowly round the pond. Twice round he went, glancing every now and then towards the cottages. Kate followed his glance. Both the green and the blue curtains were still closely drawn . . . *Now* what was he doing? . . . For as if he had suddenly decided something, he turned quickly, walked briskly to the far side of the pond, slid down the bank, and the next minute was *in* it – gum-boots and all, and making, yes, without a doubt, making towards all that remained of the lilies, the buds away out in the middle!

The pond was not deep – not more than two feet at its deepest, Mr Shakespeare had once told Kate, and as Johnny Sears himself doubtless knew too. What he evidently did *not* know – or had not sufficiently bargained for, was the depth of the mud! At each step forward he sank deeper into it. Twice he stretched out a hand to the lilies but each time was just too far off to reach them.

Unwilling to take her eyes off him for a second Kate looked towards the cottages. One of the green window curtains had been pulled back! Johnny Sears took another step, and sank still deeper. The water was almost up to his waist now. He leant forward, stretching out his hand once again in an attempt to reach the flowers. At the same moment the door of Mr Milton's cottage opened and

Mr Milton himself clad in an old-fashioned night shirt and a pair of very dilapidated carpet slippers, brandishing a stick and calling 'Thief! Thief!' came tottering down the path. A few seconds later, and the door of the other cottage opened and out came Mr Shakespeare, slightly more clothed, and about twice as active. Johnny Sears tried to turn towards the bank but by now he was well and truly anchored in the mud. He could go neither backward nor forward.

'So you thought as you'd pinch my lilies, did you, you little varmint!' was Mr Shakespeare's greeting. 'And how do you think you're a-going to get out of my pond – eh? Nice piece of mud you've stuck in there! Perhaps if Mr Milton and I were to let you a-stay in it all day it 'ud learn you a thing or two – like as "honesty's the best policy" for one?'

'I weren't a-going to pinch nothing,' muttered Johnny Sears sullenly. 'I don't want yer old lilies. I – I just fell in – that's all I done.' But this was too much for Kate. Forgetting her hiding place was a secret, she pushed her way round an elm trunk that formed the end of the little tunnel, and appeared somewhat scratched and dishevelled on the grass beside the plank bridge opposite the cottages.

'*Oo!*' she cried, pointing at Johnny Sears. 'You *frightful* story-teller! I *saw* you wade in and try to get them – I *saw* you!'

'You couldn't of!' said Johnny Sears scowling furiously, but with a shade of triumph in his voice. 'You wasn't there!'

'But I *was* . . .' began Kate.

But now Mr Milton had arrived at the pond. 'I seen him!' he cried brandishing his stick, 'from behind my winder curtain I seen him! Straight de-lib-erate to the pond I seen him go! Breakin' the Eighth Commandment, that's what you're a-doing,' he continued addressing Johnny Sears. ''Tis boys like you as ends in the county jail! "Thou shalt not steal." Haven't they learned you that? – tho' t' wouldn't surprise me if they hadn't – not these days. That girl there,' jerking his head towards Kate, 'she'd never heard tell o' Mr Poet Milton.'

By this time Johnny Sears was beginning to look rather pale. The water was cold; it was now up to his waist, and at the slightest movement he sank a little deeper. He did not cry but he looked, thought Kate, regarding him with intense indignation, very much as if he might. Mr Shakespeare stood looking at him severely.

'No need to tell you to stay where you are,' he remarked after a moment or two, 'for 'tis plain you can't do naught else. I'm fetching a rope to pull you out – and 'tis more than you deserve – a lot more – do you hear? You, John,' shouting at Mr Milton, 'you'd best a-get some clothes on or you'll catch a cold. And what'll the young lady think – you in nothing but a night shirt!' Mr Milton apparently heard for once; at all events he retreated towards his cottage shaking his stick at Johnny Sears in a parting gesture, only stopping before going inside to make quite sure the bush under the umbrella had escaped not only the birds' but that gentleman's attentions. Kate and Johnny Sears were left alone.

'Did you take them others?' he inquired after a short silence.

'Others?' repeated Kate, for a moment at a loss to know what he meant. 'Do you mean the other *lilies* – do you mean did *I* take them – *steal* them?'

'Yes,' said Johnny Sears calmly.

'How *dare* you!' cried Kate, scarlet and stammering with anger. 'How – how *dare* you even *think* such a thing!' But before more could be said, Mr Shakespeare appeared with the rope. Without much difficulty Johnny Sears was hauled out.

'And now, home you go – with a flea in your ear!' cried Mr Shakespeare giving him a little shake. 'And if I, or Mr Milton – or anyone else – catches you up to any more monkey tricks, do you know what we're a-doing? We're telling Mr Burden – that's what we're doing. Now empty the mud and the water out of they gum-boots and 'op it – *quick*!'

'Who's Mr Burden, Mr Shakespeare?' asked Kate when Johnny Sears, looking a very draggled little object indeed, and for once subdued, had ''opped it'.

'"The bobby" – the village constable,' replied Mr Shakespeare solemnly. 'There's limits there is. Boys is boys, we all know, and I've not been above pinchin' an apple or so in my time myself, but that boy's gettin' a nuisance. Impertynint too,' he added, coiling up the rope as he spoke. ''Tis his father's fault; he don't do naught to check him so it'll be a kindness if someone does – else, like as Mr Milton said, he'll end in the county jail. But whatever be you doing up so early, my dear –'tis only just gone quarter to five o'clock!'

Omitting any mention of her hiding place, Kate explained all her well meant and carefully prepared plan. 'But, Mr Shakespeare,' she ended, wondering from the beginning he had shown no surprise about the disappearance of the lilies, or indeed expressed any concern about them, 'who *did* take the lilies – who could have done? *Not one left!*' But to her intense surprise Mr Shakespeare only chuckled.

'Aha!' he said. 'I told you once afore – first day we ever met – maybe you've forgot but I ain't; I told you as old birds aren't so easy caught. They lilies were stole last year – and "once bit's twice shy" – a lot of truth in some of them old sayings – as I've a-proved many a time. But 'twas right kind of you, my dear, to try and catch the thief. And anyway –' he chuckled again – 'you seen young Johnny Sears copped fair and square! No, I took precautions,' he rolled out the word with evident satisfaction, 'not a-going to have you left with no lilies, I wasn't. So what did I do? I picked the lot last night; they'm all sitting, happy as kings, in a big tub of water away in the cool of my larder. Safe as – safe as the Bank of England – tho' that's a saying I can't say as I've proved – one way or t'other.'

'Oh Mr Shakespeare!' cried Kate. 'How marvellous! How *clever* of you to think of it, and,' she broke off suddenly and began to giggle, 'oo! won't Johnny Sears be *mad* when he finds out!'

Mr Shakespeare nodded his head. 'He'll have a tidy long walk to find any others,' he said, 'and a hot one; 'tis going to be a real scorching day by the looks of it. When are you a-going to come for them lilies – I'd leave 'em long as possible if I were you.' But Kate had stopped giggling and a look of consternation had come over her face. 'Mr Shakespeare,' she said slowly, 'I've just remembered something. In The Flower Show rules it says I've got to pick every flower in the wildflower competition my own self. I'm afraid a lily won't count if you've picked it! Oh dear, I *did* want one so much; and there isn't time now to look for any others – even if I knew where to look.'

'Dear, dear,' said Mr Shakespeare, 'does it now; does it?' They were silent for a moment or two, and it would have been hard to say which looked the more concerned, Kate or the old man. He stood for a while scratching his head, deep in thought. Then suddenly he brightened up. 'Don't you worry, lass,' he said briskly. 'You see they buds? Day like this they'll be out in an hour or so. You come along round about nine o'clock – don't be later, for we've to get our stuff to The Priory and old men like Mr Milton and me, we're not so spry on our feet as we was. You come along then, and I'll have a plank across the pond. All you've to do is step on it – and pick what you want – yourself.'

A lot of children had got up early that morning in Upper and Lower Cassington, and before six o'clock the fields and hedges were dotted with small figures with – and without – baskets. Kate's bucket came in for a good deal of admiration. Not half a bad idea that wasn't. But the few flowers she had in it were regarded very scornfully. Kate guessed what was being thought. She said nothing, but noticing the many large armfuls already drooping, thought thankfully of her store in the cool cellar of the Inn. Surely *some* of the children had had the sense to get theirs yesterday? Some of them had – as she was cheerfully informed over various garden gates when she presently walked home with her scantily filled bucket. As she came across the sweep in front of the Inn, Mrs Wildgoose was just opening the front door.

'Now what did I say!' she exclaimed, shaking a finger at Kate. 'What did I say? I was down soon after five,' she went on, 'for I've a lot to do today, and there were your gum-boots gone, and the back door *unlocked* and *unbolted*! We might have had the till robbed! An Inn's not like a private house, you know . . . I'm afraid Mr Wildgoose will be very angry when he hears . . . You must do as I tell you, my dear . . .'

Kate felt very abashed. Mrs Wildgoose sounded really annoyed; it was the first time she had ever heard her speak the least bit crossly . . .

Mr Wildgoose *was* very angry. He said it must never, never happen again, and went off down the garden without so much as a look at her flowers. Clutching her bucket, Kate crept miserably down to the cellar, the day shorn of its glory.

Part Two

By breakfast-time, however, all was cheerful again – everything forgotten and forgiven, for, as Mrs Wildgoose said, pink eyes and long faces could not possibly be allowed on Flower Show Day. Kate had said how sorry she was about the door. '*Truly*, Mrs Wildgoose, I never thought it mattered – not like in a town – not once it was light – and people in the house.' She had also explained her reasons for such early rising – and its sequel. The happenings at Pond Cottages caused a good deal of laughter but also some shaking of heads. Johnny Sears, said Mrs Wildgoose, was becoming a thoroughly naughty boy, while Mr Wildgoose, recalling the incident of Mr Plodder's cow* and other exploits of which he had heard, said in *his* opinion there was no 'becoming' about it – he *was* one. But in the excitement and bustle that followed, Johnny Sears and his misdeeds were forgotten, and Kate, happy as she had been miserable an hour before, ran hither and thither helping to collect the various exhibits. What an array there was! They filled the counter and every little table in the bar, overflowing into the sitting-room, and even into the kitchen! Baskets of fruit, trays and boxes of vegetables; eggs and cakes, jam and honey. And there were still Mrs Wildgoose's roses and carnations, and all her own contributions to come. However would they manage to get

* *Further Adventures of the Family from One End Street.*

everything safely to The Priory? The couple of wheelbarrows and little hand-cart standing in readiness outside the side door looked sadly inadequate.

'I'd reckoned on two journeys,' said Mr Wildgoose regarding these pensively. 'Looks as if it'll be more like three – if not four. We'll have to hurry!' and he began to issue instructions. He would take the vegetables first – as much as he could load on the hand-cart. Kate was to 'nip round' to Pond Cottages for her lilies, and have all her own contributions ready by the time he returned. She could then help wheel some of the lighter things in one of the barrows, and Mrs Wildgoose the flowers, bowls, vases 'and all the rest of the paraphernalia required', in the other. Elsie now arrived. She had left her exhibits at The Priory to be 'arranged' later. She was full of excitement and reported that the big tea-tent and the two marquees were already up and the trestle tables being carried in. There were also two smaller tents in process of erection; one for the judges and one, it was rumoured, for a fortune-teller. She hadn't stayed to see more, except to glance at a list of raffles – *ever* so many there were – including one of Mrs Ayredale-Eskdale's white kittens – and to look at a mysterious notice nailed to one of the trees which said 'Take a Ticket for The Dog Daisy'. No one seemed to know what The Dog Daisy was or who had put up the notice.

Whatever could it be? thought Kate as, bucket in hand, she obediently set off to 'nip round' to Pond Cottages. Not that there was much nipping about it. Past The Dew Drop Inn, up Post Office Lane, along Church Street, straggling all over the road, singly, in couples, or in groups, the inhabitants of Upper Cassington were streaming forth; some pushing wheelbarrows or hand-carts; others carrying buckets or baskets; but all laden, and all, 'Young men and maidens, old men and children' – with a fair sprinkling of elderly spinsters, mothers, grannies – and even some great-grannies – chattering like magpies!

Kate hurried shyly past them, receiving many kindly smiles and greetings, and some good-natured jokes about the emptiness of her bucket. She ran the length of Pond Passage to make up time, arriving rather breathless. But Mr Shakespeare had been as good as his word and in less than five minutes she had filled her bucket with water and standing on the plank now stretched across his pond, cut three perfect, newly opened lilies; added the ones picked overnight and was ready to 'nip' home. but Church Street and Post Office Lane were nearly deserted now, but admiring glances were cast at her buckets by the few people she met, and, 'Coo! look at *those*!' from some children emerging from a cottage fell very pleasantly on her ears. At The Dew Drop Inn Mrs Wildgoose had been busy, and Elsie had very kindly carried in the mustard-and-cress – which was heavy – from the tool-shed. Mrs Wildgoose's carnations and roses were picked, and she was busy putting tissue paper over their heads to keep off the sun. 'Though I doubt if they'll need it,' said Mr Wildgoose when he presently returned, hot but cheerful, and immediately set about re-loading his little cart. 'There's a change coming; wouldn't surprise me if it rained before we got this lot safely there!'

The day *was* changing. Away over 'the rainy quarter' the big white clouds were massed again, bigger than ever, and now moving perceptibly. There was an odd, misty look about the sun, and on the sweep outside the Inn, little eddies of dust kept blowing up and as suddenly setting again. By the time they were all ready to start – Mr Wildgoose leading with the hand-cart, Kate and Mrs Wildgoose following, each with a wheelbarrow – there was a low growl of thunder; faint and very far away but, unmistakably, thunder.

In the big marquee everyone was working like a beaver. Conversation was brief and to the point, and people spoke low – sometimes in whispers – almost as if they were in church. Very white and stiffly starched cloths had been spread on the trestle tables which lined the sides of the tent and on which space had been reserved for each competitor. A delicious smell – a mingling of fruit, flowers, and vegetables, warm canvas and newly trodden grass – was wafting about. Kate and Mrs Wildgoose worked hard, and by the time Mr Wildgoose arrived from his third, and he was thankful to say last, trip, everything was ready to be put in its appointed place, and they had had time for a brief glance at other entries.

How beautifully, thought Kate, people had arranged their things! The plates decorated with cool green leaves on which sat gooseberries, and currants, and loganberries; the trays and boxes of vegetables in beds of crisp curly parsley; the collections of onions, their stalks as neatly tied as a child's hair for Sunday-school! and the flowers! Particularly the roses and carnations and the *huge* sweet peas! Could The Dew Drop Inn do as well? No one, surely, *could* do better?

The Dew Drop Inn could, and she watched, fascinated, while Mr and Mrs Wildgoose set to work, beginning with enormous blue cabbages, and ending with Mrs Wildgoose's wedding present roses in their imposing silver bowl.

The children's entries, together with the cakes, jam, honey and eggs, and also the table decorations, were in another, smaller marquee to which Kate and Mrs Wildgoose now made their way. Here the atmosphere was even more tense. At a dozen or more little tables, the ladies of Upper and Lower Cassington, a few older children among them, were arranging flowers in a variety of bowls and vases, standing back every now and then to observe the effect; adding a bud here, snipping off a leaf there . . . Mrs Edwards hovering over a bowl of sweet peas; Miss Midgley feverishly selecting and discarding carnations and sprigs of lavender from a white enamel jug; Angela Smallpiece up to her eyes in roses and gypsophila . . . In other sections everyone was busy inspecting everyone else's contributions, the children crowded together round the handwork and models. Away at the far end of the tent in their respective jam-jars, each entry accompanied by a sheet of exercise paper with a list of names – some twenty entries in all – were the wildflowers. The briefest glance showed Kate that her collection far out-numbered any others, but, as with all the entries, numbers, not names were displayed, so there was no knowing to whom each exhibit belonged – and there were still three empty spaces to be filled. She had just deposited her jars and was arranging the finest water-lily and a large blackberry flower of which she was particularly proud, to their best advantage, when a very little boy came staggering up with a most impressive display, and a moment or two later Angela Smallpiece was beside her. 'Hullo! *You!*' was her greeting as she slapped down two large jars, attractively if rather sparsely filled, and an extremely neatly written list beside them.

'Got a water-lily, I see!' she exclaimed, her eyes darting over Kate's jars. 'And – what's that – a blackberry flower? You can't have that – it's a fruit!'

'It's *not*,' retorted Kate indignantly, 'at least it's not yet – and it's got to be a flower first,' she added in a somewhat confused attempt to refute this rough and unexpected criticism.

'Bet they don't count it,' replied Miss Smallpiece. 'And don't think you're the only one to have a water-lily, because you're not; Johnny Sears'll have one – he said so yesterday. Bet he gets first prize!' and she darted away. But before Kate had time to consider this somewhat depressing information a bell began to ring.

'You must hurry, my dear!' said Mrs Wildgoose coming up to her, 'that's the "warning" bell – another five minutes and they'll ring the "all out". Gracious me, child, you've not unpacked your cakes and jam and toys yet! Quick, give me the basket and I'll see to them. You run and do your table decoration. You're No. 5, I've left the can and scissors all ready.'

Oh what a horrible rush – and people looking on! . . . What luck to have chosen something easy – and quick! In frantic haste. Kate filled a large tin tray with water, seized her precious bucket of lilies, frenziedly snipped the stalks off both flowers and leaves, and put them to float on the water. Then diving down and fumbling in one of her knicker-legs, she produced a tiny tin frog which Mr Wildgoose had found – most inexplicably – in the bar, and put it on the largest lily leaf. Her table decoration was complete! She stepped back to observe the effect, and collided, *crash bang* with Mr Wildgoose hurrying in with the mustard-and-cress boxes left forgotten in the other marquee! At the same moment, clean, tidy, and looking as if butter would not melt in his mouth, Johnny Sears marched by, carrying a large and well-filled jar of wildflowers, followed by a small sister meekly bearing a second.

Mr Wildgoose managed to save one box, but the other slipped and fell with a crash. The box itself was undamaged but some of the mustard forming the letters was shaken out of place, and the beautifully even cress bruised and bent. But there was no time for repining; the 'all out' bell was ringing! There was only time to push back the mustard as neatly as possible, prop the boxes back to back in their appointed place, and hurry out of the tent.

Except for a few large thundery drops the rain expected by Mr Wildgoose had held off, and there had been only two more rumbles of thunder, very faint and distant; but the sun had gradually disappeared and by noon the sky had a sullen, lowering look. During dinner at The Dew Drop Inn it became so dark that for a few minutes it was necessary to turn on the electric light, and shortly before two o'clock, when Mr and Mrs Wildgoose and Kate, all in their best clothes but armed with macintoshes and umbrellas, set forth for The Priory, it looked as if Mr Milton's prophecy of 'tempest' might be fulfilled at any moment. The air was heavy; the big elms that bordered the long drive had a dark, sultry appearance, their leaves hanging limply except

when a little dusty wind sprang up and they stirred uneasily. Away behind The Priory the sky was a menacing blue-black, and The Priory itself looked strange and unreal, its grey stone standing out sharp and clear-cut like cardboard scenery against the dark sky. On the largest of the marquees a Union Jack drooped sadly.

But there was nothing drooping or sad about the company disporting itself on the smooth, newly mown lawns. Black sky or blue it was Flower Show day, and that was enough. Everyone was dressed in his or her best; everyone was gay. In couples, little groups, or family parties they strolled about, talking, laughing and admiring the splendour of 'Mr Smallpiece's' flower beds. Mrs Ayredale-Eskdale, tall and stately, moved graciously among the throng; the vicar, hatless, smiling, and besieged by questioners, doing his best to give information on every conceivable subject; but of Miss Alison Kate caught only the briefest glance, and of Lord Glenheather there was not a sign.

There was no getting near the big marquee where people were crowding and pushing in to see the exhibits. The judges' tent was closed to prying eyes, a pile of red, blue, and yellow cards for 1st, 2nd and 3rd prizes, ready to be placed on the winning exhibits, all that was visible. Close beside it was the big tea-tent, and away behind that, all by itself, was another tent, very small with green stripes. Outside it, a notice in large red letters proclaimed that for sixpence, 'Gypsy Geraldine (patronized by Royalty)' would 'be honoured' to tell your fortune. Inside it was rather dark, and except for a table, a screen, and a couple of chairs, empty. It was attracting a good deal of attention, however, and judging from the conversation, 'Gypsy Geraldine', when she should appear, seemed assured of a warm welcome!

Everywhere people were darting about with raffle tickets in aid of a bewildering assortment of charities. Mr Wildgoose recklessly contributed threepences, sixpences and even shillings, and between them he, Mrs Wildgoose and Kate, guessed the name of a large doll, the weight of a cake, and the number of tomatoes bottled in a jar; held a stake in a set of embroidered table-mats, a pair of glass vases, and an alarum clock. They also competed for the Hidden Treasure – £1 and two 10/-notes buried in one of Mrs Ayredale-Eskdale's rose-beds, first writing their names on neatly painted garden labels provided for the purpose and then pushing these hopefully into the soil beneath the rose bushes. But far and away the most popular of the raffles was one of Mrs Ayredale-Eskdale's white kittens, sleeping peacefully on a blue satin cushion in a box covered with wire netting, and the mysterious 'Dog Daisy' mentioned earlier by Elsie.

Under a large cedar tree stood Willie Sims. He was attired in a neat blue-serge suit, a brown felt hat with a red rose in the brim, and barely recognizable from his ordinary everyday self. In one hand he held a book of tickets, in the other a money box, and he was chanting, like some kind of incantation, '*Take*-a-ticket-for-The-Dog-Daisy! . . . *Take*-a-ticket-for-The-Dog-Daisy! . . . Put sixpence in the box and choose yer own number! . . . *Take*-a-ticket-for-The-Dog-Daisy . . .'

What, everyone was asking, *was* The Dog Daisy? Was it a dog – or wasn't it? And, as somebody inquired, if it *was* a dog – well, *was* it a dog? In other words was it a 'he' or a 'she'? But all Willie Sims, pausing for a moment between his chantings, could be induced to say was, 'It's a Surprise – like!'

'Well whatever it is, Willie, I'm having a ticket,' said Mr Wildgoose; 'three tickets,' he added. 'Come along, missis, choose your number, and you too, Kate.' But Mrs Wildgoose did not seem particularly enthusiastic.

'I believe you're afraid it's a bull-terrier!' said Mr Wildgoose. 'Well, we've never won a raffle yet, but you never know! What about Kate?' But Kate had never even tried. At St Mary's Church Fête at Otwell – her nearest experience to a Flower Show – raffles were not allowed,

and even if they had been she would certainly never have had the necessary threepences – much less sixpences or shillings.

Whatever The Dog Daisy was it was proving an extremely popular raffle. Willie Sims's book of tickets was half gone already! People were crowding round, and among them, rich with the wages of bird-scaring, Kate caught a glimpse of Johnny Sears. A sudden rumble of thunder, still distant but louder than before, distracted everyone's attention for a moment, and it had hardly died away before a bell was being rung and a voice through a megaphone announced that the time was now ten minutes to three. The opening ceremony would be at three o'clock precisely, and owing to the threatening weather would take place under cover in the big barn. Everyone prepared to move and Willie Sims and the Dog Daisy were temporarily abandoned.

Kate hardly recognized the big barn – last seen on the day of Mrs Ayredale-Eskdale's memorable hay-party.* Then it had been hung with flags and filled with gaily-decorated tea-tables. Now it looked bleak and empty except for a few chairs, some long wooden benches, an old table or two, and some boxes – anything in fact that could be hurriedly collected for people to sit on.

Along one side was a slightly raised platform with chairs for the judges, and a long trestle table covered with the prizes. Except that instead of books these seemed to be

* *Further Adventures of the Family from One End Street.*

mostly silver or glass, or what are sometimes collectively called 'leather goods', it reminded Kate a little of a school speech day. The front row of all was marked 'reserved' and in the middle of it sat Mrs Ayredale-Eskdale, beside her Mrs Megson, accompanied by Mrs Edwards, Mrs Smallpiece, and others who had either helped with the organizing or were donors of prizes. Other seats were being quickly filled. Mr Wildgoose managed to secure places in the third row, but Mrs Wildgoose was beckoned to by Mrs Ayredale-Eskdale and invited to a chair among the 'reserveds'.

People were crowding in now.

'I've never seen so many at the Show before!' exclaimed Mr Wildgoose. ''Course we always get a lot of Haddon folk, but these look to me from farther afield.' He sounded pleased and it was doubtless very flattering to Upper and Lower Cassington but Kate would have preferred to see someone she knew; even the vicar seemed to have disappeared! And then, suddenly, altogether – or so it seemed – were Mrs Midgley being pushed in her wheelchair by her daughter, Miss Alison assisting; Willie Sims escorting old Mrs Blossom; Mr and Mrs Digweed with their two daughters; Angela Smallpiece, resplendent in white muslin and a hat with daisies, accompanied by two incredibly elegant elder sisters; what was evidently the entire Sears family; and finally old Mr Shakespeare and Mr Milton. Mrs Midgley's chair was pushed alongside the 'reserveds' to which Mr and Mrs Digweed were also invited, and, to Kate's astonishment, Angela Smallpiece – who was provided by Miss Alison with a cushion at Mrs Ayredale-Eskdale's very feet – an honour which quickly dispelled any feelings of envy! It was gratifying, however, when the Digweed girls waved and presently squeezed along the row towards her, wedging themselves in the place she had kept for Mrs Wildgoose.

But whatever was the matter with old Mr Milton? He was stamping with his stick on the ground and muttering furiously to Mr Shakespeare, both of them completely oblivious of Miss Alison hovering near to conduct them to the last of the reserved chairs. Whatever it was, was interrupted by the voice though the megaphone – something even Mr Milton could hear – announcing that the 'Opening' was about to take place, and to much clapping and cheering, in trooped the judges preceded by the vicar accompanied by the lady referred to by Miss Alison as 'Aunt Mary', who was evidently to perform the ceremony, Mr Smallpiece bringing up the rear.

Just as Mr Wilson did not believe in long sermons, so he did not believe in long speeches. He knew well enough that all his parishioners – and their friends – wanted to hear was, who had won what. Briefly thanking Mrs Ayredale-Eskdale for the use of her grounds, her staff for their help, and the judges of their patience in what must have been a most difficult task, he introduced 'our distinguished visitor, the Honourable Mrs James Cameron', and sat down amid much applause.

Mrs James Cameron, Kate was to learn later, was Mrs Ayredale-Eskdale's sister-in-law, though for what she was distinguished was not revealed. She spoke nearly as briefly as the vicar and almost before anyone realized it, the Show was declared open! Now for the Results! . . . But no! Before the clapping and cheers had died away, Mr Smallpiece was on his feet smiling smugly and proposing a vote of thanks. Mr Smallpiece was anything but brief. Firstly, secondly, thirdly – even fourthly and fifthly – were invoked. By the time 'lastly' was reached, the audience was becoming very restive, and the clapping when he finally lowered himself into his seat again was very hearty indeed!

All this time, as people sat snug and dry in the big barn, the elements had been temporarily forgotten. Now it was noticed it was becoming very dark. The sky through the open barn doors was the colour of wet slates, and as the vicar – who always read out the prize lists – was about to begin, it was torn with a terrific flash of vivid, jagged lightning. Instinctively everyone drew in their breath and waited, tense, for the thunder that must follow, Mr Wildgoose, Kate noticed, counting on his fingers – the good old-fashioned method of estimating one's distance from a storm's centre.

'Vegetables: Section One,' began the undaunted vicar.

'Six . . . seven . . . eight . . .' murmured Mr Wildgoose, when everything was silenced by a savage, deafening roar.

There was a brief pause, then another, even more vivid flash of lightning, followed almost immediately by a ferocious ear-splitting *crack*!

'Something struck!' was heard being whispered on all sides . . . Another, but less vivid flash . . . Some small children began to wail, and Kate found herself gripping the edge of the wooden bench. 'Eight . . . nine . . . ten . . .' she heard Mr Wildgoose count, and this time the thunder when it came was not so loud. Was it moving off? she whispered, and to her relief he replied he thought it was, though he feared not for long; the storm had come up against the wind – and there was no rain – both bad signs . . . But – hush! . . . for the vicar was beginning to read again . . .

As Kate remarked later, if it wasn't *Mr* Wildgoose being read out, it was *Mrs* Wildgoose, and if this was perhaps a slight exaggeration it was not so far from the truth. First, second, third or Highly Commended, The Dew Drop Inn had won something in every single class! Sandwiched between, as you might say, were the names of many friends, though before the list came to an end it became increasingly difficult to remember who had been awarded what. One thing, alas, was certain, poor old Mr Milton who had won 'time and time again' had not got even a second prize for his gooseberries.

'I can't understand that!' whispered Mr Wildgoose to Kate. 'I saw them – far and *away* the best they were! Must be a mistake somewhere.' And a mistake it seemed there was, for as the vicar paused for a moment before beginning the children's section there was a disturbance in the 'reserveds' and there was Mr Milton standing up and pointing accusingly with his stick towards the judges.

'Excuse me, ma'am' – removing his hat and bowing jerkily to Mrs Ayredale-Eskdale. 'Excuse me, Mr Wilson, sir, but afore you starts a-readin' further, I've summat to say. Summat to say,' he repeated and his thin quavery old voice trembled with anger. As for the audience, you could have heard a pin drop!

'There's summat monstrous happened,' he continued, then paused, partly for breath and partly in order that the weightiness of his words might sink well in. The audience stirred a little uneasily; looked questioningly at each other, looked at the judges, then back at each other again. 'Summat monstrous!' repeated Mr Milton. 'Aye! *There's three of my gooseberries a-been stole* – yes, *stole*, I tells you! Fifteen I had – three over the dozen – I've got it all a-written here,' and putting down his stick he fumbled shakily in his waistcoat and produced a crumpled piece of paper. 'Fifteen; there 'tis,' and he tapped the paper with a long, bony forefinger. 'I'd suspicions,' he went on, 'long time I've had; so I took precautions. Marked 'em – that's what I done – aye – marked 'em! Crosses I put – *leetle tiny* crosses – just under the stalks. And when I go to the big tent just now – what do I find?' He paused again and a ripple of excitement passed over the audience. Nothing like this had ever happened at The Flower Show before!

'I finds,' continued Mr Milton slowly, 'I finds as there's still fifteen gooseberries on my plate. Oh yes, still fifteen. But not fifteen big juicy berries, all of 'em perfect, like as I left there. No. There's three of 'em disappeared and instead there's three little miseries –*'arf ripe and a quarter the size!*'

Murmurs of sympathy could be heard among the audience. Well I never! What next! and similar sentiments. But Mr Milton, even if he could have heard them, was not interested in sympathy; he was demanding justice. 'I knew where to look for my berries!' he continued triumphantly. 'Aye, I knew! And if you'll look in the same place, sir,' he nodded towards the vicar, 'you and the other gents, you'll see 'em settin' there – bigger nor any others on the plate. And marked – aye – all marked with *leetle crosses*! And here,' holding up another crumpled piece of paper, 'here's the entry number,' and he shuffled over to the platform and handed it up.

There was some conferring among those on the platform and then the vicar, in a very kindly voice, assured Mr Milton the matter would most certainly be 'looked into', but the children had waited a long time and firstly their prize list must be read out. All of which, Mr Milton not hearing a word, had to be relayed into his ear by Mr Shakespeare.

The children *had* waited a long time and, exciting as Mr Milton's interruption had been, they were becoming impatient. As for Kate she was longing to know – and not to know – the results, both at the same time. Now that The Dew Drop Inn had done so well it would be dreadful if it didn't win in everything. She did not hope for 'Firsts' – not even with the wildflowers now she had been seen Johnny Sears's . . . or for the mustard-and-cress now it was spoilt . . . a 'Second' perhaps;' and for the essay, untidy though it was . . . (There were no 'Thirds' in the children's classes.) As for the rest – if they could even be '*Commendeds*' . . . Mr Wildgoose, glancing towards her, asked if she felt all right? Though the thunder was definitely retreating it was very hot and stuffy and he thought she looked rather white. 'Yes, *quite* all right,' she assured him, 'only . . .'

'I believe you're *worrying*,' he whispered. 'Then *don't*. There's no need – believe me. I *know*!' But Kate had scarcely time to wonder *how* he knew – and none at all to try to believe him, before she knew herself! . . .

First in the Wildflower Competition! *First!* . . . Johnny Sears second – with only *one* flower less! . . . Angela Smallpiece 'Highly Commended' . . . It couldn't be true . . . but people were clapping and cheering; Mr Wildgoose patting her on the shoulder; Laura Digweed giving her a friendly pinch.

'Fruit or Vegetables entirely grown by candidate' . . . Johnny Sears first – with radishes and gooseberries; herself 'Highly Commended'. This was dreadfully disappointing . . . still, it was *something*, and 'Highly Commended' *was* better than just 'Commended' . . . But the lovely mustard-and-cress! . . . *Second* in the Handwork! Angela Smallpiece first . . . Now the cakes . . . and the jam . . . Oh *good*, the Digweeds First and Second for both – and she gave Laura a kindly squeeze in return for her pinch – 'Highly Commended', someone she did not know; 'Commended', Kate Ruggles . . . . *Oh!* She drew a deep breath of thankfulness. Only the essay was left.

'And now,' said the vicar, 'I come to the last competition: an essay – "My hobby, and why", and as I'm the giver of the First Prize for this I have had a rather special interest in the entries. They were pretty fair on the whole,' he continued, 'what there were; eleven among about twenty-five children over nine in the parish doesn't seem to me as many as there might be, you know! There were three of a very much higher standard than the rest,' he went on, 'and of these, one showed a lot of originality, and some very real poetic feeling.' He paused a moment and Kate almost held her breath. 'I would like to congratulate the winner and compliment her on her enthusiasm. Enthusiasm, I always think, is a great thing to have – even if we sometimes waste it on the wrong things. But,' he paused again, smiled and looked towards the back rows where most of the children were sitting, 'as one who has once been a schoolmaster (that may be a surprise to some of you!), I would like to urge the winner to take a little more trouble with her *writing*! One day she may want to pass examinations and what examiners can't read they can't be expected to pass! The First Prize, then, goes to Kate Ruggles; the Second to Mary Digweed; Highly Commended . . .' But who was Highly Commended – much less Commended, Kate did not hear. Between cheers, clapping, Mr Wildgoose's triumphant 'Didn't I tell you The Dew Drop would sweep the board!' and the fact that The Dew Drop had, Kate was completely over-whelmed!

Part Three

At Upper Cassington Flower Show, as long as anyone could remember, the order of things never varied. After the opening ceremony and the reading of the prize list a rush to the marquees to see how one's opinion agreed with that of the judges; then a hearty tea with one's friends, and an equally hearty argument about the justice – or injustice – of every award. Another visit to the marquees to confirm one's opinions, and finally the prize-giving. Later there were games or races for the children, sometimes Bowling for a Pig for the men, and, always, dancing on the lawn. But today the time-honoured custom was broken. Before anyone could be allowed in the marquees Mr Milton's accusations must be investigated, and no sooner had this been made clear to the audience than he, Mr Shakespeare – the only person considered capable of making him hear – accompanied by the vicar, the judges following, all set forth. The thunder was still rumbling in the distance and occasional flashes of lightning lit up the dark sky. It was very airless, and outside in the garden the trees and bushes were curiously still. Inside the big barn, however, it was anything but still. There was a perfect babel of conversation; people were pushing and crowding round, shaking hands, congratulating or condoling. Mrs Wildgoose was being slapped on the back to cries of 'good old Charlie!' 'Long live The Dew Drop!' 'Free drinks for all tonight,' and similar remarks, while on every side comments and conjectures could be heard as to the disappearance and the whereabouts of Mr Milton's gooseberries. Meanwhile Kate, who had privately never had any doubts that Johnny Sears was at the bottom of the matter, taking advantage of a lull in the spate of congratulations, was looking about her to see if she could see him, when she caught sight of Miss Alison making her way through the crowd towards her.

'Oh, Kate, I *was* pleased about your essay!' she exclaimed, 'and yours, Mary! And Laura's First for her cakes and jam! Such a lot of prizes between you! I kept hearing the names Digweed and Ruggles, Digweed and Ruggles, over and over again! . . . You must all come and be congratulated by my mother.' And almost before Kate realized what was happening she found herself being propelled towards the 'reserveds' and standing, all too conscious of her last encounter, in front of the alarming Mrs Ayredale-Eskdale.

'Well, little girl – I have forgotten your name but I remember your school hat and your long thin legs. And how is my white kitten faring?' she inquired kindly, regarding Kate through a pair of lorgnettes. Torn between pleasure at recognition of her precious hat, and indignation at 'little girl', Kate was momentarily unable to reply, but her affection for Cuckoo-Coo, delight in recounting his progress, and remembering that after all it was Mrs Ayredale-Eskdale who had given him to them, quickly overcame all other considerations, and she replied that the white kitten was ever so well, thank you; had grown ever so big; and that they all loved him very, very much, adding a little hesitantly, uncertain how such news might be received, that he was a good deal bigger than his about-to-be-raffled sister!

'Really?' Genuinely interested, Mrs Ayredale-Eskdale inquired what food he was given.

'Real milk – I mean not skim – or even *tinned*,' replied Kate, ticking the items off on her fingers, 'and scraps; and once a week – if Mum can afford it – Kipper Snacks. He just *loves* those!'

'And what,' asked Mrs Ayredale-Eskdale, putting down her lorgnettes and raising her aristocratic eyebrows, 'what, may I ask, are Kipper Snacks?'

Kate in her turn looked surprised. *Everyone* surely had heard of Kipper Snacks! She gravely informed Mrs Ayredale-Eskdale that these could be bought at grocers' and sometimes fish shops but more cheaply at Woolworth's.

'"Kipper Snacks"! Alison, make a note of the name,' commanded Mrs Ayredale-Eskdale turning to her daughter, 'and next time you are in Ailesford visit Woolworth's and bring back a dozen tins. Thank you, little girl,' to Kate, 'I shall certainly try them. So you have won a prize for an essay? Well done! *And* beaten my head gardener's daughter with your wildflowers, I understand? What were you thinking about, Angela,' and the lorgnettes tapped smartly on Miss Smallpiece's daisy-trimmed hat, 'to allow a town child to beat you at *that*?'

It is, of course, easy to be magnanimous when one has come out top, but even so, and although still faintly dazed at the idea of anyone ordering a dozen tins of Kipper Snacks at a blow so to speak, Kate couldn't help feeling a little sorry for Angela, who looked up, very pink in the face, from the cushion on which she was perched, and murmured something to the effect she didn't 'really'

care for wildflowers'. A remark to which – even if she heard it – Mrs Ayredale-Eskdale, now congratulating the Digweeds, made no reply.

Everyone was very kind about her prizes, thought Kate. No one seemed to mind at all she was not an Upper or Lower Cassington child – or if they did they were too polite to say so; all except one. Mrs Megson had given her a very sour look, and she heard her now muttering to Mrs Digweed about children from 'away' taking 'our' prizes, and, worst of all apparently, her, Mrs Megson's 'own' prize for Handwork. Kate felt very uncomfortable and retreated as far as possible from the 'reserveds', intending to have another look for Johnny Sears. Looking for Johnny Sears, however, or indeed anyone else proved to be like looking for the proverbial needle in a haystack, but finding Miss Alison alone for a moment she seized the opportunity to ask whether Lord Glenheather and Jaeger had returned? It seemed they had – but only that afternoon; the former, Miss Alison thought, was changing his clothes and Jaeger was shut securely in the stables for the duration of the Show.

What exactly happened in the big marquee, no one ever really knew. After what seemed an interminable time, the voice through the megaphone announced the matter in question was settled, and braving the threatening sky and the occasional flashes of lightning the company emerged from the big barn to see for themselves. Standing beside his gooseberries, now labelled 'First Prize', beaming but stone deaf – genuinely or otherwise – to all inquiries, was Mr Milton. Beside him Mr Shakespeare who seemed also to have become rather hard of hearing. In the smaller marquee the children quickly drew own conclusions, for it was soon discovered that Kate's mustard-and-cress, formerly labelled 'Highly Commended' now had a large blue card with 'Second Prize' propped against the boxes, while beside Johnny Sears's radishes and gooseberries, instead of a bright pink 'First', was a white card bearing one stark word 'Disqualified'! And if there was still anyone unable to put two and two together, outside the judges' tent stood P.C. Burden in close and earnest conversation with Johnny's father, Mrs Sears and her three small daughters standing by, the whole family looking scared out of their wits. As for Johnny himself, he appeared to have vanished completely.

But no one was bothering over-much. They were there to enjoy themselves; justice had been done and all was well. Many were making for the tea tent already; others crowded round Willie Sims, established once more under the cedar tree, while in spite of the still threatening sky, a small queue was forming outside the fortune teller's tent. Apparently 'Gypsy Geraldine' had arrived.

In the tea tent, members of Mrs Ayredale-Eskdale's staff in peacock-blue dresses and white spotted muslin caps and aprons – prominent among them the kindly Emily – assisted by other helpers, were fluttering about with plates of bread and butter, cakes and buns, and cups of tea from a huge brass urn at one end of the tent, and amid satisfied murmurs of 'it's nice to be waited on for a change', the company set to work with a will. Mr and Mrs Wildgoose, the Digweed family, Miss Midgley and Kate were all together at one of the larger tables, beside them at a smaller one, Mrs Midgley in her wheelchair, Mrs Megson, Mrs Edwards, and Miss Alison.

'Wherever can Elsie be?' asked Mrs Wildgoose who had been guarding the only remaining chair at their table against all comers, looking about her.

'Elsie, Mrs Wildgoose,' said Miss Alison overhearing the inquiry, 'is with the fortune teller! I saw her going into the tent as I came by.'

'Ah! That's where *I* want to go!' exclaimed Mrs Edwards, 'I always think these gypsies know a *lot* – and this one – "Patronized by Royalty" – she'd never dare put that if it weren't true – I'm sure she's good!'

'You'd far better keep your money, Estelle,' remarked Mrs Megson coldly, 'it's just waste of a good sixpence – that's what it is – all that nonsense. And I'm not sure as it's *right* either – not at all I'm not. I'm surprised at your mother, Miss,' she turned to Miss Alison, 'allowing it in her grounds – not to mention the vicar.'

'Oh, my mother *loves* fortune tellers!' replied Miss Alison gaily, 'and I'm sure Mr Wilson would have said at once, if he objected. It's only for fun,' she continued, ignoring one of Mrs Megson's stoniest and most intimidating looks. 'Do waste sixpence, Mrs Edwards! – though I'm sure it won't be wasted – I hear she's really *very* good!' And as if to confirm this opinion, almost the next minute, in came Elsie, all smiles and giggles, her pink cheeks even pinker than usual.

Ever so good! was her verdict. A proper gypsy and no mistake! Brown face, black straggly hair, big ear-rings, and a handkerchief over her head! All you did was sit on a chair, then she put her elbows on the table, shaded her eyes with her hands, gazed hard into a big crystal ball, and *saw* things! . . . And *what* she saw! . . . Uncanny it was! . . .

'"You work for very kind people," she said. "You work in a very old house – a house with a thatched roof." . . .

What do you think of *that*! She couldn't say rightly what my work was she said "but it's where people go in and out a lot . . . Not a shop exactly," she said, "hotel perhaps? And you've had trouble quite recent," she said, "near relative I'd say." "Oh I *have*," I said, thinking of my poor brother-in-law as died only a month last Friday! Then she said I were a hard worker . . .'

'And she said true there all right,' murmured Mrs Wildgoose putting down her tea cup and nodding emphatically as Elsie paused for a moment.

'All very good – as far as it goes,' said Mr Wildgoose, pleased at the idea of The Dew Drop Inn elevated to an hotel – if only in a crystal ball, 'but was there nothing about wedding bells and such like? Come on now, Elsie, out with it for we're all waiting to hear.'

'Well,' said Elsie, becoming if possible even pinker, and taking a gulp from the cup of tea just handed to her, 'well she *did* say as if I weren't walking out now I soon would be . . . and she told me as she thought I'd cross water one day . . . and – she couldn't say this for sure she said, but she thought I'd live to be very, very old! Then the five minutes was up! She tinkled on a little bell – might have been Dr Weston's surgery – and the next one come in. Oh, you must all go!'

'Think if I had sixpenn'orth I'd get some tips on next year's harvest?' asked Mr Digweed, 'and what about you, Charlie?' – addressing Mr Wildgoose.

But Mr Wildgoose said he had spent too much money already – indeed he was doubtful if he could pay for the tea, and no one must eat more than six cakes each, saying it so seriously that at first Kate thought he really meant it. As for Mrs Edwards she could hardly wait to finish her cup of tea, and saying she never ate anything at this time of day – bad for the figure and she on the plump side – begged to be excused, and to everyone's amusement, and a very black look indeed from Mrs Megson, hurried away to join the queue for Gypsy Geraldine.

Though she did not eat six cakes – or even three – it seemed to Kate the tea lasted a very long time. It was stiflingly hot in the tent, and the conversation – argument and discussion, agricultural and horticultural – seemed to float and flow about her like some kind of enveloping mist.

'You're tired Kate!' said Mrs Wildgoose. 'And no wonder – getting up so early! And there's not a breath of air in here, and – goodness me – it's getting on for five o'clock! It will be the prize-giving before we know where we are, and I did want to have a look at the exhibits again! And whatever's happened to Mrs Edwards – she's had time to have her fortune told twice over!' But Mrs Edwards, they learnt when they finally emerged into the fresh air, had not long gone into the gypsy's tent; there was still a small queue and she had had to wait her turn.

'Well I'm more interested in the exhibits than fortunes,' said Mrs Wildgoose and she and Mr Wildgoose were just about to set off for the big marquee, when a little boy standing near cried shrilly '*Look!*' and pointed excitedly in the direction of the big barn. There, running swiftly, but veering like a weather-cock, now this way, now that, nose close to the ground, uttering sharp, pleased little barks at intervals as he picked up and followed some trail, was Jaeger!

'Jaeger!' exclaimed Miss Alison coming out of the tea tent and catching sight of him. 'However did he get loose! Jaeger! *Jaeger!* Come *here*!' But Jaeger took not the slightest notice. Across the lawn, dodging the crowd, carefully skirting the flower beds, his tail swaying slightly in pleased anticipation, on he came. Near the back of Gypsy Geraldine's tent he suddenly stopped, stood listening, head on one side for a moment, then gave a wild yelp of delight. The next minute he had squirmed under the canvas and was inside, knocking over the screen, sending the crystal ball flying – and very nearly Mrs Edwards as well – as with short joyful barks he hurled himself at Gypsy Geraldine. Finally, in an exuberance of joy, leaping on to her lap and vigorously licking her face, thereby completely deranging the handkerchief, the ear-rings, 'the black straggly hair', and revealing to the astonished gaze of Mrs Edwards, alas, no gypsy but Lord Glenheather!

Never, said Lord Glenheather later, had he encountered anything like the wrathful indignation of Mrs Edwards! As for Mrs Megson, disapproving of her niece but doubly disapproving of what she called 'The Imposter', she had to be almost forcibly restrained from attacking him with her umbrella. Only when it was revealed that Mrs Ayredale-Eskdale had herself visited the tent, been completely taken in and was now standing near laughing about it with her sister-in-law and the vicar, was the tension eased. Everyone else seemed to be laughing too but there was no doubt Mrs Edwards was extremely mortified. Muttering '"Patronized by Royalty" indeed,' she finally lapsed into silence. Lord Glenheather, still wrapped in a Japanese dressing-gown, a large brass curtain ring hanging rakishly from one ear, and gripping Jaeger tightly by the collar, stood beside the tent looking almost as dejected. He was a kind-hearted man and was distressed that what had been intended as a mild practical joke was turning out as it had. Only Jaeger looked pleased with himself; his tail wagged gently to and fro, his nose quivered, and his three-cornered eyes gleamed with joy. It was a welcome relief when it was announced that the prize-giving would take place in five minutes' time and everyone began to move towards the big barn again.

Having divested himself of the dressing-gown and ear-ring but still holding tightly on to Jaeger, Lord Glenheather caught up with Mrs Edwards, now walking haughtily and alone. By the time the big barn was reached they were laughing and chatting like old friends.

'But what did you *say*?' asked Mrs Cameron at dinner at The Priory that evening.

'I just said I was sorry,' replied Lord Glenheather simply, 'and that I really had been "Patronized by Royalty". I *have*! I attended a shooting party – unasked and very grubby – when I was about eleven; the King was present, mistook me for one of the beaters' sons and gave me half a crown; it's one of my most cherished possessions.'

'Colin, my dear,' said Mrs Ayredale-Eskdale smiling indulgently and helping herself to a peach, 'has always had what is known as "a way" with him.'

Before everyone had reached the big barn, large drops of scattered thundery rain were beginning to fall, and as the last stragglers came running in, the deluge, which had held off so long, descended – and in no half-hearted manner! A real cloudburst! Through the barn doors the garden swiftly became almost invisible, a curtain of rain like a waterfall blotting out lawns, trees and flower beds alike. The paths were soon rivulets and the drive rapidly becoming a lake. The noise on the roof of the barn was deafening, and the vicar calling out the names of the various prize winners had to shout to make himself heard, while the congratulations of the Honourable Mrs Cameron as she smilingly presented each prize were totally inaudible.

'Beautiful prizes,' Miss Midgley had said, referring to the children's awards. They were! And those for the grown-ups too. And for once everyone seemed to have got what he or she wanted, from Mr Milton staggering under a bale of garden netting and a two-gallon watering-can, Mr Shakespeare grasping several packets of seeds and proudly shouldering the latest model in gardening forks, to old Mrs Blossom – who had won First Prize for her bantam eggs – affectionately nursing an enormous tea-cosy. The prize for the wildflowers was beyond Kate's wildest dreams! A real leather – no paper and cardboard about it – writing-case, fitted with pockets for paper and envelopes – something she had often gazed at in Otwell's most exclusive shop but never, never, expected to possess. And the prize for the essay equalled it! *The Poems of Alfred, Lord Tennyson*, bound in glowing red leather with golden lettering and gold-tipped pages! Mrs Megson's prize for handwork – a knitting bag complete with needles and balls of wool – she regarded with less enthusiasm. It was very nice, of course – and certainly representative of the donor! . . . And Mr Smallpiece's gardening basket would be very welcome at home . . . So too – if she could manage to keep it – would be the huge box of chocolates – identical with Angela Smallpiece's – the Third Prize for the table decoration, for which they had tied, and which they received standing side by side resolutely avoiding each other's eyes.

Finally the list of raffles was read. Here The Dew Drop Inn had by no means 'swept the board'; not been so much

as mentioned! Its sole supporter was Elsie with 'Elizabeth' as the nearest guess to 'Eliza' for the doll. Mrs Edwards had won the white kitten and was in ecstasies; Mr Shakespeare – which pleased everyone – ten shillings of the hidden treasure; and Mrs Megson one pound – which pleased no one – not even Mrs Megson herself judging from her face when she went to receive it.

'What did I tell you?' said Mr Wildgoose to Kate as the list neared its end. 'Never any luck with raffles – and it looks like you're the same!' But Mr Wildgoose spoke too soon. At some pre-arranged signal Willie Sims came running into the barn. He had a sack over his head and water poured off him in every direction. In his arms he carried a large dripping bundle wrapped in another sack. In it was the mysterious Dog Daisy – and Mr Wildgoose was proclaimed the winner!

'Oh dear, I hope it's not a bull-terrier!' murmured Mrs Wildgoose apprehensively and with a somewhat apologetic look at Jaeger, now lying in the most exemplary manner at Lord Glenheather's feet, a little farther up the row.

'Bull-terrier!' exclaimed Willie Sims miraculously overhearing her amid the din, and jealous for his contribution, 'it's worth ten bull-terriers!' And he pulled off the sack and revealed a shaggy, half-grown, sheep-dog bitch!

She stood for a moment bewildered by the crowd and then before Willie Sims, her new owner, or anyone else could grab her, bolted through the open barn doors. A second later, Jaeger, for whom it was obviously a case of love at first sight, had followed! Round and round, up and down the lawn, oblivious of the torrential rain they raced, the Dog Daisy, wild with joy at being released from her sack plunging madly in and out of Mr Smallpiece's precious flower beds; Jaeger, uttering delighted little barks, leaping and bounding like the Hound of the Baskervilles in pursuit. It took Lord Glenheather, Willie Sims, an under-gardener and a boy to catch them, while Mr Smallpiece stood in the doorway moaning in anguish, 'My roses! . . . My bedding-out! . . . *That Jaeger!*' until Mrs Ayredale-Eskdale called sharply, 'Pull yourself together, Smallpiece, do! Or go and *help*,' and he subsided.

Needless to say, there could be no dancing on the lawn; no bowling for a pig. Instead, it was decided to have games and dancing in the big barn. But Mr Wildgoose – to say nothing of his shaggy-haired prize – was soaked to the skin, and as he must, in any case, be back at the Inn by six o'clock for opening time, Mrs Wildgoose insisted on leaving at once. Perhaps, she asked Miss Alison, they could fetch their many prizes next day? But Lord Glenheather, who was soaked to the skin too, said he could not possibly be any wetter, and after Jaeger's behaviour the least he could do was to drive them home – likewise Willie Sims (whose beautiful blue suit now looked like black blotting paper, while the red rose had been washed clean out of his hat!). As for the prizes, there was a rug in the garage, they could put them all in that; he would bring the car round to the back of the barn and they would be back at The Dew Drop in no time.

Five minutes later, to much cheering, shouting, cries of 'don't forget – free drinks all round tonight', they all squashed into Lord Glenheather's not over-large car, and drove off through rain so heavy it was next to impossible to see to drive, and 'the like of which', Willie Sims solemnly assured them had not been equalled 'since the Flood'!

Whether there were free drinks all round at the Inn that night Kate never knew, but the noise in the bar was terrific. Even after closing-time when it was still raining fairly heavily, people stood about on the flooded gravel outside talking, talking . . . It must be midnight at least! . . . She lay listening . . . for the church clock to strike . . . Listening . . . Listening . . . But when it struck, it struck *eight*; the sun was shining, it was tomorrow – no – *today*!

6. The Concert

Part One

Today! It couldn't be . . . but it was! Of course it was! . . . It was light and the sun was shining . . . But when exactly did tomorrow become today – or today tomorrow? . . . Wasn't there a proverb that said 'tomorrow never comes'? Kate lay for a moment or so, sleepily considering these matters . . . she must ask Mr Wildgoose at breakfast. But when she eventually arrived downstairs, having dressed with frequent pauses to contemplate her prizes, breakfast was over. There was no sign of Mr Wildgoose and Mrs Wildgoose and Elsie were busy washing up.

'I let you sleep on, my dear,' said Mrs Wildgoose. 'You needed it after such a long day! It's breakfast in the kitchen this morning,' she went on, 'for the sitting-room table and half the chairs are covered with prizes; we were too tired last night to do anything about them. Here's your bowl of corn flakes, and there's one of my First Prize eggs for you when you've finished them.'

Kate ate her breakfast dreamily, thinking now of the problem of todays and tomorrows, now of her prizes, and half listening to Elsie as she chattered away to Mrs Wildgoose in the back kitchen. Elsie was very elated, both with the achievements of The Dew Drop Inn, and her own success in winning the raffled doll. The doll was apparently the very thing for her little niece's birthday next month . . . For herself of course she would have preferred the white kitten . . . Just fancy! That Mrs Edwards had announced she was going to call it after Lord Glenheather! . . .

'But it's a "she",' objected Mrs Wildgoose laughing.

'Yes!' said Elsie, 'and so we all told her, so now it's to be just "Heather" . . . As for his lordship himself – he was A One! Proper took in I was, Mrs Wildgoose, and no mistake!' and Elsie broke into a fit of giggles at her recollections of 'Gypsy Geraldine'. And what about young Johnny Sears's behaviour – what did Mrs Wildgoose think of *that?* Poor old Mr Milton! . . . But who'd a-thought an old chap like him u'd be so cute? . . . 'Right down clever I thought that was, Mrs Wildgoose!' . . . And The Dog Daisy – goodness! She'd almost forgotten! Where was it? And how did Mrs Wildgoose feel about such an addition to The Dew Drop Inn? . . .

Mrs Wildgoose was not very enthusiastic about The Dog Daisy. It was certainly better than a bull-terrier – just *look* at the way that Jaeger had behaved – but a half-grown sheep-dog about the place! . . . It was going to make a lot of extra work – Mr Wildgoose was out feeding it now. It would want exercise too and he'd enough to do already. 'If it had belonged to anyone but Willie Sims,' she concluded as she finished drying the last plate, 'we'd have said "no" to keeping it, but there – he *was* so proud of it – we just hadn't the heart! Now, let me see, what's the next thing . . . The beds – and then those prizes . . .'

It was dinner-time before Kate had an opportunity of asking Mr Wildgoose her question and then he only laughed and said all *he* knew was it seemed far nearer the weekend than it ought, what with the things he had to do, the things he hadn't done, and The Concert *on* as you might say, this very Saturday as ever was. 'As I said before, and I say again, it was a daft idea having The Flower Show so late. Instead of a nice break between it and The Concert, here we've got the two nearly on top of each other, and bless me, why couldn't we have had this lovely weather yesterday! There! now I've said all that I feel better!'

But Kate was seized with something almost like panic! For the last twenty-four hours or so she had almost forgotten about The Concert. And not only had she not yet decided which poem to recite but in none of those she had selected was she really word-perfect. It would not do to mention it to Mrs Wildgoose but she now made up her mind that today her afternoon 'rest' should be devoted to the matter. Once inside her little room, however, the sight of her prizes claimed her attention. She examined them all once again, fingering each one lovingly and sniffing appreciatively its newness and individual smell. The writing-case was by far the grandest thing she had ever owned! It was a lovely glossy chestnut-brown; soft, real, leather. It had shining silvery locks and two dear little keys tied to the handle. She picked it up again, delighting in the sharp leathery smell; then she opened it. Inside it was lighter brown and even softer leather; there were pockets with paper and envelopes; a blotter with leather corners and two little leather-covered books labelled Notes and Addresses! It was perfect! And the Tennyson in its way was as good. Shining red leather, gold-tipped pages, and, could it be an omen – a red silk ribbon lay marking the first two pages of *The Lady of Shalott*! Forgetting completely all instructions about removing the quilt and taking off dirty shoes, Kate curled up on the bed and was soon lost in the gold-tipped pages. An hour later she looked up from the story of Gareth and Lynette, her face wearing the faintly dazed expression of one who emerges from a dark cellar into strong sunlight, to find Mrs Wildgoose standing in the doorway. Camelot, King Arthur, The Round Table all vanished abruptly and Kate was conscious only of the crumpled quilt, her dusty shoes, and Mrs Wildgoose's reproving glance.

It would – of course it *would* be the one and only time she had forgotten! Happily, unlike many grown-ups in similar circumstances, Mrs Wildgoose accepted her explanation without further comment. She had come, she said, to say that The Dog Daisy was yapping its head off, driving everyone distracted; Mr Wildgoose was going to take it for a run in the water-meadows now, straight away, and would Kate care to go too?

'I thought you must be asleep my dear,' she concluded, 'we called several times!'

It was very lovely in the water-meadows – and The Dog Daisy evidently thought so too! As soon as they reached an untenanted field and Mr Wildgoose released her from her chain she raced madly round in circles uttering sharp, joyous, barks. Then, her first wild exuberance evaporated, tore wildly up and down, back and forth, across the field, snapping impartially at butterflies and wasps or jumping and twisting in pursuit of her own stumpy little tail. Finally, as they came near the river, splashing in among the reeds and lapping great pink tonguefuls of water.

Kate would have liked to linger by the river but Mr Wildgoose, consulting his watch and satisfied The Dog Daisy had covered at least four miles though he and Kate had walked barely one, said they must be getting home. The Dog Daisy, however, thought otherwise and it was a good ten minutes before, lured by sticks thrown into the river, she was eventually caught and put on her chain. Mr Wildgoose was rather silent as they walked homewards and Kate wondered if perhaps he was tired after yesterday. But Mr Wildgoose was not tired. He was wondering whether Willie Sims would be very hurt if another home could be found for The Dog Daisy.

'Now don't you go rushing off somewhere,' said Mrs Wildgoose to Kate when tea was over, 'it's very hot and you look tired.'

'I'm not a bit tired, Mrs Wildgoose,' replied Kate, faintly indignant, 'I'm only ever so worried about my poems. You see,' she went on, 'because I don't know *which* I'm going to recite it means I must know them *all*. I do wish I could see Miss Alison about them; she promised she'd help me but perhaps she's forgotten. I thought if I walked round the village I might see her.'

'I should think Miss Alison's busy with the tidying up after yesterday,' said Mrs Wildgoose. 'I'd let the poems wait till tomorrow if I were you. It's not what I call book-learning weather anyway. How about your writing a letter home now you've got that beautiful writing-case?' she added after a pause. 'It's nice and cool in here and you can have the table to yourself when Elsie's cleared the tea things away.'

Normally Kate detested writing letters; the thought of the new writing-case, however, overcame her . . . Besides, she would like them to know at home about the Show and her prizes and everything . . . There was also a faint chance she might meet Miss Alison when she went to post the letter. She glanced at the clock; half past five. The post went out at ten past six . . . plenty of time . . . But both Elsie and Mrs Wildgoose spent so long admiring the writing-case when she brought it down, it was nearly a quarter to six before she started, and though she had covered several sheets of the superior blue note-paper provided she had not nearly finished giving an account of yesterday's doings when the church clock struck the hour. Finishing off the letter in a rush she hurriedly printed a line of 'X's' for Peg, William and Cuckoo-Coo – underlining the last name several times, put it in the envelope already addressed and rushed up to her room for a stamp and her hat, then out and away to the post office. And just in time!

As she dropped her letter in the old 'V.R.' pillar box set in the wall of the post office garden, the little red mail van came round the corner from the main road. At the very same moment from the opposite direction, a small grey car drove up and, oh joy! out of it jumped Miss Alison. She had some unstamped letters in one hand and with the other she waved towards the approaching van calling, 'Ask him to wait!' as she hurried past Kate into the post office.

Having always believed that postmen – like time and tide – waited for no one, Kate rather timidly gave the message to the young man who presently appeared. To her surprise he seemed in no hurry; he grinned broadly and after collecting her letter and two others, put them in a sack in his van, took a seat on the wall, and remarked it was a fine evening. Kate agreed and was comparing his pleasant and leisurely behaviour with the gruff and hurried performance which seemed always to attend the clearing of the box round the corner from One End Street, when Miss Alison reappeared and handed over her letters, now duly stamped. The young man jumped off the wall, smiles and thanks were exchanged, and the red van drove off.

Miss Alison had not forgotten about the poems. She had in fact been on her way to The Dew Drop Inn. 'I meant to come this morning,' she said, 'but you've no idea how much there was to clear up after yesterday – the rain made everything in such a mess! Why, oh *why* couldn't it have been fine like today! I've thought a lot about the poems,' she went on, 'and it's for you to choose really, you know, but I do feel one of the shorter ones – or better still two – because they are so very short, would be best; and if, as you said, they seem a little sad, then how about one of the Lear rhymes – which are anything *but* sad, for an encore?'

'But Miss Alison,' objected Kate, 'there mightn't *be* an encore! And, and . . .' she hesitated a moment, 'well I know Mr Wildgoose thinks the Lear poems are marvellous and you like them too, and of course they are *funny*, but,' she hesitated again, 'well I feel they're sort of *babyish*, Miss Alison – a lot of them; owls and pussy cats and things . . . I'd feel ever so silly reciting about a *pussy cat*!'

'I know what you mean,' replied Miss Alison slowly. 'I think perhaps you're the wrong age for them; you'd probably like them better if you were Peg's age or quite grown up. Well, never mind them for the moment; which of the others would you choose?'

'I think "Nod" and "A Child's Pet",' said Kate slowly after some thought. 'But oh dear! *two*, Miss Alison! And – would it matter – they're both about sheep – though different kinds of sheep – I mean real and sort of made-up ones? And if there *is* an encore then I think the poem about standing and staring. It's a very country sort of poem,' she added persuasively, 'so I should think Cassington people would like it. And another thing, Miss Alison, I *know* all these – not absolutely perfectly – but nearly; if we had a Lear I'd have to learn it!'

'You lazy child!' exclaimed Miss Alison. 'No, I can't say that after all your achievements yesterday, can I? Very well, we'll keep to those two – I don't think it matters at all about the sheep – and don't you be so sure about no encore – there might even be two!' she added, 'and then you might be glad of Mr Lear after all! There, I'll write down the titles for the programme. Miss Kate Ruggles: "A Child's Pet", by W. H. Davies, and "Nod" by Walter de la Mare. Oh, one more thing. On Friday there's to be a meeting in the church hall – a sort of rehearsal really for everyone taking part. It's at six o'clock *sharp* – you won't forget, will you? And now I must go home!'

Forget! Could anyone possibly forget such an occasion? During the next four days Kate could think of little else! Her book of poems was never far away though she was certain she knew both poems and her 'perhaps encore' – as she called it to herself – backwards, forwards, and inside out. There were few other distractions. Lord Glenheather, who had been persuaded to perform some Highland dances at The Concert, was away again, Jaeger with him, and would not be back before the afternoon of the great day. The Digweed girls had gone away to stay with relatives till Friday; Angela Smallpiece to her grandmother at Haddon, and of Johnny Sears there was not a sign. Except for the resentful yappings of the tethered Dog Daisy The Dew Drop Inn was strangely quiet after all the recent bustle. The village too seemed subdued. Even Mr Shakespeare, though he proudly displayed his own and Mr Milton's prizes, was less talkative than usual. They were both coming to The Concert he assured Kate. 'Never miss The Concert, do we, John?' he shouted across the fence of bedheads to his neighbour, to which Mr Milton nodded assent and replied to the effect that though he never *heard* naught, he enjoyed seein' folks a-makin' fools of theirselves. Mrs Edwards was invisible – though by no means inaudible – Miss Midgley at the post office complaining bitterly that the piano opposite was never silent and that she was unable to concentrate on important government business as a result. Even Thomas seemed dispirited and refused to purr. Only Willie Sims went about whistling happily as usual.

'Reaction after the Show – that's what's the matter with everyone,' said Mr Wildgoose. 'We'll perk up come Saturday, you'll see!'

They had perked up by Friday evening – or so it seemed to Kate. She arrived at the church hall to be greeted by a perfect babel of noise! Everyone appeared to be shouting at everyone else and the air was rent with arguments and people clamouring for information. In one corner two young men were having a violent altercation about a duet they were to sing; in another the Digweed girls, still in their best clothes having come straight from the station, breathlessly beseeching Miss Alison their performances might not come too near the beginning of the programme; while high above the din could be heard the plaintive tones of Mrs Edwards complaining about the piano. She was sure it had not been tuned; the keys were sticky; the candle sconces rattled . . . There was a faint lull when the vicar, who was to preside over the meeting, arrived; but not for long. Mr Wilson, however, had not been a schoolmaster

for nothing! He was an expert at reducing chaos to order. In less than five minutes you could have heard the proverbial pin drop. In less than half an hour, all questions had been answered; everyone taking part assigned his or her place in the programme; Mrs Edwards satisfied the piano had been tuned last week, the keys would be cleaned, the rattling sconces attended to; the two young men pacified; the Digweeds reassured. Almost before Kate realized it, gathering up some papers in his hand, Mr Wilson was preparing to depart. They would all meet tomorrow – at nine-thirty *sharp,* please – for the programmes to be distributed and for any last minute arrangements to be made. The meeting was over.

'You have selected two very charming poems, my child,' he said catching up with Kate as they came out of the hall, 'an unusual choice; I shall look forward to hearing them. What's that – you're "ever so nervous"! Bless me, most of us are when we get on a platform – or I might add in a pulpit. Yes,' as Kate looked incredulous, 'even after forty years! But,' he stopped a moment and put a hand on her shoulder, 'I'll let you into a secret! Forget *yourself* – though I know,' and he gave a little laugh, then sighed, 'that is very, very much easier said than done . . . Well, I must be off to my supper. Good night – and God bless you.'

Kate woke early next morning. It was fine and sunny; small white clouds sailed slowly in a clear, pale-blue sky; swallows went swooping by and there were happy twitterings in the thatch above the window. Had it been an ordinary Saturday it would have been just the day for a long walk with Mr Wildgoose and The Dog Daisy, or even better, a picnic. As it was, the thought of The Concert weighed on her spirits. Though she was sure she knew her poems inside out, the thought of standing on a stage in front of all those people she didn't know – or, worse in some ways, those she did, was terrifying. She had heard the vicar's 'secret' before, but neither he nor anyone else ever gave a hint of how to set about it! She lay for a while looking at the sailing clouds, and listening to the chirpings in the thatch . . . She would say each poem and the 'perhaps encore' through just once more, very slowly, then it would be time to get up . . . When she came down breakfast was not quite ready and she wandered into the garden for a few words with the tethered Dog Daisy who, her resentful yappings quickly turning to barks of joy, leapt roughly about her, thrusting a cold wet nose into her outstretched hands. A few minutes later Mr Wildgoose appeared with an enormous bowl of bread and milk and leaving The Dog Daisy eating ravenously, they went back together to the house.

Unlike The Dog Daisy. Kate had little appetite for her breakfast – a fact which Mrs Wildgoose, who was beginning to think she would be quite glad when The Concert was over, noticed but did not remark upon; she was quieter than usual too and very soon after breakfast was over, though it was long before 'nine-thirty sharp', slipped away to the village hall. Early as she was, she was by no means the first to arrive. Through the open door came the sound of voices and of hammering and in the road outside stood Miss Alison's car from which she and a young gardener from The Priory were unloading large pots of schizanthus and pelargoniums and other greenhouse plants, reluctantly and very grudgingly lent by Mr Smallpiece who was convinced they would all be dead by next day as a result. Inside, the hall already presented quite a festive appearance. On either side of the stage stood The Priory flowers looking very impressive; chains of coloured paper and strings of little flags were strung from wall to wall; larger flags, anchored with jam jars of flowers, hung down from window sills; and a large coloured photograph of the King was festooned with laurel leaves and surmounted with two crossed Union Jacks. Chairs and benches were being dusted and set in order; someone was cleaning the piano keys and adjusting the candle sconces that had so offended Mrs Edwards; and the vicar's gardener (who was acting as stage manager) testing the lights – switching them on and off, off and on muttering and grunting disapprovingly. Punctually on the stroke of nine-thirty the vicar himself arrived closely followed by Mrs Edwards. Very soon, programmes had been distributed and everyone instructed once again in the order of his or her performance. Mrs Edwards after rippling up and down the piano with a couple of scales had announced herself satisfied, and the stage manager, though doubtful about the efficiency of the lighting – which had been known to give trouble on previous occasions – expressed his opinion it would 'hold out'.

'Then I think everything is now in order,' said the vicar. 'Good luck to you all – and let us make it the best concert we have ever had!'

Kate walked slowly back to The Dew Drop Inn reading the programme as she went.

No. 1. Mrs Estelle Edwards. Piano Solo. 'Marche Militaire' by Franz Schubert.

No. 2. Miss Doreen Smallpiece. Song. Accompanied by Miss Ayredale-Eskdale.

No. 3. Miss Laura Digweed. Violin Solo. 'Minute' by Mozart. Accompanied by Miss Ayredale-Eskdale.

No. 4. Miss Angela Smallpiece. Recitation. 'A Little Quaker Maiden'.

No. 5. Mr Larry Coote and Mr Jim Baker. Comic Song.

No. 6. Miss Laura and Miss Mary Digweed. 'Duet' by Robert Schumann.

No. 7. Miss Kate Ruggles. Two Recitations. 'A Child's Pet' by W. H. Davies and 'Nod' by Walter de la Mare.

No. 8. The Reverend H. Wilson. Sketches from Dickens.

No. 9. Mrs Estelle Edwards. Piano Solo. 'Polonaise' by Frederick Chopin.

No. 10. Lord Glenheather. Sword dance and Highland Fling. Accompanied by Miss Ayredale-Eskdale.

'Miss Kate Ruggles. Two Recitations' . . . How grand it looked! . . . 'No. 7,' said Mr Wildgoose when she showed him the programme at dinner-time, 'well that's supposed to be a lucky number! It looks like a good concert to me. I only wish I could have come, I'd dearly like to have heard you recite and seen his lordship dance but there – it's Saturday night, there's no one can take my place this year, and business is business!'

Part Two

'I can't, Mrs Wildgoose. I just *can't* eat anything!' said Kate as she and Mrs Wildgoose sat down to an early supper that evening.

'You must eat something,' said Mrs Wildgoose firmly, 'you ate next to nothing tea-time. Have a little of this nice ham now?'

'I couldn't, *truly*, Mrs Wildgoose. The whole of the inside of my mouth feels dried up, and, and, I feel sort of sick too! Just imagine if I was sick on the stage!'

'I can't imagine no such thing,' said Mrs Wildgoose and she spoke almost crossly. 'I'm beginning to think I'll be glad when The Concert's over! It's ridiculous, going on like this. You must have *something*. If you won't have any ham you must have some bread and butter. There!' And she put a large slice on to Kate's plate. But it was no good; after a couple of bites Kate put it down.

'I can eat after it's all over, Mrs Wildgoose. It says on the programme there's to be refreshments. *Please* don't make me now!'

'Well, if you won't you won't,' said Mrs Wildgoose, 'but I'm afraid you'll have to watch me,' and in a very leisurely manner she set about disposing of a plate of ham, lettuce and tomatoes, followed by some bread and cheese. Finally, as if there was no such thing as hurry in the world she selected and began to peel an apple. Kate sat watching the hands of the grandfather clock in a perfect agony of impatience. At last she could bear it no longer. 'Oughtn't we to go, Mrs Wildgoose? It's almost on the quarter and Miss Alison said the – the *performers* must be there early!'

'Now, Kate!' said Mrs Wildgoose smiling. 'How long does it take to get from here to the church hall! You know by this time, as well as I do! Five minutes at the very most. The Concert's not till eight. If we're there by half-past seven it's more than time enough. But I can see you'll give yourself no peace till you are there so you'd best run upstairs and tidy yourself while I finish my apple and then we'll be off – I've brought my hat and coat down . . . Now don't *rush*! . . . Bless the child!' . . . for Kate had flown from the room and could be heard clattering up the uncarpeted oak stairs and racing along the passage overhead.

They were at the church hall before half-past seven but even so, by no means the first arrivals. People were clustered round the door where Willie Sims was handing out tickets, and inside, the cheaper seats were nearly half full and many others already taken.

'Goodness me!' exclaimed Mrs Wildgoose, 'it's hot in here!' It certainly was; and since the windows of the church hall, which had been built for winter rather than for summer entertainment, opened only at the top, and this by means of a rather complicated system of cords needing expert manipulation, it became progressively warmer as more and more people poured in. Mr Smallpiece need have had no fear for his plants! It was as hot as any greenhouse!

'We're right in the front row!' whispered Kate with awe when they found the chairs corresponding to the numbers of their tickets. It was a privilege, however, which she soon realized had grave disadvantages. Mrs Ayredale-Eskdale and Mrs Megson among others, would undoubtedly be accommodated there. How near the stage was! The thought of standing on it and enduring their critical gaze at such short range was very unnerving. As far as Mrs Megson was concerned, however, she need not have worried for Mrs Edwards who presently arrived, resplendent in brown satin, was heard to announce, without, Kate thought, any great distress, that 'poor Auntie' was not feeling well enough to come. Mrs Edwards was resplendent indeed! In addition to the brown satin dress she had long yellow ear-rings, very high-heeled satin shoes, and round her shoulders a beautiful brown fox fur.

'She's never, surely, going to keep that fur on in this heat!' whispered Miss Midgley who had taken a seat behind them, having first manœuvred her mother's wheelchair into a place specially reserved for it in the front row. But Mrs Edwards evidently *was*! She stood now at the foot of the little steps at the side of the stage ready to open the entertainment with what she had described to Kate as 'A Gay Military March'.

As at many similar entertainments, it was more or less taken for granted that the first musical item on the programme was to allow everyone to get comfortably settled in his or her seat, and to drown the noise of late arrivals. Mrs Edwards, however, was having no nonsense of that kind! Just before the clock struck eight she mounted the little steps, sailed across to the piano, and seated herself on the red plush music stool. Not, however, until the party from The Priory who had arrived at two minutes to the hour and with a good deal of rustling settled themselves in the front row, and several pairs of heavy boots creaked to their destination at the back of the hall, would she condescend to bow, first to the vicar who was to announce each item, and then to the audience. Even when these preliminaries were over she did not start immediately. There was a screwing and unscrewing of the plush-seated stool; a lace-edged handkerchief to be deposited at the end of the keyboard; the fox fur to be adjusted. But at last all was ready, the vicar announced, 'Mrs Edwards will now open The Concert for us by playing Marche Militaire by Franz Schubert,' and the next moment Mrs Edwards had plunged into it.

It was certainly a very spirited performance, and the way in which Mrs Edwards swayed about, back, forth, and sideways on the plush-covered stool, was most impressive, while the occasional rocking of the piano on the uneven boards of the stage, if a trifle unnerving to those in the front rows, was felt by most of the audience to be in keeping with the stirring character of the music. Tremendous applause followed the last resounding chords and there were cries of 'Encore! Encore!' But Mrs Edwards was reserving her energies, and she only bowed graciously, and walked to the side of the stage where she stood hesitating, as if afraid to descend, until Lord Glenheather jumped up from his seat at the extreme end of the row and offered a helping hand.

The next item was a song about a shipwrecked sailor, rendered with much pathos by the eldest Miss Smallpiece accompanied by Miss Alison. This too called forth great applause and several cries of Encore to which Miss Smallpiece, more obliging than Mrs Edwards, responded with what she described as 'an old favourite', which, judging from the reception it received, was enormously popular. There were again cries of Encore but Miss Smallpiece had had enough and after bowing shyly with many becoming blushes, hurried off the stage.

Laura Digweed was next with her violin, also accompanied by Miss Alison. Having not long since confided to Kate she was 'sick with terror' it was a surprise to see her walk calmly on to the stage, arrange her music stand, and tune her violin all with the utmost composure, and finally to play placidly to the end of her 'piece' – apparently unperturbed even by the sight of Mrs Ayredale-Eskdale beating time with her lorgnettes!

She was followed by Angela Smallpiece, supremely self-confident, and wearing, yes, yet another resplendent muslin dress – pink this time, with small blue flowers!

But not even pink muslim and unlimited self-confidence can make up for poor reciting. *A Little Quaker Maiden* seemed an interminable poem, and long before the end there were signs the audience was becoming restive. There was much rustling of paper bags, coughing, and shuffling of feet. Kate felt encouraged; she could do better than that she told herself, and she was faintly surprised when the droning singsong at last coming to an end, everyone clapped heartily and there were even one or two calls for an Encore. To most people's relief, however, Miss Smallpiece shook her yellow curls and clutching the pink muslin completed her performance with a rather clumsy curtsey.

The next item was a comic song sung by two young men from Lower Cassington. It was no doubt an exceedingly funny song; unfortunately most of the words were totally inaudible – even in the front rows! The singers, however, so obviously enjoyed singing it, and laughed so much themselves, that the audience indulgently laughed too and at the end applauded so good-naturedly that the young men were encouraged to embark on a second song – if possible even more inaudible.

They finally laughed themselves off the stage and then it was 'No. 6 Laura and Mary Digweed. Duet' and on to the platform climbed the sturdy Miss Digweeds. They spread out their music without a sign of nervousness, drew up a short wooden bench and sitting squashed together, pounded their way through a Schumann duet. They, too, were encored, Mrs Edwards clapping loudly and crying 'Bravo! *Bravo!*' which caused them both to blush furiously, and their parents to glow with happy pride.

After some whispering together a second duet followed and though there were a few wrong notes this time everyone clapped with a will.

And now, now, it was No. 7! . . . Miss Kate Ruggles: 'A Child's Pet' by W. H. Davies, and 'Nod' by Walter de la Mare . . . and with a funny feeling in her chest, dry mouth, and damp hands, Kate stumbled her way up the steps to the stage, made her way to the middle of it and stood blinking nervously, a little dazzled by the footlights, at a terrifying sea of faces. For one horrible moment she was convinced she had lost her voice – or – worse – was going to burst into tears. Then, among the blur of faces she caught a smile from Miss Alison, a scornful glance from Angela Smallpiece, and an encouraging nod from the vicar. The smile, the glance, and the nod, was each in its way, a spur and a challenge; the next moment, in a voice she hardly knew for her own, and which seemed to come from far, far away, she had announced the title of the first poem and – suddenly the faces didn't matter any more; nothing mattered except what the poet had felt, what she herself felt, and wanted the audience to feel, about the poor pet lamb crossing the stormy Atlantic with its seasick companions.

There was a moment of complete silence when she finished and she stood looking anxiously at the audience. She knew she had made no mistake in the words – but had she said them terribly badly? . . . Was . . . was the poem too sad? There seemed to be a handkerchief or two in use? . . . But she was not left long in doubt. With the wildest enthusiasm the audience clapped and clapped and clapped – no one harder than Miss Alison and the vicar! Kate stood looking shyly down at them, twisting her handkerchief between her still damp hands; when at last the applause died down all her fright had vanished.

Happy, reassured, with almost as much pleasure as she had had from reading it to herself, she recited Walter de la Mare's lovely poem, 'Nod'. 'Softly, along the road of evening . . . His lambs outnumber a noon's roses . . . His blind old sheep-dog, Slumbersoon . . .'

No rustling of paper bags; no coughing; no shuffling of feet. Only an attentive silence . . . These poems were somehow different from those usually recited at The Concert . . . She came to the last lovely lines, 'His ram's bell rings 'neath an arch of stars', . . . and the applause when she finished was an enthusiastic as before – if not more so. Even Mrs Ayredale-Eskdale nodded approval at her and murmured something in Lord Glenheather's ear. As for Angela Smallpiece, she sat with her mouth wide open – stunned!

There was no doubt about an encore – and they even encored that – though unsuccessfully. Dazed but elated Kate made her way back to her seat. It was over! *Over!* She hadn't made a single mistake – not *one*; and they had *liked* it! . . . Now she could begin to enjoy The Concert – or what was left of it.

'You did it lovely, my dear!' whispered Mrs Wildgoose as she sat down. 'Lovely! Oh, I *did* enjoy it; you had me near tears once or twice – and I wasn't the only one! There, I mustn't talk – they're putting up the next number.'

'The next number' was the vicar's and consisted of several short but spirited sketches from Dickens in which he interpreted each character in turn. Badly done such a performance can be painful; Mr Wilson, however, was a master of the art and the audience rocked with laughter or furtively produced handkerchiefs as the case demanded. Kate sat entranced. Hitherto she had regarded the long, closely printed volumes of Dickens in the public library at home – volumes so frequently extolled and recommended for reading by her form mistress – with suspicion and distaste. But when at last the vicar stepped down from the stage, having good-naturedly given two encores, she had registered a vow: however long and closely printed, *David Copperfield, Pickwick Papers,* and *Nicholas Nickleby* should be the very first books she asked for at the library when she went home!

And now, at long last, it was the turn of Mrs Edwards. Most of the inhabitants of Upper and Lower Cassington were greatly looking forward to this performance, the rippling scales and cascades of arpeggios that had floated out morning and evening from the back of Mrs Megson's shop, to say nothing of the earlier performance, making it abundantly clear no mere beginner was in their midst. Mrs Edwards sailed as gracefully across the stage as the creaking, uneven boards would permit. The same ritual of screwing and unscrewing the music stool was repeated; the lace-edged handkerchief deposited. This time, however, she evidently decided she could not endure the heat of her fox fur. She stood up, unclasped it, and after a moment's hesitation laid it across the music stool, the head hanging down one side, the tail the other. She then sat down on it, bowed graciously

to the audience, and was waiting for the rustle of paper bags and other distractions to subside when suddenly the lights which had already dimmed ominously once or twice during the evening began to flicker and then suddenly went out. For two, perhaps three, minutes the hall was in pitch darkness, but by the time those behind the stage had groped for, found, and lit some of the candles kept in readiness for such emergencies, the lights flickered and then came on again as suddenly as they had gone out. But – what was this? For in the brief interval while the lights were off Mrs Edwards appeared to have grown a *thick, bushy tail*!

In some way the fox fur must have slipped or twisted round for now, the tawny fur blending perfectly with the brown of her dress the tail hung down behind her over the music stool, producing a very curious effect indeed! Blissfully unaware of what had happened, with another gracious smile and bow to the audience, Mrs Edwards began to play. At first the playing was smooth and calm, demanding little bodily movement from the pianist, and the tail hung limply down, but, as the music became more impassioned and she began to sway now to this side, now to that, it swayed too. She leant backwards and it dipped, forwards – and up it jerked. A softer passage followed and it seemed to droop in sympathy. Then came a succession of runs and trills and short staccato notes and it twitched and trembled; then a series of resounding chords. Mrs Edwards fairly *bounced* on the piano stool! Up and down, up and down flipped the fox tail until it seemed to the delighted onlookers as if it almost wagged with emotion!

Meanwhile, among the audience, what at first had been an exchange of amused smiles turned quickly into silent, suppressed laughter, then rapidly to laughter neither silent nor suppressed, finally into helpless gurgles and giggles. Loud and barely smothered guffaws came from the back rows. Even Mrs Ayredale-Eskdale could be seen dabbing away tears of mirth with a lace handkerchief!

Mrs Edwards, still happily unconscious of her curious appendage, played on and on . . . Up and down, faster and faster, faster and faster flipped the fox tail until, the performance coming to an end in a shattering crescendo of chords, it gave a final convulsive jerk and was still! Mrs Edwards stood up, walked to the middle of the stage and bowed, to be greeted with a perfect storm of clapping! Cries of 'Encore! *Encore!*' and the stamping of feet echoed all round the hall, while from the back rows there were shouts of 'Tally Ho!' and someone shouted, 'Good old Foxy!'

Mrs Edwards had expected applause but never, never anything like this! And – could it be possible – the light *was* very bad – people appeared to be almost hysterical, laughing and dabbing away tears . . . Would the clapping never stop! . . . It was all very gratifying . . . But – what was that – what were they calling at the back? . . . *'Good old Foxy'!* . . . Well of course one must make allowances for village manners . . . but *really* . . . her beautiful fur! . . . Once again Lord Glenheather saved the situation. He stood up, clapped loudly, and calling, 'Hush, there at the back!' said quietly, '*Please* – Mrs Edwards – an encore!' And Mrs Edwards, blushing with pleasure, murmured something no one could catch and, walking across the stage, picked up her fur, handed it to him and sat down at the piano once more.

There were some audible groans when the fur was handed over; a large proportion of the audience was longing to see the fox tail in action again. But Lord Glenheather glanced sharply towards the back rows and the next moment the hall was filled with the strains of Grieg's Bridal Procession. There was clapping when it came to an end, and several cries of encore, but nothing, nothing like the earlier triumph. Mrs Edwards couldn't understand it at all. She felt quite hurt . . . of course, it *was* only an encore, but it was usually such a *popular* piece . . . As she confided later to Lord Glenheather over a cup of coffee, she was afraid people had been more interested in her beautiful fur than her playing . . . she had distinctly heard cries of 'Foxy' and 'Tally Ho' . . .

She stood now, faintly bewildered but still bowing graciously, and it was not until the stage manager, waiting to put up the next, and last, number, had given two loud 'ahems', that she became aware of his presence. She walked to the side expecting to be helped down as before. But Lord Glenheather was not there . . . Of course . . . she had forgotten . . . The next number was his . . . Lying on his empty chair was her fur . . . She sidled down the steps, caught it up, and smiling bravely, returned to her place. Just as she reached it there was a sudden burst of clapping. Could it – could it be another encore? . . .

But the clapping was for Lord Glenheather who now appeared on the stage clad in full Highland dress. He carried two short swords and was followed by Miss Alison who, as he explained to the audience, was 'a substitute – and a very nice one – for the Pipes.'

Lord Glenheather looked most romantic, Kate thought! He had a good figure and good legs – two great assets for the successful wearing of a kilt. He was also, it was quickly revealed, a neat and nimble dancer, performing with great skill the rapid and intricate succession of steps, the cunning crossing and uncrossing of feet, with the delicate timing demanded by a sword dance! True, the swords, now lying neatly crossed in the centre of the stage, had not been newly whetted, and there was little danger from a foot misplaced. The audience, however, were not aware of this, and the dancer's feet so perilously near to the bare steel provided a pleasant thrill. The performance was made no easier by the loose and rattling boards of the stage. Unwhetted swords or not, Lord Glenheather was quite glad when it was over; and though the hall echoed with clapping, stamping of feet, and cries of encore – one enthusiast jumping up and calling, 'Do it again, yer lordship, sir, *do*! Please to do it again!' his lordship shook his head. Time, he told them, was getting on. He would keep to the programme and end his performance – and alas, The Concert, which he had enjoyed enormously – as he was sure everyone else had done – with The Highland Fling. And the announcement having been greeted with loud cheers and more clapping, Miss Alison played the opening bars of the music and the dance began.

Alas, Lord Glenheather had not allowed for the effect of his six foot two inches in such strenuous action on the already loose and creaking boards of the Upper Cassington stage! At first all went well but The Highland Fling is an active, not to say violent, dance. Under his leaps and bounds, neat and controlled as they were, the boards creaked and rattled and groaned, and Miss Alison was hard put to it to keep time on the wildly rocking piano. Unaware or unconcerned Lord Glenheather danced on. The creakings and groanings grew louder until the noise was audible even above the gay, spirited music. The whole stage quaked and shook; the piano rocked even more madly! On went the dancer, his steps swifter and swifter, his leapings and boundings more and more frenzied. Finally, gathering all his strength, with a loud 'Whoop!' he sprang high in the air in a last wild leap. As he landed on the stage there was a sharp cracking sound – the noise of splitting, splintering wood. The next minute Lord Glenheather had disappeared from view!

Half a dozen people rushed to help: the stage manager, Willie Sims and other helpers from behind the stage, Miss Alison and the vicar. But before they could pick their way over the shattered boards, Lord Glenheather's laughing face, followed by his shoulders, emerged from a large jagged hole. With the assistance of Willie Sims and the stage manager he was pulled out – none the worse except for a few bruises and scratches. Laughing still he took Miss Alison by the hand and led her to the front of the stage where to quite the loudest cheers and clapping the village hall had ever heard they stood bowing to the audience, to each other, to the audience again. Then Miss Alison returned to the piano, everyone stood up, and the singing of *God Save the King* that followed could be heard, so it was said later, even in Lower Cassington!

Over the 'Refreshments' – paste sandwiches and the buttered halves of penny buns, accompanied by lemonade or coffee – it was considered one of the best concerts for years – some insisted quite the best! Certainly they had never laughed so much! Happily wolfing sandwiches and buns, swilling down lemonade and coffee, everyone appeared delighted with themselves and everyone else – the true test of a successful entertainment! Only old Mr Milton seemed sunk in gloom and could be heard announcing loudly, ''Twill cost something to repair they' – indicating the shattered boards, and muttering darkly about increased rates. Mrs Edwards stood apart. She was deeply offended. Her fur hung over one arm and she lovingly stroked and caressed its shining hair. Every now and then her lips moved slightly and Kate standing near, her appetite now completely restored and her mouth full of buttered bun, caught the words, 'My Beautiful! "*Old Foxy*" indeed! "*Old* Foxy"! . . .' If Mrs Edwards only knew! . . .

And as Mrs Wildgoose said later – concluding what she called 'The tale of a tail' to Mr Wildgoose on their return home, she could only hope Mrs Edwards never would!

7. Lily Rose's Good Deed for the Day

Part One

'And what,' said Mr Wildgoose coming into the kitchen one morning and seeing Kate absorbed in a postcard from home, 'is the news from No. 1 One End Street?'

What indeed? For the postcard was baffling in the extreme! All it said, in Lily Rose's surprisingly neat writing – so unlike Kate's own untidy scribble, was, 'There hasn't half been a row but the cops were sports all right. Mum's writing. Love from Lily Rose. X's from Peg and William and *C.C.*' – the last mentioned being underlined three times.

What *ever* could have happened? . . . Now she'd have to wait for a letter from Mum – and that might not come for a week!

But two days later there was another letter with the Otwell-on-the-Ouse postmark. It was not from Mum, however, but – rather surprisingly – from Dad. It said nothing whatever about Lily Rose or rows or cops but it contained some most unexpected – and *very* exciting – news!

But to return to One End Street. What *had* been happening?

It began one Saturday morning – a particularly fine, sunny Saturday, and Lily Rose stood, as Kate had stood some three weeks or so ago, looking out of the bedroom window, but where Kate had visualized the orangy-coloured cottages, and the joys of Upper Cassington, Lily Rose saw only the grey-slated roofs of the house opposite, and a very dull Saturday ahead.

Lily Rose was bored. Though they sometimes quarrelled when together, she missed Kate when she was away, and she was sick to death – yes she *was* – of taking Peg and William to the Park on Saturday mornings – and sometimes Saturday afternoons too! A girl ought to have a day off from kids *sometimes*! She *ought*! And quite suddenly Lily Rose determined she *would* have a day off!

At the moment she was in charge of the house and 'keeping an eye' on Peg and William – last seen grubbing happily in the back yard – Mrs Ruggles having hurried out early to deliver some laundry. Yes, decided Lily Rose, turning away from the window, she was going to have a day off come what might, and, her excitement increasing the more she thought about it, she'd tell Mum so, fair and square, the minute she came back . . . In the meantime . . . those kids . . . ! And darting into the boys' bedroom she leant out of the window that looked over the yard. All seemed well.

'You keep good!' she called as Peg glanced up. 'I've got my eye on you!' 'Though that's an awful wopper!' she added to herself as she turned her attention to her next duty – the making of her brothers' beds.

Gosh! how untidy the twins and Jo were! Their beds . . . ! The whole room! '*Boys!*' muttered Lily Rose contemptuously as she set to work. 'My word, if I ever get married and have boys they'll *do* things – make their own beds and tidy up – same as the girls!' There were times when Lily Rose fairly *hated* boys!

'You wait a while, my girl!' Uncle Albert's young lady, now his newly wedded wife whom they were all trying to learn to call 'Auntie Winnie', had said, Lily Rose having expressed this sentiment when they had come to tea one Sunday. 'You wait; another year and you'll be walkin' out – like as not!'

Kate and the twins had giggled while Lily Rose herself had gone pink with indignation at the very idea. Mrs Ruggles had looked angry, and Mr Ruggles had said, rather sharply, 'There's plenty time for that sort o' thing. Leave her be: she's not fourteen yet – and I likes my children to *be* children.'

'Sorry I'm sure,' said Auntie Winnie, and there was a rather strained silence until Uncle Albert caused a diversion by insisting there was a wasp in his strawberry jam.

They needn't have worried, thought Lily Rose, the incident recurring to her as she cleared the best part of a Meccano set from two of the beds and a jigsaw puzzle from the third; ripped off the sheets and blankets, shook up pillows, and collected dirty handkerchiefs and torn stockings from the floor. Boys! . . . Girls were infinitely to be preferred, and today, her day off, should be spent in the company of Miss Mary Mills, a young lady her own age who shared many of her tastes though few of her trials – especially young brothers, being that object of questionable envy, an 'only' child.

Ah! – as the kitchen door handle rattled – there was Mum! And removing a public library copy of *The Boy Aviators* lying open face downwards in the soap dish on the chest of drawers, Lily Rose clattered downstairs eager to announce her plans.

But Mrs Ruggles, it seemed, had plans too.

'There!' she exclaimed, putting down an empty laundry basket. 'There! That's the last of the Beasley children's washing for a whole fortnight – going off to Devon for holidays today they are. Mrs Beasley's given me the best part of a plum cake, and close on two dozen bananas and a tinful of sugar biscuits for you children, and this afternoon I'm sitting quiet for once in my life and asking Mrs Hook in for a bit of the cake and a nice cup of tea in peace.'

Lily Rose's face (which had brightened at the mention of the sugar biscuits) fell considerably when she heard this. Without doubt it would be the Park for herself, Peg, and William that afternoon. But she had hardly opened her mouth to protest before Mrs Ruggles was announcing very different arrangements!

Her friend Mrs Mullet had, it seemed, invited Peg and Jo to spend the afternoon with her Muriel, and was calling for them shortly after two o'clock. Mr Ruggles would be out till supper-time – cleaning out the pigs and then at a meeting of the allotment holders; and if Lily Rose and the twins liked, they could take some of Mrs Beasley's biscuits and go off for a picnic. Mrs Ruggles would then have the house to herself, only William to contend with, and be able to enjoy Mrs Hook's company in peace.

Enormously surprised, and, on the whole, rather relieved to be spared the necessity of asserting her 'rights', Lily Rose rushed off to acquaint Miss Mills with the situation; and the twins arriving five minutes before dinner-time, hot, dishevelled, and full of suppressed laughter over some recent but unrevealed experience, greeted the idea with great enthusiasm. There was a meeting of The Gang of the Black Hand that afternoon, and some of Mrs Beasley's biscuits would add greatly to their welcome and prestige.

And so, shortly before two o'clock, Mrs Ruggles having extracted promises from all three that neither the river nor the railway would be visited, saw them off with a light heart and set about preparations for entertaining her friend.

'Which way shall we go?' asked Lily Rose when Miss Mills, very tidy in a clean cotton frock and carrying a basket containing her tea, joined her at the corner of One End Street. Miss Mills considered, and finally conceded she thought you got 'to proper country quickest Brightsea Road way', and Lily Rose agreeing they set forth.

It was turning into a *very* hot afternoon. The small back streets sweltered in the sun and there was a smell of stale cabbage and unemptied dustbins wafting unpleasantly about. Even when they reached the top of the town and began to walk along the raised grass-bordered path which ran parallel with the main road, past the prison, and then past trim little houses from behind whose neat garden palings small trees and bushes threw a little shade, it was scorchingly hot. Both road and footpath – as is so frequently the fate of public highways in the warmest season of the year – had recently been tarred. Little lumps of melting blackness forced their way through the gravelled surface and stuck to the feet of unwary pedestrians, while on the road itself, everything that had wheels seemed to have elected to come out that afternoon. Motor coaches, buses, lorries, private cars, and last, but by no means least, motor-bicycles went roaring by in a steady petrol-reeking stream, shaking the footpath with blasts of hot air, and every now and then throwing up tar-spattered pebbles. One hit Lily Rose on the hat, and, as she remarked, it might well have been her eye!

'Let's get away from the main road soon's ever we can,' she said and her companion agreed. They walked in silence for a little. 'There,' said Miss Mills presently, and she pointed, 'there's a turning – a side road – there away under that railway arch – I've often seen it from the bus; I think it goes to Salthaven but I've never been up it. Look, there's a gate into a field on the other side of the arch and a haystack away at the top. Let's go and sit under that – it'll be lovely and cool there, and we can easily climb the gate if it's locked.'

But when they reached the gate – after waiting nearly five minutes for a pause in the traffic to allow them to cross the road, climbing was not necessary for the gate was only latched. They opened and shut it carefully, and looking round to make sure no cows were about, toiled up the steep slope to the haystack, threw themselves down in its most grateful shade, and were soon happily chewing bits of grass and deep in the discussion of their favourite subject – what to do when they left school.

They remained occupied with this all-absorbing topic for the next hour or so, then decided they were hungry and thirsty and it was time for something in the way of refreshment. Miss Mills produced a superior-looking thermos of tea, a medicine bottle of milk, and some very neatly cut jam sandwiches. Lily Rose, who had only an old vinegar bottle which she had filled with a concoction made of lemonade-powder and water, eyed the thermos with surprise and a little envy, but consoled herself with the thought of the unquestionable superiority of Mrs Beasley's biscuits over jam sandwiches – however neatly cut!

They had just cleared a space in the hay, and set out their provisions when suddenly there was a sound of rustling – as if a heavy body – or bodies – were heaving about in the hay on the other side of the rick.

Lily Rose and Miss Mills sat up straight and looked at each other in some alarm. Cows? No, *not* cows, for a minute later came a sound of subdued whispering, and then, hair full of wisps of hay – in fact covered with wisps of hay all over, two figures in very crumpled white shorts – and what looked like under-vests, came crawling on all fours round the stack!

'Boys!' exclaimed Lily Rose to herself in disgust. Well, really! Could one *never* get away from them! But – no – these were not boys – at least what she meant by boys; they were young men.

'Say, miss,' said the first, addressing her, after glancing rather nervously around and then assuming a semi-upright position and sitting back on his heels, 'do you think you two young ladies could spare us a drink?' and he looked very lovingly at the thermos and the ex-vinegar bottle.

Lily Rose and her companion glanced at each other questioningly, both secretly flattered at being referred to as 'young ladies' and not mere 'girls' – or – worse still – 'kids'.

'Are you *hikers*?' inquired Miss Mills rather shyly.

The young man hesitated a moment. 'No,' he said, shaking his tousley head, 'no, we're *runners*. Fact is,' and he glanced round again and spoke in a low and very confidential voice, 'fact *is*, we're on a very *special* sort of race. It's like this, see. We – only runs when it's dark – so's we shan't see the others – and they shan't see us, and know how far we've got. That's one reason we're laying off here awhile, and why we can't go into a town for drinks and such, and have to rely on meeting kind young ladies like yourselves,' and he gave them a dazzling smile (he was a very good-looking young man), 'don't we, Bert?' and he turned to his companion. Bert, decided Lily Rose, was terribly shy. He blushed furiously, and could only stutter a quite unintelligible reply. Lily Rose was often shy herself; she knew the signs only too well, and she felt sorry for Bert.

'Is it a *new* sort of race?' inquired Miss Mills, 'I never heard of one like it before.'

'New?' exclaimed the first young man whose name he later informed them was Ron. 'Oh no. There's nothing new about it. It's as old – as old as – Time – yes, old as Time. Ain't it, Bert?' and he laughed. But Bert looked even shyer and muttered something no one could catch.

'Do you run without shoes?' inquired Lily Rose who, always attentive to footwear, had observed both young men had nothing on their feet but thick grey woollen socks. This time it was Ron who looked confused.

'Yes,' he said after a slight pause, 'but – but sometimes we keep on our socks – specially if we get blisters. I've got a terrible blister now; coo! chronic it is! Don't hardly know how I'm going to run tonight I don't!'

Lily Rose knew all about blisters on the feet; she frequently had them and knew how painful they could be. She began to feel sorry for Ron too – and that – alas, was her undoing.

''Course we can spare you a drink – can't we, Mary?' she said. 'And' – and this was really heroic, for her mouth was fairly watering for Mrs Beasley's biscuits, and there were only six – 'you can have a biscuit if you're terribly hungry.'

Hungry, Ron assured her, was hardly the word. 'Plates of fresh air' being practically all they had had today, and he grabbed the biscuit held out to him as if it might vanish into space and – or so it seemed to Lily Rose – swallowed it whole, while Miss Mills's sandwiches proffered with a shy invitation to 'help themselves' soon disappeared in the same lightning manner. In fact neither Lily Rose nor her companion had very much tea.

'Phew! That was good!' presently exclaimed Ron, draining the last drop from the thermos, and licking the last crumb of sandwich from his fingers. 'Wonder when we'll see our next meal, Bert! How we're ever going to run tonight without another bite of food or drop of drink I don't know! Oh for some good, juicy plums or a nice bunch of bananas!'

Lily Rose, who had been lolling back in the hay, sat up. She had been thinking somewhat along these same lines herself, and the words 'bunch of bananas' decided her.

'Tell you what,' she said, 'if you'll give me the money to give Mum for it, I could bring you some bread from home – and some lovely bananas we've got; and if Mary could get her thermos filled I'd bring that too! – you could hide it somewhere when you'd done and we could come and fetch it sometime. You could run if you had bread, and bananas, and tea, couldn't you?' she asked anxiously, 'and it would be my Good Deed for the day – I'm a Girl Guide,' she added proudly.

'My word!' exclaimed Ron, and he looked at her with real admiration, 'that's something like a good deed that is! Bread! Bananas!'*Course* you shall have the money for 'em. And *tea*! If your friend could manage that – well, grateful wouldn't be the word, would it, Bert?' Bert, as usual, said nothing but he nodded vigorously.

Miss Mills said she thought she could manage the tea – easy; they never hardly used the thermos, only if they went on a picnic, or Dad (who worked at the gas works) did a spell of night duty – and he'd only just finished one . . . Both her parents were out this afternoon, and she could make the tea in a jiffy if Lily Rose would take it . . . No, in answer to a question, she was not a Girl Guide but, rather primly, she was always glad to help anyone in trouble . . .

Ron now became very excited, and for the next ten minutes issued so many instructions that at last his 'kind young ladies' as he kept calling them, begged him to stop as they really couldn't remember any more.

Well, were they *certain* they knew what to do? And he went over the directions again from what he called 'keeping their eyes skinned' for any other runners every *inch* of the way, to – most important of all – not mentioning to *any human being* the existence of, or of anyone even *remotely* resembling Ron and Bert . . .

Yes, they understood perfectly but, objected Lily Rose, how long must they keep silent?

'Till Monday,' said Ron solemnly.

'*Monday!*' Lily Rose shook her head. That was impossible – absolutely. Her mother would miss the food at once and directly she got home she'd be asked if she'd taken it; she couldn't say 'no', and then it would be 'why?' . . . She thought she could hold out about it till she went to bed, but all next day – *never*!

Ron thought deeply for a moment. 'Sunday morning then,' he conceded, 'Sunday morning till *eight*. *Promise?*'

'*Promise!*'

'And your friend?' He turned to Mary. Mary also promised. There'd be no bother at her end, she assured him – no one would be any the wiser. But *he* must promise to hide the thermos where no one but Lily Rose or herself could find it.

Ron quickly settled this. He would put it in the hedge – there, and he pointed across the field; exactly opposite the haystack under that big tree – they couldn't miss it. He'd put some hay round it so it shouldn't be noticeable to anyone who might chance to come along.

'It's half-past five now,' said Miss Mills, who was the proud possessor of a wrist-watch. 'It will take us almost an hour to walk home. Mum and Dad will be back at seven, so if I'm going to get the tea we ought to be going.' Lily Rose also needed to time her arrival at One End Street when Mrs Ruggles would be upstairs putting the younger children to bed; and at last, with many 'good-byes' and 'good lucks', and reiterations of 'don't you worry – we won't forget', they set off homewards.

They could not have timed matters better! After many whisperings Lily Rose left Miss Mills at her door and went on to One End Street. Mrs Ruggles was, just as she had hoped, upstairs putting Peg and William to bed. Jo was invisible, and the twins absorbed in some counter game on the kitchen floor. In less than five minutes Lily Rose had secured all she needed and gone quickly out again.

It was later than Lily Rose expected by the time she reached the gate beside the railway arch and toiled up the steep slope to the haystack once again. For a brief moment she thought her friends had gone; there was not a sign of them. She was just about to call their names when, almost at her feet, Ron's head, grinning broadly, emerged through a hummock of hay!

'Gosh! for a moment I thought as you were another runner – found us out!' he said. 'Bert, it's our young lady back again!'

Lily Rose hot and panting, set down the basket, and Bert emerging from another hummock, she began to enumerate the provisions she had brought. She was a wonderful girl, Ron said, yes, wonderful!

It is always pleasing to be considered wonderful, and Lily Rose, whom no one had ever considered remotely approaching such a state, enjoyed it particularly, and fairly swelled with pride as the proofs of her prowess in catering were exhibited and applauded.

The wish was expressed that she would not 'get into trouble at home', but Lily Rose was certain 'no' because, after all she had only 'borrowed' the food – they themselves had promised to pay for it . . . And she looked at them both expectantly, adding please could she have the money now – and if possible for a bus back, because if she didn't start soon she'd be late in and then there *would* be trouble!

'Of course!' said Ron and he dived into first one and then the other of what Lily Rose supposed were pockets in his crumpled shorts. Then he looked blankly at his companion, and finally at Lily Rose herself.

'It's gone!' he said in a hollow voice. 'The money! Gone! The lot of it – the whole blooming lot! Must have fallen out the time we had to crawl under some wire . . . Well . . . I . . . I . . . don't know what to say . . .'

Lily Rose didn't know what to say either! She was thinking, sickeningly, of the cost of almost a whole loaf – and a big one at that – and six large bananas . . . And what about her bus fare – if she had to walk back she'd be most frightfully late! . . . Hadn't he got a penny even? . . . Hadn't Bert got a penny? . . . Bert said nothing but shook his head, indicating his pockets in a sort of mute appeal. As for Ron he looked almost as if he were going to cry – 'ever so mournful', as Lily Rose was to say later. Of course it must make him feel awkward . . . And once again she was sorry for him . . . But oh dear she must, she simply *must* go or goodness knows when she'd be back now she'd got to walk. It was getting dark too . . .

'Tell you what!' cried Ron slapping a hand to his forehead as if suddenly inspired. 'Tell you what – we'll *send* you the money! Be home tonight we ought. You just tell your mum as it's coming in the post. All right? See, I've got a pencil – funny I didn't drop *that*' – and he produced a tiny stub of a thing – 'look, you write your address – here – on the banana bag. There! Now there'll be no mistake! It's too bad about the bus but it's getting a bit cooler now, and if you slips off quick you'll be O.K. We shan't forget our young lady, shall we, Bert?' he said as Lily Rose with a final reminder about the disposal of the thermos, prepared to go, and he held out a hot and sticky hand and clasped Lily Rose's which was hotter and stickier still. Bert said nothing but he too held out a hand. It shook rather and though equally sticky was, surprisingly, cold. Lily Rose said she would never forget *them*, and wished them both the best of luck, and hoped, if they were ever this way again they'd look in at No. 1 One End Street.

Ron seemed to be overcome with something between a cough and a sneeze but Bert looked shyer than ever. Lily Rose stood hesitating for a moment; then she snatched up her empty basket and ran quickly down the field.

Part Two

'Well that's an extraordinary thing!' exclaimed Mrs Ruggles beginning to busy herself about preparations for supper, and she stood gazing into the bread bin in the back kitchen where very much less than half of a large loaf the baker had delivered that morning was lying. 'I never used up all that bread tea-time! Why, I didn't cut off above four slices at the most – along of Mrs Hook saying as she were never a one for new bread; that I'm certain of. It's very odd, that is! And look at those!' and she pounced on Mrs Beasley's bunch of bananas dangling from a hook in the larder, 'I do believe some of them's gone too! Twenty there were – exactly four short of the two dozen – I counted them particular! Twenty – That I remember *distinctly*! There's never twenty there now!'

Most certainly there were not. Three times Mrs Ruggles counted them, and each time the answer was fourteen – no more, no less.

'It's those boys, I'll be bound! *John!*' she called through the open door to the kitchen. '*Jim!*'

'Yes, Mum?' answered two shrill voices.

'Come here!'

The twins sitting on the floor engrossed in a game of Snakes and Ladders looked at each other. What now? What hitherto undetected sin was about to be disclosed? They got slowly to their feet.

'Come, hurry!' called Mrs Ruggles.

'What's up, Mum?' asked John peering round the doorway, Jim leaning over his shoulder.

'Have either of you two been in here after those bananas – and the bread?'

'No!' chorused two indignant voices, and two red heads were vigorously shaken.

'What about that Bates boy – you had him in here this evening?' (In moments of crisis or indignation, Mrs Ruggles always prefaced the name of any suspected or unwelcome character by 'that'.) Both twins rushed loyally to the defence of their friend.

'*Sam?* He wouldn't do a thing like that!'

''*Course* he never took nothing! He never even went *near* the back kitchen anyway!'

'Then it must have been Lily Rose – or that Mary Mills,' said Mrs Ruggles, 'for there's no one else come in; and Jo's been upstairs with his nose in a book ever since he was back from Mrs Mullett's. And where *is* Lily Rose – I saw her come in when I were putting Peg and William to bed.'

'She went out,' said John briefly, 'and anyway she don't eat bananas, leastways not above half a one – you know she don't, Mum – says they make her fat. And Mary Mills didn't come here – we saw her when we came home – leaning out of her window.'

'Perhaps it was Cuckoo-Coo?' suggested Jim hopefully.

'Don't be ridiculous!' said Mrs Ruggles sharply, 'as if a small kitten could eat the best part of a loaf of bread and six bananas! Well . . . it's a mystery to me, and I only hopes as you two are telling the truth!'

'We've *said* we are,' muttered John sulkily, and full of offended dignity the twins retreated into the kitchen again.

'Listen,' said John, and he lowered his voice. 'Lily Rose was in there –' he jerked his head towards the back kitchen. 'She's gone out, and – she took a basket with her – I saw it! Where's she *gone*?'

And they stood looking at each other, their eyes widening, Snakes and Ladders totally forgotten.

Lily Rose hurried breathlessly along the footpath by the main road. The air was hot and still and dusk was changing slowly to darkness. Some belated rooks went flapping and caw-cawing overhead, and here and there little stars the size of pin-heads were beginning to show in the clear sky. On the road itself, the traffic was not much less than it had been in the afternoon for though there were fewer buses and lorries there were now streams of cars. Family parties returning from the sea, and young men and maidens in sports cars went roaring by, motor-bicycles dodging perilously in and out amongst them. Every now and then a coach-load of excursionists, all singing and shouting at the tops of their voices, whirled past; the footpath shook and the glare from the headlights was dazzling. Stealthily the darkness was increasing, the daylight fading. Whatever *was* the time! There'd be the most frightful row when she got home . . . Out till dark made Dad angry enough – much less after! Perhaps with luck, he wouldn't be back yet – those meetings sometimes lasted ages . . . But now an awful thought struck her! Suppose they'd gone round to Mary's to see if she was there! What would Mary say – what *could* she say? . . . And what, for that matter, was she herself going to say when she *did* get in? . . . Well – what was *true*; only that she'd tried to help someone; and if she *had* taken food from the house it was only sort of *borrowed* – they'd promised, honest, to pay for it (it was just a bit of bad luck they'd lost the money the way they had but they *were* going to send it, hadn't the one called Ron written down the address special on the banana bag). And anyway, above everything else, it was her Good Deed for the day! . . . She couldn't help being so late because that again was on account of the money getting lost; she'd have been home in splendid time, if she'd been able to take the bus . . .

Poof! she was hot – and tired! Must have walked miles today . . . Talk about blisters on the feet; she'd be lucky if she got home without one! . . . Ah, at last, the lamp posts were beginning. Lily Rose felt a little better. She didn't anyway much like being out in the country all alone when it was nearly dark even if it *was* on the main road . . . Now came the beginnings of houses . . . now the prison . . . another five minutes and she'd be at the main cross-roads; then a quick run down the back streets and she'd be home! . . . She plodded on, getting stickier and stickier, and more and more breathless with heat and hurry. It was almost dark now . . . Coo, what luck! There was a policeman on point duty at the cross-roads – they didn't always have one – and the traffic was being held back. She slipped quickly across. Now at least it was down hill nearly all the way! And puffing and blowing, her heart thumping with exertion and anxiety, Lily Rose ran homewards through the sultry and sparsely lit back streets.

Supper was on the table and it was after half-past eight. Mr Ruggles had said not to wait for him – he might be kept at his meeting – but where was Lily Rose? At first annoyed, but now beginning to feel uneasy, Mrs Ruggles glanced anxiously up and down the street. It was getting dark. 'Another ten minutes,' she said, drawing the curtains, 'and if she's not in, you John, you run round to those Mills and see if she's there.'

'O.K., Mum,' said John who relished any excuse that provided the smallest respite from bedtime. 'Coo! are those the bananas? Aren't they whoppers? Can I have one – please?'

'Thanks to whoever *took* them,' replied Mrs Ruggles tartly, 'there's only enough for one each instead of two – and not that till you've ate up your bread-and-marg. – and look sharp about it – it's getting on to bedtime. And you, Jo, if you've finished, you go on up now – and no reading in bed – do you hear what I say? You've never stopped reading since you come in – you'll be saying as your eyes hurt next.'

'It's *The Boy Aviators*,' put in Jim as Jo muttered something and then pushed back his chair and stumped sulkily upstairs. 'He can't put it down – no one can, not once they've started it! I wish more people would write books like that! Honest, Mum, you ought to read it!'

But Mrs Ruggles was not listening. Her eyes were fixed on the clock . . . close on nine . . .

'If you've finished, John, you run round to those Mills now; straight there, mind, and straight back.'

'O.K., Mum.'

'And stop saying "O.K." – *do*!'

'O.K. – sorry, Mum – all right,' said John, and he scuttled off.

In not much more than five minutes, to Mrs Ruggles's surprise, he was back.

'You've been quick!' she exclaimed. 'Is Lily Rose there?'

'No – she's not. But, Mum –'

'Who did you see?'

'I saw Mary – she was up at her window, sniffing away – hadn't half been crying, I should think! Mum, listen!'

'Did she say when she saw Lily Rose last?'

'No. Mum – *listen* – *do* – it's *terribly* exciting! *There's two prisoners escaped from the prison!* I met old Mr Towner – Tony's grandfather – Tony was with us this afternoon.

"Not seen any suspicious-looking characters when you was out, did you?" he said. Gosh! If only we *had*!'

'What's that you're saying?' said Mrs Ruggles sharply. 'Two prisoners got out? *When?*'

'Mr Towner didn't know – only as the cops was out looking for 'em, and people helping. Coo! Mum – I expect *that's* where Lily Rose is – helping to look! Oh, can't Jim and I go out and look too! Oh, Mum, *can't* we?'

'Don't talk so stupid!' cried Mrs Ruggles. 'The idea! And get off to bed now, both of you. Oh my goodness me, and that girl not in! I wish your Dad would come!'

'I expect he's helping to look too!' said Jim consolingly.

But just as he and John had reluctantly started to go upstairs there were footsteps outside, and the next moment the latch lifted and in came Mr Ruggles.

Mr Ruggles was not in the best of tempers. He had had a hot and tiring afternoon cleaning out the pigs, and the meeting of the allotment holders concerning a dispute about a right of way, had been prolonged and stormy; nothing settled, and, so far as he could see, no one any the wiser.

'Another two prisoners escaped!' he remarked lugubriously, hanging his cap on a hook on the kitchen door, and he drew up a chair and sat down heavily beside the supper-table.

'That'll be the third lot got out this year,' he continued, 'any more, and the Governor'll get the sack I shouldn't wonder! Why,' noticing his wife's agitated countenance, 'why, Rosie – what's up? You're never going to tell me as they've been *here*! Thought we'd had our share with the tiger and all!'*

'I don't know whether they've been here or they haven't,' replied Mrs Ruggles rather uneasily. 'And that's a fact. It's true there's food missing – It's Lily Rose I'm worried about – she's not come in, Jo, and look at the time!'

It was Mr Ruggles's turn to look disturbed.

'What's that?' he said sharply. 'Lily Rose not *in* – at this hour – it's after nine! Really, Rosie –'

'Now don't you go a-blamin' me!' cried Mrs Ruggles angrily. 'With the best will in the world I can't keep my eye on six children at once! She was around when I were putting Peg and William to bed – that's all I can tell you. I only knows as if she isn't back in the next five minutes we ought – one of us – to go down to the police station – oh, have your cocoa first, Jo! And a bite of something . . .' as Mr Ruggles got to his feet and made for the door. 'Have your cocoa *do*!'

'"Cocoa"!' exclaimed Mr Ruggles, 'do you think I'm drinking *cocoa* while a girl of mine's out and there's escaped prisoners running around loose!' And taking his cap from the hook where he had just hung it, he was about to put it on when the door handle rattled and the next minute, breathless and almost purple in the face with exertion, Lily Rose stumbled into the room!

Lily Rose stood leaning against the door, panting, exhausted.

* *Further Adventures of the Family from One End Street.*

'And where,' demanded Mr Ruggles, 'where, my girl, may I ask have you been – a-comin' home this time of the evening?'

'Yes – where indeed!' echoed Mrs Ruggles, her anxiety giving place to anger. 'And perhaps,' noting the empty basket Lily Rose had put down, 'perhaps you can tell me if you know anything about the best part of a loaf of bread and six of Mrs Beasley's bananas that's disappeared from the larder?'

'Oh, Mum!' gasped Lily Rose, still trying to get her breath, and now on the verge of tears, 'I've only *borrowed*

them – truly I have, and, and they're going to be paid for – the money's being sent – *honest* it is. It'll be all right. I know they'll send it – they've got the address written down ever so careful.'

'Now what's all this about?' demanded Mr Ruggles. 'Who's "they"? Have you been a-pinching food for someone? Answer me. Sharp now!'

Lily Rose began to cry. 'I – I can't,' she wailed. 'I can't. Not till tomorrow, anyway, I can't . . . I've promised – I . . .'

'What do you mean "not till tomorrow"? You'll tell me now this minute or –' began Mr Ruggles when he was interrupted by a thunderous knocking on the door. 'Drat it!' he muttered. 'Here – come away from the door,' and he pushed Lily Rose aside and opened it. Outside on the step, displaying a very angry countenance indeed, stood Mr Mills, and beside him, weeping loudly, his daughter Mary.

'Evenin', Ruggles,' he began curtly. 'So this,' and he glared furiously, 'this is what comes of lettin' my little girl play along of yours! Nice goings on I must say!' Then as Mr Ruggles stood regarding him in some amazement, 'Yes, nice goings on,' he repeated, and, his aitches deserting him as his indignation increased, 'Tea under 'ay stacks with 'ikers! All the same, I suppose,' he continued, 'if it 'ad been these 'ere prisoners what's escaped! And our good thermos – where's that got to I'd like to know? That thermos, let me tell you, 'as got to be returned – and sharp too or –'

'Here, less of it!' interrupted Mr Ruggles angrily, as Mr Mills paused for breath. 'You keep a civil tongue in your head!'

'And suppose you come *inside*,' suggested Mrs Ruggles icily, ''stead of standing there bawling away for all the neighbours to hear! What's this?' she demanded when, pushing the weeping Mary before him, Mr Mills had somewhat reluctantly complied, and the door was firmly shut, 'What's this about hikers? And are you trying to tell us as our Lily Rose has stole your thermos? You'd better be careful, Mr Mills, what you're a-sayin' of, yes you better! And you, Mary,' she went on, 'stop making that hullaballoo – *stop* it! We can't hear ourselves think!'

But Mary was past stopping anything. The shock of finding that Dad had elected to do night duty for a friend, and the thermos was needed that very evening, combined with her mother's scandalized fury at the enormity of having shared tea and sandwiches with unknown young men, had unnerved her completely. She continued to weep unrestrainedly.

Mrs Ruggles turned to Lily Rose. 'What *is* this about a thermos?' she demanded. 'Answer me – do you hear!'

'I didn't take it, Mum!' wept Lily Rose now completely dissolved in tears, and sniffing miserably, 'leastways I did . . . but . . . but not for keeps . . . I – I know where it is and it's all right. Tomorrow . . .'

'There!' interrupted Mr Mills triumphantly, 'she's took it! I told you so! I *knew* our Mary wouldn't tell a lie!'

'You speak proper to my missis!' shouted Mr Ruggles now thoroughly roused, 'and before anything else, what's this about hikers and hay stacks – let's get that clear. We've a right to know what's happened before you begin accusin' one of our kids of pinching things! Let's have it now!'

'Very well,' said Mr Mills, 'you can!' And he proceeded to give his version of the afternoon's adventures. 'Leadin' my girl astray – that's what it is,' he concluded. 'And now, where's our thermos?'

'Well it's not *here*!' snapped Mrs Ruggles. 'Lily Rose, have you, or have you not took it? And if you *have* – where is it?'

'I haven't *stolen* it!' cried Lily Rose. 'I've *told* you!' And suddenly she, also, lost her temper. She hated everyone! Particularly she hated Mr Mills. As for Mary! . . . Mary had 'told' – told on Ron and Bert!

'I haven't *stolen* it!' she repeated, 'I've *said* so!' and she stamped her foot with fury. *'I haven't, I haven't, I haven't!'*

'That'll do now!' cried Mr Ruggles sharply. 'That's enough! Be quiet – *at once*! I'm doing no more arguing,' he continued. 'If Mills here insists as we've got his thermos he can come along of me to the police. Yes, I'm going, straightaway; and you, Lily Rose, you'll come along too.'

'Dad – Jo!' exclaimed Mrs Ruggles catching him by the sleeve, 'You're never –'

'Leave me be, Rosie,' replied Mr Ruggles shaking her off, 'I've an idea. I think as the police may be quite pleased to see me – and Mr Mills and his daughter. As he's just said himself, might have been escaped prisoners under the hay stack. Well, so it might. And afore I worries about a thermos I'm making sure it were or it weren't!' And putting on his cap he opened the door, beckoned Lily Rose to follow, and went out.

Mr Mills hesitated a moment. He glanced at Mrs Ruggles then said abruptly, 'Come, Mary!' And without another word, followed by his still-weeping daughter, he joined Mr Ruggles and Lily Rose outside in the street.

Everything in the police station was very shiny, and polished, and *hard*. The floors, the walls, the bench they sat on. Even the jaw of the constable in charge looked like granite, and his face and neck had a well-scrubbed-and-no-nonsense-about-it appearance. Mr Ruggles and Mr Mills between them had stated their business, and a fat sergeant, whom Lily Rose knew well by sight, had been summoned. He asked many questions, wrote ponderously in a shiny black-backed notebook, and then plodded heavily away to confer with some higher authority. The hard bench seemed to get harder every minute. No one spoke, and there was no sound but the ticking of a huge clock on the wall, an occasional sniff from Miss Mills, and the scritch-scratch of the policeman's pen as he made mysterious entries in an enormous ledger. Lily Rose gave a little shiver. How awful if you'd really done something dreadful . . . waiting and waiting . . . Ron and Bert! . . . Could they really be the missing prisoners like Dad seemed to think? . . . She just couldn't believe it – *didn't* believe it . . . 'Dad,' she whispered, afraid to speak aloud in such an awe-inspiring atmosphere, '*Dad!*' . . . But at that moment the door opened and there was the fat sergeant again. 'This way, please,' he said and beckoned to them. Lily Rose went cold all over, and clutched Mr Ruggles by the arm. Whatever was going to happen! . . . Were they being taken to the cells, which she had once been told were located down below in the basement! . . . What would they . . . But before she had time to imagine anything more, the sergeant opened a door almost opposite labelled 'Detective Inspector Kivell', said briefly, 'In here, please,' and shepherded them all into another shining and polished apartment. Behind a table sat a very important-looking gentleman indeed. He wore a neat grey suit and a large pair of horn-rimmed spectacles. On the table, beside a pile of big ledgers and a telephone, stood a vase of roses and a large silver cigarette box. A real toff, said Lily Rose to herself. Next to a judge almost, she wouldn't wonder. Now Dad 'ud be nervous . . . And she glanced apprehensively at her father.

But Mr Ruggles was not in the least nervous. His blood was up and at the moment he had no fears of toffs, Detective Inspectors, or anyone else. It was the voluble Mr Mills who appeared to be struck dumb, and before he could collect his scattered wits, or indeed anyone open their mouths to say anything, Mr Ruggles had plunged headlong into what he had come to say: Might not Lily Rose's acquaintances under the hay stack be the escaped prisoners? As to Mr Mills's 'to-do' about a thermos . . . 'My girl may have acted foolish,' he concluded – 'I'm not saying as she didn't; but she's not a thief, and,' with a glance at Mr Mills, 'no one's a-going to say as she is!'

The Detective Inspector was very kind. He listened patiently until Mr Ruggles came rather breathlessly to the end of his speech, then asked the sergeant to bring forward chairs. He even offered cigarettes from the silver box. Then he questioned first Lily Rose and then Miss Mills, listening gravely to all they said and occasionally making a note on a blotting pad in front of him; then Mr Mills (who had refused a cigarette and sat throughout the interview on the extreme edge of his chair, nursing his cap and glaring angrily at everyone in turn); and lastly Mr Ruggles himself. Finally he turned to the sergeant.

'Who was on duty at the prison cross-roads this evening, Sergeant?'

'Braund, sir.'

'Is he back?'

'Yes, sir; just come in, sir.'

'Send him in here.'

It is commonly supposed that it is only to the old and ageing that policemen look young. Perhaps it was the absence of his helmet, or his very fair hair, but even Lily Rose was struck with the youthful appearance of the constable who entered the room. However, youthful or not, P.C. Braund showed no nervousness in the presence of his superiors; he stood smartly to attention, and answered all questions clearly and with dispatch.

Had he, while on point duty, noticed a couple of young men in running-clothes – white shorts and vests? asked the Detective Inspector. P.C. Braund had. In fact one had called out, as they ran past him, 'Seen any others ahead, Serg?' (The compliment of 'Serg' – though this he did not reveal to the Detective Inspector – having particularly impressed the incident on his mind.)

'Did you,' pursued the Detective Inspector, and he spoke slowly and impressively, 'did you happen to notice if both young men were barefoot – or at least without shoes?'

'I can't say as I did, sir,' replied P.C. Braund regretfully. 'There was a mort of traffic,' he added, more as a statement of fact than as an excuse for lack of observation. The company on the chairs looked at each other at the unfamiliar expression, but the Detective Inspector noted it, and smiled to himself: like P.C. Braund he, too, was from the West Country. He remained silent for a moment, frowning down at his blotting-pad. Then he looked up. Something in his expression struck the constable.

'You're not saying, sir, you're not saying as they were the escaped prisoners!' he exclaimed.

'I'm afraid I am,' said the Detective Inspector drily.

For a moment the room seemed to be full of a kind of stunned silence. Lily Rose stole a look at P.C. Braund. He was blushing to the roots of his very fair hair; blushing as badly as poor Bert had done . . .

But the Detective Inspector was speaking . . .

'As you may know,' he said, addressing them all, 'the Territorials have been in camp near here this last week; some of them have been practising cross-country running; these prisoners were out with a working party this afternoon – they may have seen them and thought they might pose as runners themselves – in their underclothes – and get away with it. And so,' he added, 'they might have done since none of us were alert enough to spot them. However, thanks to your promptness in coming here,

Mr Ruggles, I don't think they'll get very far now. We've alerted every police station, and there's a watch on all road junctions . . .'

Mr Ruggles sat grinning with satisfaction, but P.C. Braund drew a hand across his forehead and almost groaned.

'And to think,' he said slowly, 'to think one of 'em even *spoke* to me, sir!' The fat sergeant looked down his nose and his lips twitched slightly.

'Don't take it too hardly, Constable,' said the Detective Inspector smiling, 'considerably senior staff to yourself have been taken in over this. And,' he added kindly, 'I was on the main road myself this evening – and there *was* a mort of traffic!'

P.C. Braund looked at him gratefully. He seemed about to speak when the telephone rang. The Detective Inspector picked up the receiver and a brief conversation consisting mainly of yes – yes – where? – when? followed. Then he rang off. 'They've got them,' he said quietly. 'Once again, I must thank you, Mr Ruggles, for so promptly contacting us. Dear me – *whatever's* the matter?' For Lily Rose had begun to cry.

'Oh, oh!' she wept. 'Oh, *poor* Ron and Bert! Oh, what will they do to 'em! Oh, I can't bear it!' And she burst into noisy sobs, while Miss Mills who had never completely stopped sniffing, began to cry again in sympathy.

'Give over – at once!' said Mr Ruggles angrily, giving Lily Rose a little shake, 'and stop acting like a baby! Stop it now – do you hear what I say.'

'And you too, Mary,' said Mr Mills sharply, 'stop it!'

'I shouldn't worry your heads about Ron and Bert,' said the Detective Inspector. 'They're a couple of real ne'er-do-wells. And they'll only get what they deserve – probably a good deal less,' and dismissing the sergeant and P.C. Braund he stood up and began putting some papers together. The interview, so far as he was concerned, was over.

But it was not over for Mr Mills. 'And what about my thermos!' he demanded angrily. '*Whoever* took it *I* want it back! I'm due on duty at ten o'clock and it's close on it now!'

He had hardly finished speaking when the door opened. 'Almost like a conjuring trick,' as Mr Ruggles was to say later, and in came the sergeant again. In his hand was a thermos flask.

'The missing property I think, sir,' he said, addressing the Detective Inspector. 'Just been brought in. Along of,' he consulted a notebook in his other hand, 'two pairs black prison shoes; one quarter pencil; one paper bag with writing on same, containing banana skins. All found in hedge bordering . . .'

The Detective Inspector held up his hand. 'And now,' he said, Mr Mills having identified and received his flask, and completely, if somewhat grudgingly exonerated Lily Rose of stealing it, 'suppose you two gentlemen shake hands? That's the spirit,' as Mr Mills and Mr Ruggles somewhat sheepishly complied. 'Come, Sergeant, you and I must be getting along. Bless me! What's the matter *now*!' For Lily Rose had dissolved into tears yet again!

'The bag!' she wept, 'they left the bag – with our address! Now they'll never send the money for Mum like they said; never, *never*!'

'Well, I expect we can settle that,' said the Detective Inspector. 'It wasn't so very much, was it?'

'Oh *yes*,' replied Lily Rose, doing her best to blink back her tears, 'there was more than half a big loaf – that 'ud be sixpence – quite – and, and the bananas – they're about tuppence each, 'praps more – and I took *six* of 'em.'

'Would two shillings cover it?'

'Cover it?'

'Be enough?' And feeling in his pocket the Detective Inspector produced a two-shilling piece. But here Mr Ruggles intervened. 'It's very kind of you, sir,' he said, 'but I'd rather she didn't take it – thanking you kindly all the same.'

'Oh come,' said the Detective Inspector. 'Let it be *my* good deed for the day. *I* used to be a Boy Scout. Scouts always help Guides – don't they, Miss Ruggles?'

'I – I don't know,' said Lily Rose smiling rather damply.

'But I do!' said the Detective Inspector moving towards the door; and the sergeant springing forward to open it for him. 'Good-night,' he said and was gone.

8. Week-End Arrivals

Part One

'It doesn't say a single *word* about Lily Rose, or a row, or cops!' said Kate when she finished reading the letter from Mr Ruggles referred to at the beginning of the last chapter. 'But it's about something ever so exciting, Mr Wildgoose – and there's a message for you and Mrs Wildgoose in it. You'll never guess what so I'll read it!'

'Have thought for some Time,' wrote Mr Ruggles in his large, sprawly writing with no commas anywhere and with capital letters in the most surprising places, 'as its about my Turn for a Holiday so have worked a stiffish bit of Overtime and got some days Owe me week end after next. Now your Mum and Lily Rose and William are all going to Uncle Albert's for Whole Day Saturday then and Mrs Mullett having Peg and Jo which means Twins Alone Here so have thought how about me and them all coming to The Dew Drop Inn for a little stay. Another thing is as Sid Watkins is Taking a Load Ailesford way and would bring us along that far in his Lorry. So you Ask Mrs

Wildgoose if she will please to write and say if she and Mr Wildgoose is Agreeable also Terms and would be pleased to give a hand in garden if required. It will be a nice change specially If Fine but no one can't Arrange *That*! Your Loving Dad.'

'Well, that *is* a lovely surprise!' said Mrs Wildgoose, ''course they can come – can't they, Charlie?' Mr Wildgoose nodded and said he was only too pleased, adding that Mr Ruggles couldn't have chosen a better moment – the Early Victoria apples would be ready then and he'd welcome a hand with the picking. And – had she and Mrs Wildgoose *forgotten* – 'week-end after next' was The Fair! 'And if there's anything your young brothers'll enjoy it's that! When I was a nipper I used to fairly live for it from one year to the next! And I still enjoy it, I don't mind telling you – Lighthouse, Dodgems, Swing-boats, Hoopla and all! Well, I must be off and give The Dog Daisy her breakfast,' he concluded, brushing some crumbs from his pullover on to the tablecloth as he got up. 'You write today, missis, and don't bother about "terms",' he added as he went out – 'we'll settle all that when they come.' But Kate found this faintly worrying. She felt sure Mr Ruggles would rather know – in case he hadn't enough money saved, 'specially' as she tried to explain to Mrs Wildgoose, 'with The Fair and all?' Mrs Wildgoose was very understanding and said she would write the letter just as soon as the dinner was in the oven and Kate could run along with the letter and catch the twelve o'clock post. She had hardly finished speaking, however, when there was a loud knock at the front door.

'Now whoever can that be this time of day!' she exclaimed and she bustled into the sitting-room and peeped through the window curtain. 'Gracious me – it's Lord Glenheather – and he's got that Jaeger dog with him! Run out quick, Kate, and make sure Daisy's still tied up, for if the two of 'em get together they'll be chasing all over the flower beds!' And she hurried away to welcome her visitor.

'Good morning, Mrs Wildgoose,' said Lord Glenheather removing his battered-looking felt hat which had reminded Lily Rose so strongly of a badly made pork pie.* 'I've called to see if your husband can spare me a few minutes? . . . He's in the garden? . . . Then I'll go straight there if I may? But I don't want to bring my dog into the house – he's very dirty; perhaps your young visitor, if she's about, would

* *Further Adventures of the Family from One End Street.*

keep an eye on him for me?' Mrs Wildgoose, who had been regarding Jaeger's feet and legs which were plastered with slimy black mud as if from recent immersion in pond or ditch, with no favourable eye, was grateful for this consideration, but before she could reply, a small voice said suddenly, 'I'll hold him, mister!' And there, almost invisible since the day of The Flower Show, stood Johnny Sears who seemed to have appeared silent and spook-like from nowhere!

Lord Glenheather regarded him somewhat doubtfully. 'Do you think you can – he's pretty strong, you know.'

'He'll stay along of me,' said Johnny Sears confidently. ''Ullo, Jaeger! 'Ullo!' and he held out a grubby but ingratiating hand. Jaeger strained forward on his lead and sniffed it, then sniffed again in evident approval. Johnny Sears came a step nearer and was soon being sniffed appreciatively all over.

'You see!' he said proudly, 'likes my smell he does!'

Mrs Wildgoose looked extremely disapproving but Lord Glenheather laughed. 'Well, here you are,' he said, 'here's the lead – mind you hold on to it – *tight* – and with both hands.' And taking off his odd-looking hat he followed Mrs Wildgoose through the hall of the Inn, down the passage by the kitchen, and out into the garden.

The Dog Daisy, tethered by a long chain to her winebarrel kennel, was eating her breakfast at her usual furious speed while Mr Wildgoose stood by regarding her in thoughtful silence. The Dog Daisy was not, alas, proving a very happy acquisition to The Dew Drop Inn. 'She was a dear thing' (Mrs Wildgoose); *'sweet'* (Kate); and 'a nice little beast' (Mr Wildgoose); and though docile enough with the ducks and hens, having been, as Willie Sims put it 'reared along side 'em', she was neither house-trained nor garden-trained – particularly the latter. Cabbages and young seedlings to The Dog Daisy were so many objects to be dug up, borders slept on, flower beds rolled in; windfall apples specially designed for her amusement. The choicest flowers would be found with their heads bitten off; neat little heaps of weeds scattered to the four winds, and bone-burying holes dug in the lawn. Mr Wildgoose strongly disapproved of keeping a dog on a chain but after a week or so of The Dog Daisy's gardening depredations he felt there was nothing else to be done and for the greater part of the day she remained tethered. Every evening, however, he or Mrs Wildgoose had tried to find time to give her a run in the fields. But here, alas, yet another flaw in her character was revealed; she ran sheep! Sheep were in her blood as you might say; for generations her shaggy ancestors had been working dogs on farms; she had only to sight a sheep and she was off, like an arrow from a bow. Had he had the time Mr Wildgoose felt sure he could train her, but he had not, and for anyone to own a sheep-running dog in a community of land-owners, farmers, and smallholders was asking for trouble; for the landlord of The Dew Drop Inn it was unthinkable. Willie Sims's feelings would be hurt, but The Dog Daisy he was afraid would have to go. The question was, *where*? And then, as he told Mrs Wildgoose later, he had looked up, and there, like an answer to prayer – as perhaps it was – stood Lord Glenheather, announcing that he had come, in the truest sense of the expression, '"to see a man about a dog". Two dogs, actually,' he added with a laugh.

Rumours of The Dog Daisy's behaviour it seemed had penetrated even the thick walls of The Priory. Lord Glenheather was returning in a few days to his native land; he could 'do' with another sheep-dog on his farm, but, much as he liked the beast, he could not 'do' with Jaeger. To put the matter in a nut-shell, would Mr Wildgoose be willing to consider an exchange?

'Miss Ayredale-Eskdale tells me you have a liking for bull-terriers,' he continued. 'Jaeger is house-trained, more-or-less garden-trained, and he doesn't, surprisingly, run sheep – or cows – though pretty nearly everything else – including fowls, which I see you keep, though he *is* improving slightly in that respect. A very lovable animal,' he added, 'no doubt about that – and with patience – more patience than I admit I possess, he could be made obedient. He also wants exercise – plenty of it.'

'And that, your lordship,' said Mr Wildgoose after a short silence in which he seemed to be thinking deeply, 'that would be the difficulty – that and the missis,' he added slowly. 'Bit prejudiced-like she is,' he explained, as Lord Glenheather looked slightly surprised, 'don't care for the breed.'

'But otherwise – apart from those two objections,' asked Lord Glenheather, who seemed to be thinking deeply too, 'would you like to have the dog?'

'I would, my lord! I would indeed!' said Mr Wildgoose fervently. 'I'd be proud to own him. He's a beauty! It's just as I said, the exercising – and the missis.'

'Would it help, do you think,' said Lord Glenheather, and he looked hard at Mr Wildgoose, 'if I had a little talk with your wife?'

A smile spread slowly over Mr Wildgoose's face. 'I think it might, your lordship; I think it might.'

'It can't do any harm!' said Lord Glenheather.

'No, it can't do any harm,' agreed Mr Wildgoose. And they stood looking at each other for a moment in silence, fellow conspirators. Then, 'I'll go and call her,' said Mr Wildgoose.

There was no doubt, as Mrs Ayredale-Eskdale had said, Lord Glenheather had 'a way' with him. 'Before I knew where I was,' said Mrs Wildgoose later, 'I'd said "yes" about that Jaeger dog!' Actually she had demurred a good deal but as she confided to Kate, 'I just couldn't bring myself to disappoint Mr Wildgoose. A dog like he's wanted so long for the asking as you might say! And pedigree too! I didn't feel I'd a right.' She had made one stipulation, however: that should Jaeger kill fowls or be in any way beyond control, he might be given away. Lord Glenheather agreed readily, but hoped it would not be so. 'And about exercising him, Mrs Wildgoose,' he began, but at that moment Mr Wildgoose came running from the house.

'Excuse me, your lordship, but could you come – there's something very interesting happening!' And he led the way to the sitting-room where he and Kate had been watching from behind the window curtains. On the gravel sweep outside Johnny Sears and Jaeger were parading up and down. Twelve paces forward, twelve back; then *'sit!'* commanded Johnny Sears and Jaeger sat. A pause, then *'Up!'* said Johnny, and Jaeger obediently stood up. Over and over the performance was repeated. Jaeger, his tongue hanging out, panting with heat but never once failing to obey.

'Well I never!' exclaimed Mrs Wildgoose peering over Kate's shoulder, 'who'd have thought it? That naughty little boy!'

'He's always been good with animals,' said Mr Wildgoose with grudging admiration, and looking anxiously at his guest for a clue as to how the talk had gone.

'He certainly seems able to deal with Jaeger,' said Lord Glenheather, managing to convey while Mrs Wildgoose's

back was still turned that all was well. 'There's your "exerciser", Mrs Wildgoose! What's his name – Johnny Sears? Well, I hope Johnny Sears will continue with his good work because your wife, Mr Wildgoose, has decided bull-terriers aren't so bad after all! I'm leaving early on Monday morning,' he went on smiling at Mrs Wildgoose who shook her finger at him and protested that she had 'never said no such thing your lordship!'. 'I'll bring Jaeger along on Sunday afternoon, and fetch "Daisy" at the same time if I may? In the meantime, if Johnny Sears is willing he can come along to The Priory now, and discuss the further training of Jaeger!'

Five minutes later after a drink which Mr Wildgoose had insisted on providing to celebrate the event, Lord Glenheather took his leave. Beside him, head in air, hands in pockets, strutted – no other word can describe it – Johnny Sears, while at their heels, meek and docile as an old sheep, trotted Jaeger!

For the rest of the day Mr Wildgoose seemed to go about in a kind of dream, breaking out every now and then into little snatches of song.

'Just in the Seventh Heaven he is!' murmured Mrs Wildgoose fondly. 'Well I only hope we don't regret this Jaeger dog!'

Mr Wildgoose was indeed happy, and to his great relief Willie Sims had not been hurt by the news; on the contrary, he seemed rather elated at the idea of The Dog Daisy in such aristocratic company. As for Kate she was so excited she could not be still for two minutes. Dad and the twins coming, The Fair coming, and now Jaeger coming! It was almost *too* much. 'I'm so happy I'm nearly crying,' she announced to Mrs Wildgoose.

'And it's just what you will be before the day's over if you go on the way you are,' was her somewhat damping reply.

Meanwhile, at No. 1 One End Street the reply to Mr Ruggles's letter was being awaited rather anxiously. The date he had selected for his holiday had not met with at all a favourable reception.

'Really, Jo!' exclaimed Mrs Ruggles who was alone in the kitchen busy with a large pile of ironing when he arrived back with the news, looking, as she later expressed it, to her friend Mrs Mullett 'as perky as a dog with two tails'. 'You've known for weeks as that outing to Albert's been arranged for that very Saturday! . . . What about it? . . . There's this about it – it means as the twins'll be alone all day, and if we've said once we've said a dozen times – ever since that tiger business – as we'd leave none of the children alone in the house ever again! . . . What's that? *Take* 'em – Take the twins to *Albert*'s! Well really! . . . They weren't asked for one thing – if Albert had wanted 'em he'd have said so. It's a party for me and Winnie to get better acquainted, and for Lily Rose to meet Winnie's young sisters again – the ones as were bridesmaids along of her . . .'*

* *Further Adventures of the Family from One End Street.*

'Oh, come off it, Rosie,' replied Mr Ruggles sighing wearily, 'and don't be so hasty. You don't *listen*! I never said take the twins to Albert's. What I were going to say but you didn't give me time to say it, were *I'd* take the twins with *me* – always provided as Mr and Mrs Wildgoose will *have* 'em.'

'And if they won't?' asked Mrs Ruggles shortly.

'Then I'll – I'll take 'em out somewhere for the day – Brightsea perhaps,' replied Mr Ruggles firmly. 'They won't be on their own here anyway, that's certain,' he added taking out his pipe and beginning to fill it.

'Well I don't know as I'm particular set on their going away like that,' objected Mrs Ruggles pausing for a moment in her work. 'There's their clothes to think of for one thing – grown out of pretty nearly all they've got these last few months they have – and torn the rest. Hi! don't you sit on those sheets!' as Mr Ruggles began edging towards the wicker arm-chair, 'and don't start your pipe up yet awhile or there'll be complaints the washing smells of smoke – Here, let me clear 'em away if you *must* sit down.'

'So long as the boys is clean I can't see as how they'll want much else but what they wears here,' muttered Mr Ruggles whose happiness in the thought of his holiday was rapidly evaporating.

'That's as may be,' retorted Mrs Ruggles removing the sheets, 'but I'm not having my boys go to Mrs Wildgoose looking like summat off a dust dump. And you'll need some tidying up yourself!'

'Well let's leave it be till we knows whether we're going or no,' said Mr Ruggles settling himself sulkily in the arm-chair and reluctantly replacing his pipe in his pocket. How women did fuss and make difficulties! 'And don't say nothing to the twins – nor any of 'em,' he added, ''case it don't come off.'

But when Mrs Wildgoose's kind letter with its thoughtful postscript to 'be sure to bring old clothes' arrived, most of these worries were forgotten, while Mr Watkins's kind offer of free transport as far as Ailesford left money to spare for other necessities. New face flannels and tooth-brushes were bought; jerseys washed; stockings mended; trousers pressed. There were several visits to the little shop at the corner with boots and shoes accompanied by earnest entreaties that the repairs be ready in good time, while Mr Ruggles himself 'went a bust' as he put it and recklessly purchased a new cap, a pair of socks, and two collars. He also bought a large blue bandana handkerchief. This he displayed with great pride, condoning his extravagance to Mrs Ruggles by pointing out that not only would it look well in his breast pocket on arrival at The Dew Drop Inn, but take the place of a collar if and when required. Peg and Jo who looked upon The Dew Drop Inn almost as their own property, nearly shed tears as they watched all these preparations taking place, Jo going so far as to consider stowing away overnight in Mr Watkins's lorry. Even Lily Rose, who had no leanings towards country life, felt a little envious, but quickly consoled herself at the thought of the infinite superiority of a day at Uncle Albert's. As for the twins, their excitement knew no bounds; they were continually shouting, whistling, or clattering up and down stairs until Mrs Ruggles felt she would be thankful to have them out of the house for a couple of days, and even more thankful, back to school on their return. Never, she said to herself, had the holidays seemed so long; truth was, they were far *too* long – anyway as far as mothers were concerned.

But at last 'THE DAY' as the Saturday of departure had come to be called arrived, and on a perfect summer's morning exactly at a quarter to seven as promised, Mr Watkins's lorry turned into One End Street and drew up outside the door of No. 1.

At first it looked as if there was not room for so much as a packet of sandwiches, much less the bulging suitcase which stood just inside the kitchen door, one fair-sized man, two boys, and an assortment of coats, carrier bags, and brown-paper parcels. Mr Watkins's 'Load' consisted of someone's furniture and what are termed 'household effects'. Bundles of bedding huddled against each other; tables and chairs, their legs in the air, stood lashed to other tables and chairs; a dresser and a book-case back to back as if no longer on speaking terms. The most surprising objects were herded together! In a large zinc tub a carpet sweeper lolled indolently against a pink satin cushion. A coal-shovel and a rolling pin stood side by side with a feather brush and an umbrella inside an enamel jug. On a chest of drawers were two bedroom basins in one of which reposed three books and an electric stove, while the other was filled to the brim with an assortment of photograph frames and flower vases. There was a pair of steps; a bird cage but no bird; an ironing table; and several large packing cases labelled 'Fragile' with straw sticking out from their lids. Wedged into any remaining space, rolls of carpet and linoleum reared upward like stunted factory chimneys.

'It's all right!' cried Mr Watkins observing some consternation on the faces of his prospective passengers, and he switched off his engine and jumped out, banging a door loudly enough to wake all the neighbours who had not already got their heads out of their windows. 'Plenty of room! You and that suitcase, Mr R., and all that junk,' and he pointed rather scornfully at the carrier bags and brown-paper parcels, 'alongside of me, and the two nippers *here*.' And turning to the lorry he jerked away a piece of sacking that shrouded some object towards the front of it and revealed a small upholstered settee. 'There you are! There's your seats! And if you travelled in a Rolls you wouldn't travel softer! Ready now? Then up you go!' And somewhat to Mr Ruggles's astonishment, for Mr Watkins was no prize-fighter of a man, and the complete bewilderment of both twins, first Jim and then John, each clutching a coat and various bags and parcels, was swung up over the edge of the lorry and dumped down on the settee. Cautioning them to mind their heads on the chair and table legs jutting out behind, Mr Watkins next assisted Mr Ruggles to climb in with the suitcase and other packages. He then leapt into the driving seat banging the door even more loudly than before, and started up the engine. A few moments later to the accompaniment of a very strident hooter he was backing the lorry down One End Street and out on to the main road.

From the door of No. 1 Mrs Ruggles, William in her arms, Lily Rose and Peg, waved and shouted affectionate good-byes. Only Jo was missing. Fiercely determined not to shed tears in front of his brothers but utterly defeated by the sight of the lorry, he had retreated upstairs and was watching from behind the bedroom-window curtains.

To John and Jim, travelling in Mr Watkins's lorry was vastly superior to any Rolls. They sat wedged together on their settee, clasping their coats and various packages, blissfully happy, their only regret the journey was not to be longer. They would have liked to travel all day – and all night too. As far as Land's End . . . North Wales . . . Aberdeen . . . they vied with each other in naming the remotest places they could think of. All the same they were quite pleased to get

out and stretch their legs when, after driving for about an hour along the main road, Mr Watkins turned off down a lane, drew up on the grass under a large oak tree, switched off the engine, and announced 'Breakfast time!'

Never had bread and margarine, cold bacon sandwiches and tea tasted so good! The air smelt fresh and dewy, and apart from the twittering of birds and the distant drone of traffic away on the main road, there was not a sound. Mr Ruggles presently produced his pipe and leaning against the trunk of the oak tree sat puffing away in great contentment, while Mr Watkins, his cap tilted over his eyes, his arms behind his head, lay on his back smoking a cigarette. The twins wandered off along the lane, peering earnestly into the hedges in the hope of finding a late birds' nest. But all too soon Mr Watkins levered himself up and announced it was time to be moving. Knives and crockery were collected, paper bags and scraps of food neatly buried, and soon they were all on board again and out once more on the main road.

There was plenty of traffic moving now; Mr Watkins, however, was a good and careful driver though apt to become very impatient if held up unduly in long queues of vehicles. He would then make up for any time so lost by driving at what Mr Ruggles considered a dangerous pace, and in his opinion it was largely due to indulgence in one of these spurts that the accident which presently occurred took place.

They had been speeding along on a clear stretch of road after a long hold-up in a stream of traffic, only to find on rounding a bend, another procession ahead of them – a string of large lumbering wagons and gypsy caravans – what looked like an entire circus on the move. Bringing up the rear was a dilapidated little car towing a small van with heavily barred windows looking something like a cross between a hen house and a horse box. As the lorry came roaring round a bend, both these vehicles, without warning, suddenly stopped. Fortunately Mr Watkins kept his head. There was a horrible screeching of brakes, a frightful bump, and the sound of cracking, splintering wood as the front of the lorry came to rest against the back of the van. Mr Watkins was jerked against the steering wheel; Mr Ruggles thrown forward against the windscreen. The twins, too tightly wedged to move much, were jarred and shaken, while the basinful of photographs and flower vases slithered off the chest of drawers and fell with a crash into the zinc tub.

Muttering very unseemly language, Mr Watkins climbed down to investigate the damage. At the same time a little man with a pointed beard, his eyes wide with terror, emerged from the dilapidated car while from the barred windows of the van issued the most sinister roars and growlings. The van itself was cracked and splintered from its impact with the lorry, but still legible, printed in large white letters were the words 'Caution!' 'Keep away!' 'Wild Animal Within!'

'There's a proverb,' remarked Mr Ruggles recounting their adventures later in the day, 'as says as nothing happens except what you don't think will; that's not the words exact – but near enough. And looks to me like it's true!' he added.

There was a good deal to be said for Mr Ruggles's observation. To have had an escaped tigress at one's kitchen window only a few weeks ago* was surprising enough, but to encounter it again on the king's highway, and then have it as a travelling companion! . . . Few people, after all, set off on a short journey across the English countryside expecting to conclude it in such company! Never, in his wildest dreams – or perhaps nightmares would be a more appropriate word, had Mr Ruggles conceived such a situation! And yet that was what had happened, and less than twenty minutes after the crash there he was, with the twins, suitcase, parcels and all, squashed into a small dilapidated car driven by a foreign gentleman speaking little and strange English, while behind rumbled a van containing the self-same animal! It was a good thing, he kept reflecting, Mrs Ruggles was not there to witness this transformation scene! Perhaps he had been foolish to agree, but everything had happened so quickly there had been little time for consideration.

Slightly dazed as he was from his contact with the windscreen, he had recognized the little man with the beard at once, and was well aware, without any warning white letters, of what was in the van. Jumping down from the lorry he had looked quickly to make sure the twins

* *Further Adventures of the Family from One End Street.*

were all right, and then the little foreigner, Mr Watkins, and himself, barely a word spoken between them, but all sharply aware of the danger and urgency, had lashed a piece of wood with stout cord – both miraculously produced from somewhere by Mr Watkins, to the back of the shattered van. Even so, it was not until words of cajolement or command in some strange tongue had been murmured through the barred windows and the alarming noises within had ceased, that Mr Ruggles began to breathe freely again. Mr Watkins, however, now that the danger was over, seemed concerned only for himself and his lorry; at any moment something might come round the bend and crash into the back of it. By now some of the drivers and occupants of the various wagons and caravans ahead had come running up, and after some argument the car and van were pushed twenty yards or so up the road. Mr Watkins himself followed in the lorry, the twins to their furious indignation, still imprisoned on their settee, but craning their necks and shouting to know what was happening. They, also, had recognized Signor Pelli, as the little foreigner was called, but they could hardly believe their ears when it was presently revealed that he and his famous tigress Thelma, together with some other members of the troop ahead, were on their way to join a fair at Upper Cassington, though Thelma herself, it was disappointing to learn, was not to appear in public, owing to a strained foot.

To the impatient Mr Watkins it seemed as if they were all going to spend the rest of the morning standing about gossiping. He sat in the lorry frowning angrily and full of the gloomiest forebodings ... His employers would demand an explanation – probably compensation – for the damage done ... Before he knew where he was he would be involved with the police ... questions would be asked, statements taken; the fact that he had been carrying passengers revealed ... At any moment, what he called 'some interfering cop' might appear round the corner ... the sooner he moved off the better! The best thing he could do was hurry on quickly to Ailesford, have the damage repaired there and no one any the wiser. It was only a few miles now and the Ruggleses were to have left him there in any case and find a bus to Upper Cassington ... Judging from the conversation, some of the outfit ahead – as he contemptuously termed the caravans and wagons – seemed to be going there too ... They all appeared very matey; let them go along together ... And before Mr Ruggles, 'fair mazed' as he later expressed it, 'what with tigers and all', had grasped much more than the possibility of trouble with the police – a matter always worthy of attention and respect – Mr Watkins had bundled out the suitcase and parcels, lifted down the twins and driven away!

And so it came about that just as Kate, who had been standing in the sun outside The Dew Drop Inn watching a cavalcade of mysterious-looking wagons and gaily-painted caravans rumble past and come to anchor on the near-by Green, decided it was nearly time to go to the bus stop to welcome her father and brothers, a shabby little black car, towing a small battered van went rattling by. It too came to rest on the Green. A moment later, to her intense astonishment, its doors opened and out of it stepped Mr Ruggles followed by the twins.

Part Two

The fine, warm morning was turning into a very hot afternoon. In spite of the wide-open windows, the party seated round the table in The Dew Drop Inn sitting-room, replete with boiled beef and carrots, jam tarts, and bread and cheese, looked flushed and drowsy. A large empty tankard of beer stood beside Mr Wildgoose, another by Mr Ruggles, and bottles of fizzy lemonade, drained to the last drop, in front of Kate and the twins. For almost the first time since the guests' arrival there was a lull in the conversation. Kate sat smiling happily, glancing now at Mr Ruggles, now at the twins. How very clean and tidy they all looked! And how quickly Dad had lost the shyness which so often overcame him – like herself – 'in company'. He and Mr Wildgoose seemed to have taken to each other on sight . . . And so they had. Mr Wildgoose admired enterprise, and he always enjoyed a good laugh, and the account of his guests' somewhat unusual journey had caught his fancy. Mr Ruggles for his part had never felt more quickly at home than with his host and hostess. He was also enchanted with The Dew Drop Inn, its garden and orchard, all of which Kate had insisted on showing him within half an hour of his arrival, at the same time bombarding him with questions about home and receiving in return all the family news from Lily Rose's adventures with the police to Cuckoo-Coo's prowess with a rat, and the tardy William's sudden rapid progress in talking.

'Says all your names proper now he does,' said Mr Ruggles proudly. 'Your Mum's ever so pleased – beginning to think he never would, I believe she was!' As for the twins, they sat with the sun glinting in their red hair, their eyes bright as a robin's with excitement, delighted with everything, and on their very best behaviour. Mrs Wildgoose sat smiling too, pleased at the practical appreciation of her cooking and the happiness around her. Away in a patch of cool shadow by the grandfather clock lay Jaeger. His ears were pricked and his eyes fixed on the door, for this was his hour for exercise and at any moment Johnny Sears should appear.

Jaeger had been at The Dew Drop Inn nearly a fortnight now and was rapidly becoming a different dog, as Mr Wildgoose told Miss Alison when she called one morning for some duck eggs.

'A different dog – that's what he is. And – credit where credit's due – most of it's due to young Johnny Sears.'

But if Jaeger was a different dog, Johnny Sears, in the process of reforming him, was becoming a different boy. True, he had less time now for teasing and bullying other children, and for trespassing on and damaging other people's property. A little talk too, with P.C. Burden and a warning to Mr Sears concerning his son's behaviour might have helped. Not that Mr Sears had acknowledged any shortcomings on the part of his offspring. 'As I told the copper,' he announced to various friends in the village, 'he's a good boy really, my Johnny – it's just what he *does*!' A remark which caused the vicar to smile a little grimly, and sent up a snort of indignation at Pond Cottages.

Whatever it was, Johnny Sears seemed to be becoming a more agreeable child if not exactly a model of politeness. Twice a day – after breakfast and mid-day dinner – he presented himself at The Dew Drop Inn, announcing gravely he had called for Jaeger 'for training and exercise', and Mrs Wildgoose, glancing now at the clock, was just on the point of remarking, 'Young Johnny Sears is late today,' when suddenly Jaeger jumped up, ran over to the door and stood, head to one side, uttering pleased little whines. A moment later there was a knock on the front door. Jaeger barked and Mr Wildgoose called through the window, 'Come in, Johnny, come in!' and in a matter of seconds the door handle rattled and in came Johnny Sears.

He stood for a moment gazing a little owlishly through his large spectacles, surprised at the assembled company, while Jaeger leapt exuberantly about him, sniffing and licking and altogether beside himself with joy. Introductions and explanations followed, the three boys, after the manner of their kind, regarding each other in stolid silence with expressions of hostility mingled with curiosity.

'He's a big dog for you to manage, sonny,' remarked Mr Ruggles kindly, at which Johnny Sears looked scornful but made no reply.

'Can we come along with you?' asked John presently, speaking for both twins.

'No,' said Johnny Sears briefly but firmly, 'you can't. He,' indicating Jaeger, 'won't learn proper if there's people watching. Come on, Jaeger! *Time!*' and taking a chain from his pocket he clipped it on Jaeger's collar, looked round the assembled company, and remarking, 'Good-bye, all,' Jaeger prancing beside him, went out, shutting the door after him.

'I'm afraid he's a bad-mannered little boy,' said Mrs Wildgoose by way of apology to her guests.

'But improving,' said Mr Wildgoose, 'and it's a fair marvel what he's done with that dog!' and he was about to recount Jaeger's past history to Mr Ruggles – who had been expressing admiration for him from the moment of introduction, thereby still further endearing himself to Mr Wildgoose, when Mrs Wildgoose interrupted. It was getting on for two o'clock; it was Saturday, no Elsie to help, and had Mr Wildgoose forgotten there was washing up to be done? Mr Wildgoose had. With a rather rueful glance at Mr Ruggles he offered to assist, and Mr Ruggles, fervently hoping his services would be rejected, politely did so too. But Mrs Wildgoose said firmly she wanted no men in her scullery today, thank you; she and Kate would manage between them. What would please her most was for *all* menfolk – and she glanced affectionately at the twins – to take themselves off and sit in the garden out of the way. And exchanging happy if rather sheepish grins, and followed by the twins bursting with pride at being referred to as 'menfolk', Mr Wildgoose and Mr Ruggles went thankfully away.

Kate had been arranging in her mind to spend the afternoon introducing the twins to her various friends in the village, for Mr Wildgoose had murmured something about the possibility of a picnic tomorrow. There was also an invitation from Signor Pelli to visit Thelma and have other peeps behind the scenes on the strict understanding they kept right away *today.* These plans she now disclosed to Mrs Wildgoose. But Mrs Wildgoose had plans of her own. Mr Ruggles was going to help Mr Wildgoose pick the Early Victoria apples; later she would make a tart with some of them but what she really needed were blackberries to go with them – 'One of my specialities, blackberry and apple tart is,' she explained, 'and I'm sure you'd all enjoy some blackberry jelly! Willie Sims tells me the hedges in the water-meadows are fairly dripping blackberries! How about you and the boys picking me some? You can visit your friends after tea,' she added as Kate looked a little disappointed, 'and in this hot weather some of the older ones'll be better pleased to see you then, I'd say. And talking of tea,' she added, 'I've an extra special one today so if you decide to go don't be late for it! There, I think that's all. I'll just wash down the sink and you run out and see whether the twins would like to go.'

The twins were delighted with the idea; water-meadows suggested a river and that was always to be welcomed . . . They could paddle, and . . . But Mr Wildgoose quickly shattered these hopes.

'No going near the river,' he announced though no one had so much as mentioned it, and Mr Ruggles nodded agreement, holding up a warning finger and extracting reluctant promises.

When they had gone, each carrying a basket neatly lined with newspaper – blackberries, according to Mrs Wildgoose, 'staining something terrible', he turned to her and Mr Wildgoose and said shyly, 'I must thank you for what you done for my Kate. She looks a different girl – that she does!' Mrs Wildgoose blushed with pleasure and it was hard to say whether she or Mr Wildgoose looked the more pleased.

It was scorchingly hot in the water-meadows. The sun blazed down and everything quivered in a haze of heat. But 'coo-*er*!' as Jim exclaimed, '*the blackberries!*' The high hedges did indeed seem dripping with them. They hung in trails and clusters, huge, luscious and juicy; black and shiny as jet. Kate and the twins set to work with a will, though for a time for every dozen blackberries that found their way into Mrs Wildgoose's newspaper-lined baskets, at least two dozen were consumed in refreshment. In some maddening way too the very best seemed always just out of reach, or unapproachable except through a thicket of nettles. But they picked away valiantly, ignoring the heat, scratched hands, and nettle-stung legs, vying with each other in finding the biggest and juiciest specimens. When the church clock struck four the baskets were almost full.

But at last Kate cried, 'Phew! I can't pick a single one more I'm so hot – and I'm sure we've got enough now – we must have picked *pounds*! It won't be tea-time for an hour yet,' she went on, 'so where'd you like to go? It would be coolest away over there' – she pointed across the meadow – 'beside what they call *The* Stream.'

'I'd rather go to the river,' objected John. 'I wish we hadn't said we wouldn't!'

'Well we *have*, so you're not going,' retorted Kate in her firmest elder-sisterly tones. John made no reply; actually he did not mind much where they went so long as it was near water.

The Stream when they reached it proved to be almost as good as a small river; it was about eight feet broad at its widest point and at this time of year less than two feet deep. It flowed swiftly but smoothly, curving in and out between beds of rushes and the now faded and seeding pink willowherb; alders, willows, and a black poplar or two grew along the farther bank. They set down the heavy blackberry baskets and the thick jerseys the twins had long since discarded, pulled off shoes and stockings, and splashed across to where a small group of trees formed a miniature wood, cool and inviting. Here, on the exposed roots of a big willow, they sat for a while, their feet in the stream, dabbling their hands in it and every now and then splashing their hot faces with the cool clear water. Presently a woodpigeon cooing plaintively behind them attracted their attention and they turned away from the stream and crept quietly in among the trees, trying to catch a glimpse of it until, startled by something, with a frightened cry and a loud flutter of wings it flew off. When they turned back to the stream once more, cows were strolling by on the opposite bank and one, more inquisitive than the rest, was investigating the jerseys and the blackberry baskets.

'Cows!' exclaimed Jim who was a little in front of the others.

'Cows won't hurt you!' said Kate with the scorn born of nearly six weeks of country life.

'That's not a cow, you sillies!' said John sharply from behind her. 'It's a *bull*!'

It was undoubtedly a bull, though not a very large one. It had knocked over one of the baskets now and the grass was strewn with blackberries. As they approached, it moved nearer the bank, then nearer still, finally taking up a stand with its forefeet planted firmly on John's blue jersey, regarding them with a fixed, unblinking stare. Would it suddenly charge – dash into the stream, up the bank and into the trees after them . . . It looked very much as if it might . . . Kate was frightened. Cows were safe enough; a bull was quite another matter . . . 'Always respect a bull,' Mr Digweed had impressed on her more than once; 'it's only a fool that doesn't,' and Mr Digweed *knew*.

'Quick!' she cried to the twins. '*Quick!* Climb up this tree. It can't reach us there!' The next minute the three of them were wriggling and squirming their way among the branches of a large willow. The bull, however, remained where it was – staring stonily. And it continued to do so.

Minutes passed. It was very uncomfortable in the willow tree – hard and scratchy and slippery; spidery sort of insects tickled one and it was impossible to scratch for to do so meant endangering one's hold. Presently the church clock struck a quarter to five.

'We'll be late for tea,' said Kate mournfully, 'and Mrs Wildgoose has got an extra special one . . .' But the bull seemed content to remain standing on John's jersey and staring at them for the rest of the afternoon. It just flicked its tail and shook its head every now and then to keep off the flies, but otherwise never moved an inch.

'I've got cramp!' announced Jim presently. 'Gosh I have! . . . I can't hold on much longer!' And it is probable he would not have done, but all at once there was the sound of whistling and of approaching footsteps. Then suddenly the whistling stopped. A voice said, 'Oh, *there* you be!' and behind the bull appeared the figure of Mr Sears the cowman. As for the bull, it merely turned its head, gave the mildest of mild bellows, and as he came nearer turned and muzzled gently against him! A moment later to the intense disgust of Kate and the twins, Johnny Sears, brandishing a long stick, came running up.

''Ullo!' he exclaimed stopping and staring first at the blackberry baskets and then at the three figures huddled among the branches of the willow. 'What's you all doin' up there – birds-nesting?'

'We're getting cool,' replied Kate with dignity.

'Garn!' said Johnny Sears laughing derisively. 'You're scared – that's what you are! They're scared of William, Dad! Hi! Come, William . . . C-oop, C-oop . . .' and still laughing he pulled a wisp of hay from his pocket, holding it out to the bull and walking slowly backwards as he did so. And 'William', turning away from Mr Sears and without so much as another glance at Kate and the twins, followed slowly after him.

Mr Sears, his head on one side, stood watching proudly until both boy and bull disappeared through a gate at the far end of the meadow. Then he turned to Kate and the twins who had scrambled down from the willow tree and were preparing to wade back across the stream.

'You've no call to be scared of William,' he remarked. 'He's only young yet; eleven months come Monday.'Tis second time this week though he's a-lifted his stable bar and follered the cows out after milking. Have to be a-ringing of him, we will.' Then, with a glance towards the overturned baskets, 'Upset your berries proper he has! Ah well, plenty more to be had,' and with this attempt at consolation, and a warning to 'be sure and shut the gate, mind' he turned on his heel and went whistling away.

Kate and the twins picked up what they could of the blackberries and John's now very muddy jersey; put on their shoes and stockings and walked homewards, hardly knowing whether they were more surprised that a bull should be called William – a name so firmly associated in their minds with that of their baby brother – or the manner of its departure.

9. The Fair

Part One

'You must be one of those as is lucky with their weather,' Mr Wildgoose remarked to Mr Ruggles next morning at breakfast, and the day certainly seemed full of promise. 'It's a funny thing,' he went on, 'but it's always fine for The Fair. We've had cloudy days and showery days but I can't remember one real soaker.' Mrs Wildgoose said for goodness' sake not to boast or the wind would change or what she called 'one of those wireless depressions' come along. But Mr Wildgoose shook his head and said it was 'set fair till Tuesday or he'd eat his hat'. Willie Sims, in whose weather predictions Kate placed even more confidence than Mr Wildgoose's, had said much the same yesterday. So too had the occupants of Pond Cottages when she and the twins had visited them the previous evening. They had also announced their intention of coming to The Fair – much to the surprise of the twins who had both privately decided Mr Milton must be ninety-nine at least and Mr Shakespeare not far off it.

'Plenty of life in us old dogs yet,' Mr Shakespeare remarked as if guessing their thoughts. 'We both enjoys a turn on th'osses and Mr Milton he's still got a good eye for the Hoop-La! John! You show 'em what you won last year!' he shouted, and Mr Milton took them into his tiny sitting-room and pointed proudly with his stick at a large blue vase covered with some very improbable yellow roses which occupied pride of place on the mantelpiece. Kate had never seen the inside of Mr Milton's little house before and she would have liked to linger and look more closely at other treasures; some medals in a case; a curious shell, and a framed Sunday-school certificate; but the twins were clamouring to see where Johnny Sears had stuck in the mud, and there were still the farm and post office to be visited. Mr Digweed had been very consoling about the encounter with 'William', saying again it was always best to be on the safe side where bulls were concerned, and at Kate's special request good-naturedly taken them to see his own, a lusty, full-grown Jersey. It stood rubbing its ringed nose against its stall bars, snorting and pawing the ground, and looked crossly at them with fierce bloodshot eyes.

The visit to the post office was a great success, the twins enchanted with Thomas, and on their very best behaviour.

'*Dear* little boys,' said Mrs Midgley after they had said good-bye and Kate lingered behind for a moment. Kate had never really considered her brothers in this light before and was finding it difficult to reply when Mrs Midgley added, 'But a handful, I'll be bound,' which solved the problem, for this, she could truthfully assure her, was 'exactly what Mum always said'.

'And now,' said Mr Wildgoose getting up from the table from which a couple of dozen sizzling sausages, as many pieces of toast, and nearly a whole section of honey had disappeared, 'it's all hands to the pump – or rather the apple trees – again.' For even after two hours of picking yesterday the Early Victoria trees were still what Mr Ruggles described as 'smothered'.

'And there's near as many apples in the grass, I'm afraid,' said Mr Wildgoose as they went into the orchard. 'They're very early apples, these; by rights they should have been picked a week or more ago,' and even as he spoke there were several 'plop-plops' as overripe fruit fell into the long grass under the trees.

'The twins'll pick up all o' they,' said Mr Ruggles, and for some time the twins did. They also helped to steady ladders, and fetch and hand up empty baskets. After a time, however, these activities began to pall; they also had plans of their own, and when Kate, who was helping Mrs Wildgoose to clear away the breakfast, called through the kitchen window that Johnny Sears had come for Jaeger, they suddenly made a rush for the house. On the way they stopped for a moment and held a whispered conversation, then hurried through a side door from the orchard, emerging on to the sweep outside the Inn just as Johnny

Sears came out, Jaeger prancing beside him on a chain. Rather self-conscious 'Hullos' were exchanged, then, 'Can we come with you?' asked Jim.

'No,' replied Johnny Sears firmly, 'you can't. I told you "no" yesterday,' and he prepared to move off.

'Could you,' asked John leaning against one of the trestle tables by the door, his hands in his pockets and assuming a very casual air, 'could you make a *tiger* do things like you make Jaeger and – and – William?'

Johnny Sears looked surprised. 'A *tiger*,' he repeated, staring hard at John through his large glasses. 'I dunno. I never thought 'bout it. I never seen a tiger anyway –'cept in a book.'

'Well there's a tiger away over there,' pursued John jerking his head in the direction of the Green and enjoying the surprise on Johnny Sears's face, 'leastways a tiger-*ess*. It's called Thelma and Signor Pelli – that's the man as it belongs to – takes it out on a chain – same as you do Jaeger!'

'How do *you* know?' asked Johnny Sears, staring harder than ever.

'Well they're both sort of friends of ours,' replied John loftily.

'What do you mean – sort of friends of yours?' objected Johnny Sears. 'The Fair only come yesterday.'

'*Ah* – but we come *with* it!' said John triumphantly, if not very grammatically, and proceeded to relate with relish their experiences on the road and Thelma's visit to One End Street. 'We're going to see her now,' he concluded.

Johnny Sears was obviously impressed; there was also little doubt he, too, would like to see the tiger, even if trying his skill with it might be asking rather much.

'Can I come along of you?' he asked meekly after a short silence. The twins exchanged glances.

'Well I don't see why,' said John slowly, 'you wouldn't let *us* come with you and Jaeger!'

'That's different,' retorted Johnny Sears quickly. 'I told you – he won't do like I say if there's people watching. It's *quite* different.' It began to look as if Johnny Sears was going to have the last word after all. The twins conferred together for a moment.

'We'll have to think about it,' said John at last in good imitation of his parents when approached on some weighty matter, 'it won't be this morning anyway,' he added, and they both walked off in the direction of the Green leaving Johnny Sears staring sulkily after them.

Among the huddle of vehicles drawn up on the Green nothing was stirring. The doors of all the caravans were firmly shut, the little window curtains drawn. It looked very much as if everyone was still asleep and some children loitering about reported loud snores; evidently among The Fair folk Sunday was very definitely a day of rest. No one so much as mentioned a tiger. The twins said nothing, presently wandering off together looking at everything.

None of the caravans and wagons gave an inkling of their contents; only on the tiger van when they eventually found it, now more securely mended, hung a warning in freshly chalked white letters: 'Danger! Wild Animal Within!

Keep Away!' The van itself was wedged in between two big caravans; it was also partly hidden by Signor Pelli's dilapidated little black car, which was perhaps the reason why the loitering children had not discovered it, and knew, no more than Johnny Sears, what was sleeping so calmly in their midst. For sleeping Thelma must be; not a sound was to be heard, and of Signor Pelli there was no sign at all. And then, quite suddenly, tethered dogs lying quietly here and there beneath caravans began to growl and then to bark, and peeping round the little car the twins saw Johnny Sears and Jaeger.

Johnny Sears had his back towards them and was talking earnestly with a group of children, but turning quickly he saw the twins and the next moment, led by him, the whole party was pushing its way in and out among the vans and wagons towards them.

The already barking dogs barked louder, others joined in. Heads were poked out of one or two caravan windows and some very unseemly language floated about. Now Jaeger, ears pricked, and sniffing the air, began to bark; a big, deep, excited bark ... There was something – something very unusual near at hand ... All The Fair dogs barked in return, louder and louder as the approaching children drew nearer; others, away in the village, joined in. Suddenly the door of a near-by caravan flew open and out stepped Signor Pelli, looking a curious figure in orange pyjamas with a flowered shawl draped around his shoulders. He brightened at the sight of the twins but frowned heavily at the other children, while the sight of

Jaeger, now rearing up on his hind legs and straining at his chain in the direction of the tiger van, seemed to rouse him to fury.

'Take 'im away!' he screamed, his black eyes flashing and his little pointed beard twitching with anger. 'That 'ideous dog! Take 'im away! Quick! Do you 'ear me? The very sight of 'im would upset my Thelma! Take 'im away! Quick!'

Whether or not Johnny Sears was prepared to obey, he was powerless. Jaeger was pulling with all his might.

'Take 'im away!' screamed Signor Pelli again. 'The 'ideous brute!' But at that moment Jaeger made a sudden leap towards the tiger van. The chain jerked out of his hands, Johnny Sears fell forward on his face, narrowly missing the mudguard of the car. Signor Pelli screamed; the watching children screamed; the barking dogs barked louder still. Doors opened, heads were thrust out of windows and people shouted, while from within the tiger van itself came a loud and sinister *roar*!

'Now, *now*! What's all this?' said a voice audible even above the din, and there, elbowing his way towards the storm centre, was P.C. Burden.

In less time than it takes to tell, Jaeger, still on his hind legs, sniffing and pawing at the door of the van, was recaptured, and he, Johnny Sears, and all the children being briskly shepherded towards the road. Only the twins, described – by Signor Pelli to their great pride and satisfaction – as 'young friends of mine, these – the others *no*!' were permitted to remain.

And they remained some time. In fact they only arrived back at The Dew Drop Inn, very much to Mr Ruggles's annoyance, as Mrs Wildgoose was dishing up the dinner.

'I'm listening to nothing,' he said firmly as they began excitedly to pour forth their morning's adventures, 'nothing. Not till you've a-been and washed and tidied up of yourselves – and look sharp about it.'

But – how unfair grown-ups could be sometimes! Even when they returned, still bubbling with excitement, but hands washed and hair more or less brushed, to find everyone seated round the table, Mr Ruggles only said, 'Stop chattering now and give folks a chance to eat their food.'

The twins subsided, for they were hungry themselves and wanted their own dinner, and Mrs Wildgoose's plates of cold tongue, crisp lettuce and big juicy tomatoes looked particularly inviting. So too did the huge tart containing part of their labours of yesterday, which reposed in the middle of the table flanked by a large jug of cream. And – oh kind Mr Wildgoose! In front of each of them a bottle of real ginger pop in a cool stone jar! But at last Early Victoria – and other apples – the main subject of conversation, came to an end. Nothing remained of the tongue, lettuce, and tomatoes; less than a quarter of the huge tart; the ginger pop was drained to its last drop, and Mr Ruggles turned to his sons.

'Well now! And what have you been up to?' he inquired. Again how unfair! Why 'up to'?

'We haven't been *up* to anything,' said John a little resentfully, 'but we've had a *very* exciting time!' and he proceeded to relate their adventures, Jim putting in a word here and there when he considered his twin was not giving full measure. It seemed that when P.C. Burden had led Jaeger, Johnny Sears, and the other children away, Signor Pelli had allowed the twins to look through the bars of his van where Thelma, now quietened down and lying peacefully on a bed of straw, had twitched her whiskers and blinked up at them '*just* like Cuckoo-Coo, Dad, when he's been woke up sudden – like from half-asleep.' And that, it seemed, owing to her strained foot, was, alas! all they or anyone else might expect to see of Thelma.

There would be very many other things to see, Signor Pelli had assured them, and he had introduced them to various friends, all of whom had apparently promised at least one free ride, swing, or throw at their respective entertainments.

'There's Dodgems, Dad, and Chairaplanes, and Swing Boats, and Hoop-La . . .' John began ticking the items off on his fingers.

'And a Lighthouse Helter Skelter, and a Shooting Gallery, and Coconut Shies,' put in Jim, 'and a Joywheel! Signor Pelli thinks the Joywheel's the best of all,' he went on. 'It's like an *enormous* gramophone record; you sit on it and it goes round and round, faster and faster, simply *flinging* people off, but if you *can* stay on you get a prize, and,' he added triumphantly, 'he's told me a way you can – but I'd to promise not to tell anyone – not even John!'

Kate opened her eyes very wide at this – the twins always shared everything – particularly secrets. But the next moment John was announcing he, too, had a secret.

There was to be a conjuring performance and he and the conjurer, whose name was Mr Bean, had had a long talk; he had even been invited inside Mr Bean's caravan and shown – coo-*er*, no end of queer things! 'You all wait and see what happens tomorrow!' he concluded mysteriously. 'You won't half be surprised!' . . . and he became suddenly convulsed with giggles.

'Well you certainly don't seem to have wasted any time,' said Mr Wildgoose laughing. 'I asked young Johnny Sears when he brought Jaeger back what all the noise on the Green was about. "Dogs barking at Jaeger" was *his* tale. I've told him not to come for Jaeger this afternoon, my dear,' he went on turning to Mrs Wildgoose, 'I've a fancy to take my own dog out for once, and Mr Ruggles here would like to see a bit of the countryside so we're off for a walk – anyone else who wants to come – hands up!' And he looked round the table. Three pairs of hands instantly shot up. Only Mrs Wildgoose smiling placidly behind the remains of the blackberry-and-apple tart, kept hers in her lap. The arrangement would suit her very well, she said, for, as she explained to Mr Ruggles, she never washed up on a Sunday.

'I'll just clear away and then have a nice rest in the garden, so off you all go and tea'll be ready when you get back. Bless me, if I don't believe that Jaeger dog understands every word that's said!' For Jaeger had come across from his favourite place by the clock, put his head on Mr Wildgoose's knee and was looking up at him out of his three-cornered eyes, his tail wagging to and fro in pleased anticipation.

But in the end only Mr Wildgoose, Mr Ruggles, and Jaeger went for the walk. They all set off together but had barely passed the Green where, except for a few wispy threads of smoke from some of the caravan chimneys, there was little more sign of life than in the morning, when a car hooted, slowed down, and came to a halt beside them. In the front seat sat two ladies while the back seemed to be filled with suitcases.

'It's Mr Ruggles and the *twins*, isn't it?' said a voice, and a head in a very pretty straw hat poked through one of the windows.

'Miss Alison!' cried Kate while Jaeger uttered pleased little barks and tugged at his chain in a frenzied effort to reach the car, Mr Wildgoose trying to hold the chain with one hand and take his hat off with the other, being nearly pulled over in the process.

'How did I know?' asked Miss Alison when the visitors had been properly introduced. 'Because nothing ever happens in Upper or Lower Cassington without somebody knowing it. The important thing is, how long are you staying? Oh dear' – when Mr Ruggles replied rather shyly they would be going 'along of The Fair folk – somewhere around four or five o'clock Tuesday morning.' 'Oh dear,' she repeated, 'I know Kate would have liked you all to see the white cats . . .'

It seemed they had visitors at The Priory and more were arriving tomorrow . . . she would be busy in the morning fetching them from the station . . . oh *yes* – in reply to Mr Wildgoose – she was coming to The Fair – that was a thing that could *never* be missed! She glanced round at the back of the car. 'I could take you, Kate, and the twins, to see the cats, straight away, this minute, if you'd like to come and could squeeze in among my friend's luggage, but I'm afraid there isn't a corner for you, Mr Ruggles. I *am* sorry.'

Mr Ruggles said not to bother about him – thanking you kindly all the same, adding that, 'in a manner of speaking', he'd promised to go along with Mr Wildgoose and the dog . . . the twins would like it fine though if she'd really room for them . . . So Kate and her brothers scrambled in and were driven off perched on the suitcases, and Mr Ruggles, Mr Wildgoose and Jaeger continued on their way.

By six o'clock that evening the Green presented a very different appearance. The smoke from the caravan chimneys was no longer thin and wispy but thick and curly. 'The Fair folk' were up and very much about their business. Wagons were being unloaded, booths and tents put up. There was much hammering and good-natured shouting and laughing. On the fringe of these activities, speculating amongst themselves as to each fresh erection, their eyes bulging with curiosity, were half the children of Upper and Lower Cassington and a fair sprinkling of their elders, while away across the road under a small chestnut tree against which he had propped his bicycle, stood P.C. Burden, hands on hips, benevolently but watchfully surveying the scene.

Inside The Dew Drop Inn Mr Wildgoose and Mr Ruggles sat puffing contentedly at their pipes after a hearty tea; in his favourite corner, stretched out like a dead dog, lay Jaeger sleeping off the effects of a six-mile walk; Kate and the twins, who had spent a good three-quarters of an hour in The Priory stables with the white cats, were arguing as to how soon, if ever, Cuckoo-Coo might be expected to attain to the splendour and elegance of his parents; and Mrs Wildgoose was looking out of the window wondering whether with visitors to look after she would be able to attend church that evening. Then the clock struck the hour. Mr Wildgoose jumped up from his chair, knocked out his pipe and muttering 'Bless my soul! Opening-time in half an hour,' hurried away to the bar, while Mr Ruggles said shyly, and somewhat to Mrs Wildgoose's surprise, that if convenient and not too late to tidy up a bit, he had 'a mind' to go to church; Kate and the boys – looking at each other in turn – might care to come too? The twins shook their heads vigorously. They had 'arranged' to visit Signor Pelli again and see Thelma fed. Kate after a little hesitation said yes, and presently in the golden glow of early evening, the elm trees casting long shadows across the road and the sound of the church bells mingling with the shouts and hammerings on the Green, she and Mrs Wildgoose and Mr Ruggles set forth.

When they returned, an hour later, the Green was a very gay sight indeed! The big roundabout was up and beneath its red and white striped canopy could be seen the gilded posts supporting the painted and dappled horses. Away behind it, gleaming white, was the Lighthouse Helter Skelter, and behind that the stands for the swing boats. A few booths and strings of brightly coloured little flags were also up but the daylight was beginning to fade now; here and there a light shone in a caravan window, appetizing smells wafted about and men began to climb the little steps leading to open doorways for their supper. The onlookers, who had doubled now in number, were being joined by all those who had been in church, and presently the vicar himself arrived. Coming to speak to Mrs Wildgoose he was introduced to Mr Ruggles and was soon hearing of his strange manner of arrival and the presence of Thelma. Like Mrs Ruggles, Mr Wilson did not approve of wild animals behind bars,* but he accepted Mr Ruggles's invitation to visit Signor Pelli, and Mrs Wildgoose having said she must return to get the supper, Kate went with them. She was surprised to learn that Mr Wilson intended having what he called 'a turn' at some of the amusements tomorrow, and even more surprised, on arrival at Signor Pelli's van, to find the twins, accompanied by Johnny Sears, absorbed in watching Thelma dispose of a lump of meat the size of a leg of mutton, the three of them all apparently the firmest of friends!

Part Two

Either from excitement and anticipation, or the noise from the Green, everyone woke earlier than usual at The Dew Drop Inn next day. It was a perfect September morning.

* *Further Adventures of the Family from One End Street.*

A thin mist lay on the fields; the flowers in the garden were heavy with dew, and everywhere myriads of spiders' webs sparkled in the sun. Immediately after breakfast Kate and the twins raced over to the Green where a crowd of children had already collected, to be joined immediately by Johnny Sears who had been lying in wait for them and for whom it was obvious Thelma had become an irresistible attraction. More booths and some tents had gone up, and there was even more shouting and hammering than yesterday. Everyone was busy, and onlookers – children in particular – were definitely unwelcome. Even Signor Pelli, who was helping some friends, when Kate and the twins finally pushed their way towards him, said crossly: 'We haf no time for you now so please to *go*. This afternoon we welcome of you – all of us, but now we do *not*,' which though perhaps not the best English was only too clearly understood. They wandered round a little longer, getting in everyone's way, until Johnny Sears announced it was time to call for Jaeger and they all walked back to The Dew Drop Inn, Johnny with a twin on either side, Kate following behind and regarding them with some amusement.

Mr Wildgoose had been what he called 'in two minds' whether to insist the twins should accompany Johnny Sears and Jaeger this time if they wished, but on reflection decided that while one boy and a dog might keep out of mischief, three boys and a dog were very unlikely to do so. Johnny Sears went off alone but with instructions to double the usual time, for there would be no afternoon walk for Jaeger today.

It was still only half-past nine; a long morning stretched ahead, and seeing his host and hostess were busy, and anxious to keep his family out of mischief, Mr Ruggles expressed a wish to see the village and some of Kate's friends, and promising to be back for dinner 'twelve sharp', he presently set off, taking his family with him.

Although The Fair was not supposed to open until one o'clock, long before dinner was over at The Dew Drop Inn the big roundabout was turning and music pouring forth from the Green.

Kate and the twins, who had lapped up their pudding with incredible speed in order to be there at the earliest possible moment, now sat waiting in an agony of impatience while Mr and Mrs Ruggles finished theirs and began to embark in a leisurely way on biscuits and cheese. At last the twins became so fidgety that Mr Wildgoose took pity on them.

'How about you three going on ahead? Hi! Wait a minute,' he cried as they all leapt from their chairs and prepared to rush from the room.

'Here's a tanner each to spend.'

'And here,' said Mr Ruggles fumbling in his pocket, 'is one apiece to go with it.'

'And – wait a minute, wait a minute!' cried Mrs Wildgoose above a chorus of 'Oo's' and '*thank* you's', and she produced a rather squashed-looking black leather purse from her pocket – 'here's three more – for luck!'

'Coo!' exclaimed Jim as they stood for a moment outside on the sweep, 'one and six each! And we've still got two shillings left from Lord Glenheather's money.'*

'I've some left he gave *me*,' said Kate, 'but I want to keep it for presents for Mum and Lily Rose and Peg and Jo; but I've got the shilling I told you I found at The Priory and a shilling Dad gave me before I came away. *Three and six each!* We ought to be able to go to everything in The Fair for that! Come on! *Quick!*' And they raced towards the Green.

How exciting it all looked now everything was up! How mysterious the striped tents and booths, their gilded supports shining so dazzlingly in the sun; how gay the painted caravans, the gleaming white Lighthouse, and the hundreds of little flags fluttering everywhere in the slight breeze that had sprung up! Officially open or not they were by no means the first arrivals and the noise was already deafening. The big roundabout was turning to the strains of *The Lambeth Walk*; the Chairaplanes to *Rule Britannia* – with variations. On several of the stalls and in caravan doorways, gramophones were playing marches and jazz, waltzes and popular songs, while the proprietors of the various amusements shouted lustily through megaphones.

'Who's for the Lighthouse? Tuppence a time on the Lighthouse! . . . Swing on the swing boats. Anyone for the swing boats? Threepence a swing! . . . Dodgems!

* *Further Adventures of the Family from One End Street.*

Dodge 'em on the Dodgems! Sixpence a ride! . . . Shooting! Try your skill, gentlemen! Five shots a penny! . . . Coconuts! Who wants a coconut? Three shies a penny – children half price! Coconuts! Coconuts! . . . Hoop-La! Who's for the Hoop-La! Six rings for tuppence! Wonderful prizes! Hoop-La! . . . Hoop-La! . . .' Only the Joywheel, to Jim's great concern, remained inert; something apparently wrong with its machinery.

Adding to the confusion, the owners of the various booths and stalls were also proclaiming the merits of their wares.

'Toffee! Old-fashioned toffee! All home-made! Penny a bag! Twopence with nuts! . . .' And there, presided over by a stout lady in purple velvet and a hat with feathers, was a stall selling nothing but toffee. Great giant *slabs* of it – Treacle, Nut, Almond . . . The twins' eyes grew rounder and rounder as they gazed; it was hard to believe so much toffee could exist! Next to it was a stall devoted entirely to peppermints! Sticks of peppermint rock, bright pink, plain or striped with white, and varying in size from the usual candle-like proportions to pieces eighteen inches long and thick as rolling-pins! There were bullseyes, pink and white, and black and white; big ones, little ones, and medium sized; there were also huge three-cornered lumps, fawn colour with rich brown stripes. People were buying them eagerly.

Another stall had artificial flowers . . . 'Button-hole, sir? . . . Bouquet for the lady, sir? . . .' There were goldfish in glass bowls; tortoises; canaries in cages . . . People selling things on trays also added to the din. 'Balloons! Who wants balloons? Buy the kiddies a balloon! . . .' There were trays of collar-studs; bright paper and tinsel balls that danced up and down on elastic; and, most fascinating of all, little dolls, their arms and legs of springy coiled wire ending in hands and feet of what looked like dried putty. There were also little dogs with fluffy bodies and twitching wire legs and tails.

'Fourpence! All a-fourpence!' shouted their vendor, jerking them up and down by elastic attached to their necks, so that they danced and leapt about in a very realistic manner indeed. 'All on the waggle-waggle! All a-fourpence on the waggle-waggle! Buy a dancing doll or a little lucky dawg . . . Fourpence! . . . Fourpence! . . .'

It was all faintly bewildering. But – three and sixpence each to spend! Kate and her brothers stood looking at each other for a moment but there was really no question where to start. In a flash the twins were buying toffee, Kate pink and white bullseyes. She also bought a dancing doll.

'For William,' she said but it was no sooner handed over to her than she knew she would never part with it and . . . well, perhaps William would *really* prefer one of those little balls . . . 'Jumping Ball, missie? Only tuppence! Choose yer own colour. Tuppence . . . Thank you, missie . . .' Gosh! Eightpence gone already!

'Oh, come *on*!' grumbled the twins, 'or the Dodgems'll be full up!'

But before they had got half-way to the Dodgems there was Mr Wildgoose calling and beckoning to them from beside the big roundabout. It had stopped now; people were getting off, and they could see in addiction to horses there were bears, brown and polar varieties, and some skittish-looking ostriches. There were also Edwardian kind of motorcars painted green and red, with no tops and old-fashioned horns. *The Lambeth Walk* was giving place to *The Eton Boating Song*, and a gentleman wearing small gold ear-rings, a red and white spotted handkerchief about his head and looking a cross between a pirate king and a pierrot, was waving his arms about and shouting, 'Take your seats, ladies and gentlemen! Take your seats! Threepence a time; take your seats!'

'Come along,' called Mr Wildgoose. 'Who's for the roundabout?' and the next minute Mrs Wildgoose and Elsie, followed by Miss Midgley from the post office, were climbing on board a green motor-car and Mr Ruggles was straddling a benevolent-looking ostrich.

'Up you come, you three!' cried Mr Wildgoose to Kate and the twins. 'No – keep your pennies.' And he hauled them on board. 'Which do you fancy – horse, bird or bear?' The twins privately fancied a motor-car – particularly the driving seat, but people were pushing and crowding on and the roundabout was beginning to move. Kate quickly chose a horse, Jim another, and John a polar bear.

'Full up now!' shouted the pirate king. 'Full right up!' and the next minute they were off, slowly at first but gradually faster! . . . Round and round, round and round: faster, faster, and faster! . . . Men shouted, women screamed, children yelled. Mr Wildgoose who had leapt into the driving seat of the green motor-car tooted wildly on the horn . . . Faster still! . . . High above the watching crowds . . . Kate clung tightly to her horse. It was grey with a silky white mane – a fairy horse! . . . She was a princess in disguise . . . Jim's was brown with big black spots and fiery red nostrils; a snorting war horse and he a Crusader. John's bear had a chain collar which he grasped tightly; he was an Arctic explorer who had captured and tamed it . . . Faster, still faster! . . . The crowd below had become just a collection of blurred shapes now . . . They were riding away, right out of the world . . . But soon the music began to play more softly, the pace to slacken a little: then a little more. *The Eton Boating Song* came to an end; now they were travelling quite slowly . . . A moment later they had stopped . . . they were back in Upper Cassington. People were clamouring to get on for the next round and the pirate king was beginning all over again. 'Take your seats, ladies and gentlemen. Take your seats!'

Kate slid off her fairy steed, giving its neck a shy little pat. It had seemed so *very* real . . . The twins scrambled down, Mr Ruggles climbed from his ostrich, a rather sheepish grin on his face, and Mr Wildgoose gave a last hoot on the car horn and assisted his passengers to alight.

'Take your seats, ladies and gentlemen! Take your seats! . . .' And there was Mr Shakespeare climbing on and turning to help Mr Milton who was being levered up from behind by Willie Sims; old Mrs Blossom being assisted into a red motor-car with the Digweed family; Johnny Sears astride an ostrich and two of his small sisters clinging together on a brown bear . . . Now Miss Alison with some of the guests from The Priory arrived; the lady they had seen yesterday, and two tall young men. The roundabout was beginning to turn. To cries of 'Be careful there! Be careful!' from the pirate king they scrambled on, packing themselves into the last of the empty motor-cars.

The party from The Dew Drop Inn stood watching as the roundabout gathered speed and they all went whirling by. Mr Milton, very dignified, erect as a trooper and staring fixedly ahead on a black and white horse, Mr Shakespeare beside him on a brown one, regarding him a little anxiously from time to time . . . Mr Digweed hooting every time he passed them; Laura and Mary waving madly and Mrs Digweed and old Mrs Blossom clutching wildly at their hats. Johnny Sears, evidently finding his ostrich rather slippery, was clasping it tightly round the neck, while his sisters clung together on their brown bear, the smaller of the two looking frightened and a little tearful.

Round and round, faster, faster and faster they whirled, then gradually slower, finally coming to a stop with the party from The Priory exactly in front of Kate and the twins.

From then onwards it was what Miss Alison called 'One giddy round – in every sense of the word'. She introduced her friends, and the lady and the two tall young men – who all seemed to be enjoying themselves enormously and to have unlimited sixpences – joined with her in inviting Mr and Mrs Wildgoose, Mr Ruggles, Kate and the twins to sample almost everything in The Fair, Mrs Wildgoose refusing one or two of the more strenuous amusements and going over to the Inn to make sure all was well and Jaeger, left shut in the kitchen, up to no mischief.

Another turn on the roundabout, joined this time by the vicar, who invited Willie Sims and one or two others to join him in one of the motor-cars; then the Lighthouse, Swing boats, Dodgems and Chairaplanes – the Dodgems, from which the two young men could hardly be torn away, and Chairaplanes – surely the nearest thing to flying? – being by far the most popular. Then the coconut shy, the shooting gallery – a pink and green striped tent where little celluloid balls bobbed up and down on jets of sparkling water, and the Hoop-La!

Mr Ruggles won a coconut at the very first attempt and was loudly applauded by the two young men who were both unsuccessful but managed to shoot down several little bobbing balls, presently emerging from the tent, one with a bright green china vase and the other with a decorated biscuit tin which they presented to Miss Alison and her friend.

The Hoop-La was doing a roaring trade, the prizes particularly inviting though arranged with some fiendish cunning so that the little wooden hoops invariably just failed to encircle them. Mr Milton tried hard to repeat his last year's success but only managed to capture a packet of chewing gum which he transferred to his pocket with a grunt of disgust, and Mr Shakespeare had no luck at all. Nor had old Mrs Blossom who spent recklessly in an attempt to secure what she called 'a little atadgy case' which had greatly taken her fancy. Miss Alison won a china dog; one of the tall young men a packet of cigarettes, and both Mr Wildgoose and Mr Ruggles tried hard, but with no success, for a case of tea-knives on which Mrs Wildgoose had set her heart. Rather to everyone's surprise – and certainly her own – the only member of the party to win a substantial prize was Kate, who somehow managed to encircle a glass bowl containing a minute goldfish. The twins, who had both coveted this and had had several unsuccessful tries for it themselves, were consumed with envy and astonishment. *Kate!* who couldn't ever throw anything – even a ball – properly! . . . But their own triumph was at hand. At intervals, all the afternoon, Jim had kept looking anxiously in the direction of the stationery Joywheel. Now, standing on a chair and fairly bellowing into a megaphone to be heard above the din, its proprietor was announcing all was now well with it. 'Who's for the Joywheel? Starting right away! Try your luck, ladies and gents! Try your luck! Only threepence a ride and the best prizes in The Fair! Whoever stays on to the end wins one! Try your luck on the Joywheel!'

'Come on, Dad!' cried Jim pulling Mr Ruggles by the hand. '*Come on!*' But by the time they managed to push through the crowds, the rest of the party abandoning the Hoop-La! and following in instalments, it was 'Full up now! Full *right* up!' and there, raised a few inches from the ground, in a large roped-off square, covered with what looked like linoleum, was the Joywheel, looking just as Jim had described it, like a huge gramophone record except that it was made of stout polished wood.

Away in a corner behind the ropes stood a stall covered with alluring prizes, toys, sweets, china – everything just a little outsize. An enormous, almost orange-coloured teddy bear with a pink satin bow round its neck; huge circular tins of toffee the size of wheelbarrow wheels; giant teapots and jugs. Sitting or squatting on the Joywheel itself, their faces grim with determination to win one of these trophies, were the first competitors – all men and boys. 'Ready?' bellowed the voice through the megaphone. 'Then off we go!' And 'off', as Mr Ruggles presently remarked, was the right word!

The Joywheel revolved slowly for a second or two, but was soon spinning round at a terrific speed. One after another, off shot the competitors to the huge delight of the spectators, the few who remained whizzing round at a still more furious pace, hair on end, eyes glazed or closed with giddiness, and hands feverishly trying to get a grip on the slippery polished wood. Soon only three remained; then two; then only one. But when the Joywheel finally stopped it was empty!

All over the roped-in square the dazed competitors were lying about or painfully picking themselves up, while the one who had stayed on longest, a youth of about sixteen, was being quietly sick in a corner. Mr Ruggles silently drew Jim's attention to this but Jim was not to be put off by any nonsense of that kind. He had his secret; he had also glimpsed those mammoth tins of toffee! And away on the other side of the square stood Signor Pelli waving encouragement.

'Well I can't say as it's my idea of amusement,' said Mr Ruggles, 'but you go if you like.'

But if not Mr Ruggles's idea of enjoyment it seemed to be that of a great many other people; there was no lack of competitors and Jim had great difficulty in squeezing on at all, much less securing a seat at the centre which was 'the secret', imparted by Signor Pelli, for success – a secret Jim soon began to suspect was shared, alas, by many. Three times he tried to secure the coveted spot only to be pushed aside and thrown off very early in the proceedings, once landing rather painfully against the hob-nailed boots of a burly onlooker. The only consolation was that, centre place or not, no one had so far managed to stay on until the wheel stopped. For the fourth round, however, he managed to pick himself up very quickly and somehow scramble on almost before the wheel had stopped turning, and with a good-natured push from one of the tall young men who had now arrived – and who also seemed to know the secret – secured the centre place. Even so, it proved very difficult to stay in it. He was already feeling giddy and people were pushing and squashing up against him, half suffocating him.

'Put your *head* down, press *hard* with your hands – and shut your eyes *tight*!' whispered a voice in his ear. It was the tall young man again. Jim looked at him gratefully. 'O.K.,' he whispered back, and obeyed. Round and round, round and round they whirled. Jim began to feel more and more giddy and, suddenly, horribly sick, but he kept his eyes tightly shut and gripped hard with his hands on the slippery wood. Gradually the pressure of bodies against him seemed to slacken . . . Had they been thrown off? He longed to look . . . Now someone – the tall young man perhaps? – put a hand on his thigh and seemed to be holding him in place . . . now it was withdrawn . . . and now the wheel itself seemed to be slipping away from him . . . slipping . . . slipping . . . Then suddenly it gave a great jolt and stopped.

There was a loud burst of shouting and cheering. Timidly Jim opened his eyes. *He was alone on the wheel!* But had it really stopped? Sky, people, everything, was spinning madly round.

'Off yer come, sonny! Off yer come!' called a voice. 'You've a-won all right! Off yer come!' *Won!* Sick, dizzy, but utterly triumphant, Jim tried to get to his feet, wobbled, and fell down. The next moment the proprietor stepped forward on to the wheel, picked him up, and tucking him under one arm like a parcel, dumped him down on the grass outside the roped-in square.

'There y'are,' he said gruffly. 'Well done! And there,' taking something from under his other arm, 'there's yer prize.' Sick and giddy as he was, Jim turned eagerly to look at it. On the grass beside him was *a large plush monkey*! He sat staring at it for a moment, then pushing it away, burst into tears!

Mrs Wildgoose, who had only arrived in time to witness the last round – 'or I'd have stopped him going at all – nasty dangerous thing – not fit for small boys' – was convinced he must be hurt. Mr Ruggles too was a little concerned; the twins were not given to tears. But apart from a few bruises and scratches, it was only Jim's feelings that were hurt. A monkey! *A toy monkey!* And all those huge tins of toffee! . . . 'It's – it's for a *baby*!' he sniffed, feeling he was behaving rather like one himself, and doing his best to rub away disgraceful tears.

'Perhaps they'll let you change it, my dear,' said Mrs Wildgoose consolingly and looking round for the proprietor.

But the Joywheel was in action again and there was no getting near him.

'It'll do fine for William anyway,' said Mr Ruggles picking it up. 'The boy's all right' – he turned to Mrs Wildgoose, 'bit over excited-like, that's all. Get up, lad, and stop acting silly,' and he held out a hand.

'Anyway you *won*!' said John regarding his twin admiringly. That was true and clutching Mr Ruggles's outstretched hand Jim got rather shakily to his feet, felt better, and was beginning to take some pleasure in his achievement when John suddenly grabbed him by the arm. 'He's starting!' he cried, 'Mr Bean – my conjurer! *He's starting!* Come on, all of you! Come quick, *please*, because we *must* sit in the front row!'

Perhaps it was only by comparison with the blazing sunlight outside but it seemed rather dark in the conjurer's tent. Few people had arrived, however, so there was no difficulty in securing front seats. Away in the cheaper ones sat Johnny Sears, his two small sisters, and Mrs Sears with the youngest on her lap, and in the same row but as far away as possible from them, Mr Milton and Mr Shakespeare. But very soon all the hard, uncomfortable benches filled up; a gentleman in evening dress appeared before the green star-spangled curtains of the stage and announced 'Professor Beano The World Famous Conjurer' and the curtains parted to reveal John's friend Mr Bean, clad in a garment resembling an over-large dressing-gown, patterned with signs of the zodiac. In one hand he held a small white wand and on his head was a tall pointed hat like a fire extinguisher, green and spangled like the curtains – in fact it looked suspiciously as if it had been made from a piece left over from them. He had a long white beard, and wisps of white hair stuck out from beneath the pointed hat, but John, having seen all these aids to disguise, had no difficulty in recognizing his friend. He sat tightly wedged between Mr Ruggles and Mr Wildgoose, outwardly calm, but inside his trouser pockets his fists were clenched – the nails biting into the palms with excitement.

Standing beside Professor Beano on the otherwise completely empty stage was a small bamboo table. On it was a shiny top hat, a glass of water, a large green silk handkerchief, and a folded newspaper. Nothing else whatever but an expanse of bare boards. Yet in five minutes the stage was about as tidy as the twins' bedroom at One End Street on a Saturday morning! Accompanied by a rapid flow of conversation, Professor Beano performed trick after trick. He tore the newspaper into fantastic shapes: into chains of figures; into animals; into well-known personalities. He extracted a couple of rabbits and a hedgehog from the top hat – and there was no doubt they were real ones, for the rabbits went lolloping about the stage and the hedgehog promptly curled itself up into a tight ball. He made flowers grow in the glass of water, and changed the green silk handkerchief into half a dozen white cotton ones, and then into a string of coloured flags. He smoked a cigarette and blew fire from his mouth in a most alarming manner. Finally he asked for the loan of their watches from various members of the audience. 'You, sir,' pointing with the white wand at old Mr Milton. 'Would you oblige me?' But old Mr Milton – indicating he was deaf and the question being repeated – not only flatly refused but could be heard advising others to refrain too.

'Allow me to inform you, sir,' said Professor Beano regarding him coldly, 'that I have performed this trick in front of Royalty and that a gentleman in the Prince of Wales' suite lent me his watch. What is good enough for a gentleman in the Prince of Wales' suite should surely be good enough for you!' To which Mr Milton – miraculously hearing – replied bluntly, 'Well, t'aint and that's all t'is to it,' and sat with one hand inside his coat, clutching tightly at his watch as if Professor Beano might spirit it away by a mere glance. Other members of the audience, however, proved more helpful, and though in spite of John's whispered 'it's quite all right *really*,' neither Mr Wildgoose nor Mr Ruggles were prepared to oblige, three or four watches were handed over and popped into the top hat. This was then placed in the centre of the stage, and the white wand waved over it. There was a short pause and then Professor Beano suddenly leapt high in the air descending with all his weight on top of the hat! There was a dreadful crunching kind of sound and it seemed to everyone, not least their owners, that the watches could hardly be anything but smashed to smithereens. There was a horrified silence, broken only by a thin cackle of laughter from Mr Milton. But it was laughter short-lived, for a moment later

Professor Beano was triumphantly restoring the watches, whole and unblemished, to their respective owners – *plus sixpence*, and further comments from Mr Milton – if any – were drowned in a storm of clapping and applause!

How *was* it done? *How?* But there was no time to consider, for Professor Beano was announcing the next, and last, trick. John sat up, very alert indeed, and almost before Professor Beano had finished announcing that he required the assistance of two children from the audience – one boy and one girl – was out of his seat and doing his best to scramble on to the stage. There was a brief pause and then, encouraged by his example, a sudden stampede of children – foremost among them Johnny Sears.

'Two! I only want *two*!' cried Professor Beano holding up a protesting hand. 'One boy, one girl! This one,' pulling John on to the stage, 'was first . . . Now a girl . . .'

'*You* go,' whispered Mrs Wildgoose to Kate, but Kate shook her head vigorously. The next minute, however, she was almost sorry, for there was Angela Smallpiece showing a great deal of her immensely long legs, being hauled on to the stage to cries of 'Up you come, my dear,' and 'Easy does it!'

'Now, Ladies and Gentlemen,' began Professor Beano, standing in the centre of the stage, John on one side of him, Angela Smallpiece on the other. 'I'm sure there's many of you here keeps hens, and what's more, you'll agree as sometimes those hens don't lay like they ought. Now I keep only *one* hen – but I get all the eggs I want, all the year round – and *exactly* when I wants 'em. And all by a little magic! You don't believe me?' – and his eyes swept over the crowded benches – 'then just watch – watch *very* carefully! Now! . . .' He clapped his hands and an attendant appeared with a couple of chip baskets such as are used for soft fruit. 'You see these baskets, Ladies and Gentlemen – full of air and emptiness,' and he handed one to John and one to Angela with instructions to turn them upside down and show everyone this was indeed so.

'Now,' the air and emptiness having been fully demonstrated, 'Now, Ladies and Gentlemen, I am going to ask my two assistants here to hold these baskets tightly and securely for they are soon going to be heavy! *They are going to be full of eggs!* Grip hard, my dears,' to John and Angela. 'Ready? Then here we go!' and he tapped three times with his little white wand on the now empty table, murmured some unintelligible words, put it down and stretching up his right arm, appeared to draw something from the air above him, held it up for the inspection of the audience, then placed it in Angela's basket. It was an egg! Next he did the same thing with his left arm, putting the egg in John's basket. Then up and down, up and down, more and more quickly shot his arms. Eggs were being handed to John and Angela more quickly than they could put them in the baskets. In their excitement they dropped one or two and any doubts as to their not being real eggs were quickly dispelled. Very soon the baskets were full but still the Professor continued to stretch up his arms, cause eggs to rain down from nowhere and hand them to his assistants.

Little heaps of eggs lay about on the stage and on the bamboo table. The audience sat spellbound. But at last Professor Beano stopped and clasping his hands to his chest stood making the cackling noise of a hen that has just finished laying and is proud of it. Then, smiling widely, and to the enormous delight of the audience, from under his zodiac-patterned robe he drew forth a black and white speckled hen! He stood holding her for a moment, then bowed, and amid terrific applause walked off the stage. In a few seconds he was back, minus the hen, but holding under either arm an enormous box of chocolates.

'For my assistants!' he said presenting one to John and one to Angela Smallpiece and taking a hand of each in his, while the audience clapped and clapped and clapped again, he stood bowing and smiling until the green spangled

curtains were at last pulled across the stage; then he stepped behind them leaving the two children alone with the baskets of eggs and the chocolate-boxes.

A tired but very happy party gathered in the sitting-room of The Dew Drop Inn that evening. It had been a wonderful holiday, declared Mr Ruggles. There was only one thing wrong – it was over much too soon.

'We'll none of us ever forget The Dew Drop and all you done for us,' he went on, 'nor yet that gentleman lying over there by the clock!' And he added a little wistfully that if Mr Wildgoose ever felt like 'parting' with Jaeger, and he, Mr Ruggles, could manage the keep and licence money – well, they knew where to write. 'Though what my missis 'ud say to summat his size in our little kitchen's more than I like to think of!'

'You'd best say good-night and good-bye at the same time,' Mrs Wildgoose had said after decreeing early beds for all; and though Kate had done so she had fully expected to wake when Mr Ruggles came to call the twins shortly before four o'clock, but she was sleeping so deeply that she never heard a sound. Shoes in hand, by the light of a torch, Mr Ruggles and the twins crept down the dark, creaking passages and stairs. Past the open kitchen door where, curled up in front of the stove, Jaeger had not so much as growled but like an exemplary watch dog, discerning friend from foe, merely opened one sleepy eye and thumped lazily with his tail on the floor. In the kitchen passage, as silently as possible, oddments were forced into the already bulging suitcase; shoes put on, and bags and bundles – including John's basket of eggs which he was proudly taking home for Mrs Ruggles – and Jim's monkey, which the proprietor of the Joywheel had refused, alas, to exchange, collected. Silently the back door was unlocked, Mr Ruggles relocking it and leaving the key and the torch in a place arranged overnight with Mr Wildgoose. Silently still, with never a word spoken, they tip-toed over to the Green where lights were shining palely in the misty darkness.

Some of the larger caravans and all the big wagons had already gone, but the engines of most of the others, and Signor Pelli's little black car, were running and all ready for departure. Speaking in a hoarse whisper someone bundled them into one of the caravans, stowing away their belongings; someone inside handed them sausage rolls and cups of scalding tea. Almost at once the caravan lurched forward, spilling the tea and rocking slightly as it moved over the unevenness of the Green to the high road, to rumble through the mist and darkness to Ailesford . . . Then good-byes, good wishes, many, many thank-you's and here's-to-the-next-times . . . A five-minute wait at Ailesford station; a sleepy, rather hungry journey, the sky lightening every minute; a milky mist rising from the fields with here and there the blurred velvety shapes of cattle . . . All change! A short, cold wait surrounded by milk cans . . . Then off again, and as the town clock struck seven Mr Ruggles and the twins stepped on to the platform at

Otwell-on-the-Ouse. Just after it chimed the quarter they turned into One End Street, and ten minutes later, fortified with a very hurried cup of tea and with a couple of bacon sandwiches in his pocket, Mr Ruggles, his brief holiday over, went back to work.

10. The Holiday Ends

KATE'S HOLIDAY was rapidly coming to an end. She tried not to remember this too often, but one morning at breakfast she was so silent that Mr Wildgoose inquired what was the matter.

'It's only, Mr Wildgoose,' and she spoke in a low, tragic, voice, 'that less than a week now, and it will be the Last Day!'

'Goodness gracious me!' exclaimed Mrs Wildgoose, 'it sounds like The Judgement at least!' while Mr Wildgoose agreed there was certainly a very end-of-the-world flavour about it. 'Anyway,' said Mrs Wildgoose decidedly, 'it's not going to be a *sad* day. I've got a plan in mind. You've said as you wanted to buy some little presents to take home with the money Lord Glenheather gave you? There's not much choice here in Upper Cassington so how'd it be if we went a little expedition, you and I, to Ailesford that afternoon? There's one or two things I want to get myself,' she went on. 'Let's see; it's a Tuesday. I'll get my baking done Monday, then we can have dinner early and catch the two o'clock bus; that will give us plenty of time for our shopping. And we won't come back for tea – we'll have it at the nice teashop in the Square and catch the five-thirty bus back. There! what about that?'

'Oh, Mrs Wildgoose it would be lovely!' cried Kate. 'I do awfully want to get something for Mum and Lily Rose – and Peg too if I've enough money left. If I haven't, she'll have to share with Jo – I'm giving him the goldfish I won at the hoop-la!'

'Very well then,' said Mrs Wildgoose, 'that's settled so cheer up for there's still plenty of days left and many things to enjoy.'

Of course there were, and Kate felt a little bit ashamed when she remembered various delights ahead. A picnic with the Digweeds; a farewell tea with Mrs Midgley and her daughter – not to mention Thomas; and a visit to The Priory where what Miss Alison called 'A parting present' was waiting to be called for. What this could be Kate had no idea.

'Looks to me,' said Mr Wildgoose, 'as if you'd better buy a suitcase when you're in Ailesford – for how Kate is going to get what she's accumulated here – books, shoes, prizes, goldfish-in-a-bowl and I don't know what else – into the one she brought, is a mystery to me. Of course,' he added, assuming an air of deep thought, 'she could pack the goldfish I suppose and take the bowl separate.'

'Oh, go on with you!' said Mrs Wildgoose and Kate laughed. All the same it *was* going to be rather a difficult piece of luggage to manage! But after her visit to The Priory, though she was no nearer its solution, the rest of her packing problem was solved, for Miss Ayredale-Eskdale's parting present turned out to be exactly what Mr Wildgoose had suggested – a suitcase!

A suitcase of one's very own! Kate felt almost grown up as she walked back from The Priory with it. Miss Alison had rather apologized for its appearance, saying it was only a cheap one and wouldn't stand much knocking about and was just to hold all the new belongings. She could not, of course, know how immeasurably superior it was to any suitcase that had ever crossed the threshold of No. 1 One End Street, or what it felt like to have one all to oneself. But better than any suitcase was her promise that if she was ever at all near Otwell to come to One End Street and make the acquaintance of Mrs Ruggles, Lily Rose, and William; 'and then,' as Kate said, 'you'll have seen us all!'

Tea with the ladies at the post office, Thomas sitting up to the table in his own special chair, the same as last time, was a very happy occasion, and before she came away, Mrs Midgley produced a surprise present – a little framed snapshot of Thomas himself looking 'everything a cat ought to be' – and more – thoughtfully regarding a border of carnations in the post office garden.

But perhaps the happiest of the remaining days was that of the picnic arranged by Mrs Digweed – even though Angela Smallpiece and Johnny Sears were among the guests. To begin with, it was held by the river – a joy in itself. Mr Digweed drove them all there in his car, some of the party and the many bags and baskets containing the tea in a trailer behind, its rollings and lurchings when they reached the bumpy, rutty cart track across the water-meadows – judging from the squeals and giggles – apparently adding enormously to the enjoyment of its passengers.

It was a perfect September afternoon; hot but not too hot, quiet and still. Everything seemed enveloped in a benign mellowness as if the earth, content, its harvest yielded, was taking a well-earned rest before bracing itself for the turbulence of autumn and the long endurance of winter. Hardly a ripple showed on the placidly flowing river except every now and then when a fish rose, snapped at a fly and disappeared again, leaving ever-widening circles on the smooth surface; or once, when a water-rat dived 'plop' from its hole in the bank.

A couple of moorhens swam happily about among the reeds, their tiny red feet paddling hard against the lazy current. Blue-green dragonflies skimmed by, and the willow trees, under which they presently had tea, were full of little cheeping bird noises. And what a tea it was! Everything, almost, home-made. New crusty bread – so different from the same commodity sold in bakers' shops that it was hard to believe it was the same food! Butter, and thick clotted cream from the farm's Jersey cows; jam – strawberry, raspberry, and gooseberry, made by Mary and Laura; what was known locally as 'Lardie cake' – something resembling a flat outsize bun with spices and currants inside and sugar on the top; and to finish up, late juicy greengages from the farm orchard. And as they sat or lay about, replete and happily silent in the cool green-grey shadow of the willows, Kate thoughtfully chewed a blade

of grass, more convinced than ever of the superiority of farming over all other callings.

It was a really happy party. There were no quarrels and everyone was friendly. Johnny Sears seemed a different boy, while Angela Smallpiece, either so impressed with the catering or learning at last to grow up gracefully – or perhaps both – was neither rude nor boastful. They played games, climbed about the willows, and hunted – unsuccessfully – for mushrooms. But the shadows grew longer, the sun lower in the sky and all too soon Mr Digweed arrived with the car and the now empty trailer bumping and pitching more violently than ever behind him.

As they drove homewards, singing and laughing, a thin mist began to rise from the river and presently the water-rat that had dived earlier came out of his hole, eyes bright, whiskers twitching, and had a picnic of his own among the bread and cake crumbs.

But the Last Day drew nearer and nearer and eventually arrived. Most of the morning was spent in good-byes – and there were even more presents! A tiny chip basket containing the last of old Mr Milton's blackcurrants. 'A little souvenir-like,' said Mr Shakespeare presenting it on behalf of them both. 'Should have been *gooseberries* but they're all finished now,' and he winked one of his bright blue eyes very meaningly, while Mr Milton apparently heard for once for he muttered darkly, '*Aye!*' There was a big box of eggs from Mrs Digweed, while Mrs Edwards, when Kate eventually summoned up sufficient courage to go up the steps to the little shop – enormously relieved to find no sign of Mrs Megson – seemed overflowing with goodwill and produced a bar of nut chocolate 'to eat in the train, my dear – but we won't tell Auntie!' She was full of good wishes for the new term at school even going so far as to say Kate was a credit to state education. It is always pleasant to learn one is a credit to something even – as in this case – when one is not quite sure what is meant. Moreover, Mrs Megson's shop was certainly the last place where one expected compliments, and Kate couldn't help thinking of her first visit of all there.* Had it not been for the eggs and the basket of blackcurrants she would have jumped the entire flight of steps as a sort of celebration. Instead, she thanked Mrs Edwards and said she must go, for dinner was early today because she and Mrs Wildgoose were going to Ailesford to shop.

'Well, ta ta,' said Mrs Edwards, 'and good luck. You may see Auntie in Ailesford,' she added, 'she's going shopping

* *Further Adventures of the Family from One End Street.*

too.' That was a pity, thought Kate as she walked back to The Dew Drop Inn with her gifts, and she could only hope fervently that she and Mrs Megson might not patronize the same shop at the same moment.

Punctually at two o'clock Kate and Mrs Wildgoose were ready and waiting at the bus stop. Kate wore her Sunday dress and school hat and carried 'Mrs Beasley's present' and an umbrella, for Mr Wildgoose had not much 'cared' for the look of the sky at dinner-time. Mrs Wildgoose was also in her best attire and armed with an umbrella and a large shopping basket.

Last Day or not, Kate was looking forward to the trip, and by great good fortune the two front seats of the bus when it came were vacant so that she and Mrs Wildgoose had a beautifully clear view of the road and countryside. It also went very much more slowly than Lord Glenheather's car had done, stopping frequently to pick up and to set down passengers. There were stops too of considerable duration at various villages while parcels were handed in and handed out at what were evidently officially appointed places. These transactions were accompanied by a great deal of conversation. Messages from friends were delivered, inquiries answered about others, and at each and every stop, invariably and without fail, there were comments on the weather – yesterday's, today's, and tomorrow's, so that it was hardly surprising that the time allotted by the bus company for the eight-mile journey – which had been covered in Lord Glenheather's car in something like twenty minutes – should be an hour. Fortunately Mrs Wildgoose and Kate were in no hurry and they enjoyed looking about them, pointing out matters of interest to each other and agreeing that none of the villages was, as Kate put it, 'half a quarter as pretty as Upper Cassington'.

The countryside had changed a lot in the last week or so, the fields, shorn and pale with stubble, with here and there a piece of newly turned plough. Hay- and straw-stacks were dotted about and thatching was in full swing. Every now and then they passed a little group of stacks, some newly thatched, others still untidy mounds, a ladder reared against them, and on it the thatcher himself busy with comb, pegs and twine, reducing chaos to order with swift, incredible skill. The cottage gardens were full of laden apple trees, large yellow dahlias like miniature suns, and prim pink and mauve asters. There were blackberries and sloes in the hedges, and the hips were beginning to turn from green to the hunting-pink which precedes their flaming October scarlet. From back gardens thin blue smoke rose from innumerable little bonfires; over everything there was the faintest hint of autumn.

At last the outskirts of Ailesford were reached and they were rattling along narrow, twisting little streets with old and crooked houses, to the bus station. Otwell-on-the-Ouse was an old town so Kate was used to narrow streets and crooked houses, but Ailesford was much older and its streets were even narrower and more twisting and its houses still more crooked. It also boasted, which Otwell did not, a market square, and here she and Mrs Wildgoose made their way.

They walked all round it, very slowly, twice, gazing earnestly into every shop window, Mrs Wildgoose marvelling now and then at the many things for sale which as she put it 'folks could do without and never know the difference'. Even so, Kate could not make up her mind what to buy. She had six shillings and ninepence halfpenny; it had seemed an enormous sum when she left Upper Cassington and certainly more than she had ever had to spend on presents before, but now it somehow did not seem as if it would buy very much.

'How about Woolworths?' suggested Mrs Wildgoose who was beginning to get a little footsore. 'It's not far – just down the high street.' But Kate would have none of Woolworths for, as she explained, whenever she bought presents at home it was always there, and she wanted Mum and Lily Rose to have something 'special'.

'Then I think we'd better try MacAndersen's,' said Mrs Wildgoose, 'they've a big Fancy Department – you'll surely find something there and while you're looking round I can get one or two things I want for the house.'

MacAndersen's was a draper's, bigger and grander than anything of its kind in Otwell. There were several 'Floors' and 'Departments' and the profusion in the one labelled 'Fancy Goods' was almost overwhelming.

'I'll leave you here to make up your mind,' said Mrs Wildgoose, 'while I go and buy the drying-up cloths and dusters I want, but don't go moving away or else we'll lose each other.' And so saying she disappeared through an archway where a notice in gilt letters said 'Blankets and Household Linen'.

Kate prowled up and down among the Fancy Goods, becoming more and more undecided and bewildered. There were a few toys among them, and she stood for a long while fascinated by a little pyramid of dolls about four and a half inches high. She would have liked to pick one up and examine it but they were very precariously balanced and she did not dare. There was also a very severe-looking lady serving behind a neighbouring counter, and a stout gentleman in a black coat and striped trousers standing near, apparently absorbed in examining his nails but who she was sure was watching everything that went on. She walked round and round the display stand, examining the little dolls from every angle, liking them more and more. They were clothed only in a kind of muslin vest but they had the most attractive faces and thick, shining cropped hair that looked almost real. One of the dark ones reminded her very much of Peg. And they were only ninepence! If she had any money left after Mum's and Lily Rose's presents she would buy one for her. But before anything else she *must* decide what these presents were to be.

She was turning reluctantly away from the little dolls when she heard a well-known voice and there, not a dozen yards away, was Mrs Megson laying in stocks of knitting wool. She was sitting down, her back to Kate, arguing about something. Kate retreated hurriedly to the extreme end of the department. A moment or two later, in a small alcove she had not noticed before and where she was invisible to Mrs Megson, she had found what she knew at once was exactly the present for Mrs Ruggles. 'Special

Reduction!' read a notice, 'A Real Bargain! Kosi Kumfy Slippers, slightly faded, reduced from seven shillings to three shillings and elevenpence halfpenny!' And there was a whole pile of velvety bedroom shoes, brown, black, bright blue, pink, or green, with fleecy-looking cottony linings, soft and white like a rabbit's tail.

It was very difficult to know which colour to choose, and Kate had just decided on brown, which was always a good colour for not showing the dirt, and seemed also to show the fade marks less than the prettier pinks and blues and greens, when Mrs Wildgoose returned. She fully approved of the purchase, agreeing with the young assistant who had stood very patiently waiting while Kate made up her mind, that the slippers were indeed a bargain. It now only remained to find something 'special' for Lily Rose. The kindly assistant was most helpful and finally solved the problem by producing a bright green comb with two hair slides to match, all stitched neatly on to a card which said 'A Present From Ailesford'. And since, according to Kate, Lily Rose was 'always' losing hair slides and 'forever' breaking combs, it seemed in every respect a very suitable gift. 'And I've still got tenpence left, Mrs Wildgoose,' she said as they stood waiting while the parcels were being neatly wrapped up. 'I saw some of the *sweetest* little dolls just now – they were only ninepence, and one was *so* like Peg I'd like to buy it for her. The only thing' – and she lowered her voice – 'Mrs *Megson*'s in there – at the wool counter – but perhaps we could wait till she's gone?'

'There was no one there when I came through just now,' said Mrs Wildgoose, 'she must have gone.' Happily this proved to be the case, but even so, they were not able to look at the little dolls in peace. Mrs Wildgoose was very taken with them and agreed that the one Kate pointed out had certainly a great look of Peg. The assistant in charge of this department, however, was not kind and helpful like the one who had just served them. She was, in fact, exactly the reverse. She was the severe-looking lady Kate had noticed earlier. She stood grimly and unhelpfully by, saying sharply – though Kate was only *pointing* – 'Please do not touch the goods.' And when, after many regrets that she had not enough money to purchase more than one doll, Kate summoned up sufficient courage to ask for the one resembling Peg, it was insisted that all were 'precisely alike', and that to take one from the middle of the pyramid in which they were arranged was 'next to impossible'. But Kate was determined to have the one she wanted, and Mrs Wildgoose, saying as tactfully as possible, 'the expressions did seem to vary quite a lot,' with a very bad grace it was eventually extracted. Mrs Wildgoose wandered away to look at some wool while Kate paid her ninepence and waited meekly in a frosty silence for her small parcel to be wrapped up and handed to her. A new customer was admiring the dolls as she stopped to have a last look at them on her way to join Mrs Wildgoose and to wish once again she had been able to buy a pair – twin dolls in a family that possessed twins would have been so *very* satisfactory!

'Goodness gracious me!' exclaimed Mrs Wildgoose when having lingered to look at various goods on the way, they eventually reached the ground floor where a clock announced ten minutes past four, 'how the time does go! But I could do with a cup of tea,' and she was just about to push open the big swing doors to the street, when a voice said, 'Excuse me, madam!' and there stood the stout gentleman in the black coat and striped trousers Kate had noticed earlier in the Fancy Department. 'Would you and your little girl mind coming with me a moment,' he said. 'This way, please,' and he waved a fat hand towards a glass-fronted door labelled 'Manager's Office' in large gold letters.

The shop was full of people and all those near enough to hear stopped what they were doing and turned and stared. Among them Kate saw Mrs Megson, her eyes fairly popping out of her head with curiosity.

Mrs Wildgoose was so surprised that except for looking to make sure Kate was coming too she followed the black-coated gentleman without a word. 'I just couldn't imagine what he wanted,' she said later, 'it seemed almost as if I were in a dream!'

But once on the other side of the glass-fronted door it was very clear there was no dream about it. Beside a table, her hands clasped primly in front of her, was the disagreeable assistant. Her mouth was pursed up, her eyes cast down, and she looked, if possible, even more disagreeable than before.

'I'm afraid I don't understand . . .' began Mrs Wildgoose. 'What did you want . . . what is it all about?' But the black-coated gentleman held up a pudgy hand and said coldly, 'One moment, please. Now Miss Smithers,' addressing the severe assistant, 'is this the child?'

Miss Smithers glanced briefly at Kate. 'Yes, Mr Nowell,' she replied, 'It *is*.'

Mr Nowell turned to Mrs Wildgoose. 'Now, madam; firstly, is this your little girl?'

'No,' replied Mrs Wildgoose, still faintly bewildered, 'she is not. She is . . .'

'But you were shopping together?'

'Certainly. Certainly we were – she's a little friend staying with me. But – what *is* this all about, please – why have you asked us to come in here?'

'If you will be good enough to ask your little friend to open her *umbrella*,' replied Mr Nowell speaking slowly and with great deliberation, 'perhaps you will see.'

'*Open her umbrella!*' exclaimed Mrs Wildgoose. '*Whatever* do you mean!' and she passed a hand over her forehead. It was very stuffy in the little office and the feeling of being in a dream had begun to come over her again! '*Open her umbrella!*' she repeated, and she looked in a bewildered way at Kate who looked back equally bewildered. And then, suddenly, a light dawned on Mrs Wildgoose.

'Are you suggesting,' she asked, and her voice shook with anger, 'are you suggesting the child has *stolen* something!'

'I simply asked you, madam, to ask her to open her umbrella,' replied Mr Nowell.

'Then I refuse,' said Mrs Wildgoose. 'I never heard such impertinence! If you want it opened you must open it yourself. Give it to him, Kate.' And Kate, looking guilty enough to have burgled half the shop, so crimson in the face was she with fright, anger, and indignation, thrust the umbrella furiously into Mr Nowell's fat hands.

There was a moment's silence and then, holding it as if it were some dangerous weapon that might at any moment explode, Mr Nowell slowly and very cautiously opened it. Plop! Down fell something on to the rich turkey carpet of the office and four pairs of eyes were instantly focused on it. It was a small, fair-haired doll! There was a short, terrifying silence, broken only by the severe assistant clearing her throat, and then Kate burst into a storm of tears.

'I didn't take it!' she sobbed. 'I didn't! *I didn't!*'

'Of course you didn't, dearie,' said Mrs Wildgoose putting an arm round her, 'I know that! Hush! Don't cry so!'

'I'm sorry, madam,' said Mr Nowell, and he picked up the doll, 'but Miss Smithers – this lady here who served you, *saw* her take it.'

'Well, not exactly *saw* her, Mr Nowell,' simpered Miss Smithers.

'That was what you said originally,' said Mr Nowell sharply.

'If I may *explain*, sir,' said Miss Smithers haughtily, 'it was like this. The child had no sooner left the department than I noticed there was a doll missing. I'd put it a little to one side when I re-arranged them after serving her so I remembered it particularly. Her umbrella was gaping open and it's my belief she knocked the doll into it – *deliberately*. You will remember a customer went off with some handkerchiefs that way last week! And I may add,' she cleared her throat, 'that the child had remarked *more* than once while I was serving her she would like a second doll. And she was walking round and round the stand for I don't know *how* long before madam, here,' indicating Mrs Wildgoose, 'came.'

'That is so,' agreed Mr Nowell. 'I saw her myself. Children,' he turned to Mrs Wildgoose, 'are – er – often tempted, and I am sorry to inform you we have experienced a very great deal of shoplifting just lately; so much so that we feel we really must . . .' But before he could say more there was a sharp knock at the door.

'Open it, Miss Smithers,' he commanded and Miss Smithers sailed forward to comply. Outside, very breathless and rather agitated, stood the young assistant who had sold them the shoes and the present for Lily Rose.

'What is it, Miss Perkins?' said Mr Nowell irritably. 'Come in and shut the door after you. What is it you want? Cannot you see I am engaged?'

'I'm sorry sir,' gasped Miss Perkins, 'but it is rather urgent – I couldn't come before – I was serving.' She paused for breath. 'I saw it all happen, sir – about the doll I mean – the little girl never took anything! There was another customer – as she walked by she knocked one of the dolls over – quite by accident – and it fell into the child's umbrella – it was open a bit. I called out but nobody heard and I couldn't leave my customer who was a very deaf old lady and Miss Smithers had gone before I'd finished serving her. The little girl *certainly* never took the doll, sir!' And she paused again for breath.

Except for the sound of Kate's crying there was silence. Miss Smithers regarded her colleague very coldly indeed while Mr Nowell, the doll still clasped in his fat hand, stood looking most uncomfortable.

'And now,' said Mrs Wildgoose turning to him, 'I think you owe us an apology! I never heard such a thing! It's just as well my husband's not here – he'd have something to say to you! Don't cry any more, Kate my dear, everything's quite all right. And thank *you*, miss,' she turned to Miss Perkins, 'I shan't forget it.'

'Thank you, madam, I'm glad it's all right. May I go now please, Mr Nowell?' Mr Nowell, who was now the one to look bewildered, nodded. 'And you go too, Miss Smithers. And another time be more accurate in your statements, please.' And with an expression that boded ill for her colleague and a muttered 'I'm sorry I'm sure, madam,' to Mrs Wildgoose but not so much as a glance at Kate, Miss Smithers followed Miss Perkins out of the glass-fronted door. Mrs Wildgoose and Kate were left alone with Mr Nowell.

'I apologize, madam – I do indeed – and to the little girl but – er – you see how we are placed . . . so many . . . er . . . thefts lately . . . and . . . er children, you know . . .' His voice trailed sadly away; Mrs Wildgoose was so obviously not listening.

'I'm not leaving this building,' she said firmly, 'until you've said all that again, outside, in front of all those shoppers. Come, Kate,' and she turned towards the door.

Mr Nowell, doll in hand, sprang forward to open it. 'Oh, most certainly, madam . . . Most certainly . . . of course.'

And to Mrs Wildgoose's surprise, and satisfaction, he did! He went even further, asking for both her name and Kate's and saying that a statement would be made in the local paper to the effect that a mistake had been made. 'In the meantime,' and he looked almost timidly at Kate, 'perhaps the little girl would accept the doll as a gift?' And though between 'little girl' and the whole horrible experience, Kate felt more like throwing it at him than accepting it, the thought of twin dolls for Peg and also the sight of Mrs Megson hovering on the edge of the crowd overcame her, and with a somewhat hesitant 'Thank you' she took it from him.

'And now, my dear,' said Mrs Wildgoose when at last they emerged into the street, 'what we both need is a nice cup of tea and something to eat. Dry your eyes and put your hat straight and forget all about it. Dear, dear, dear, what a thing to happen – and on your last day too!'

But in the oak-panelled calm of The Marigold Tea Rooms the worst of the horrible episode began slowly to fade. For a time Kate was very quiet and as white as she had been pink before, but soon, fortified with strong tea and the most alluring-looking cakes, she began to feel better, and when she suddenly looked up, smiled broadly and said, 'Coo! I bet Mrs Megson wasn't half mad it wasn't true!' Mrs Wildgoose knew things were all right again.

Mr Wildgoose was very indignant when he heard what had happened, and said firmly that if Mr Know All – as he insisted on calling him – did not keep his word about the notice in the local paper, he, Charles Wildgoose, would have something to say.

'And to think,' said Mrs Wildgoose, 'that it never rained a *drop* and we needn't have taken umbrellas at all – much less that old one that never *will* stay shut!' adding that it was not often Mr Wildgoose was wrong about the weather.

'And if he may say so without boasting,' replied Mr Wildgoose kissing her, 'he wasn't this time; we had two sharp showers – ask Jaeger there, who had his walk cut short and now wants his supper – like myself.'

'It's never supper-time?' exclaimed Mrs Wildgoose. 'My goodness me – it's after seven! I'm all mixed up with the time today and no mistake; seems to me we've just had tea!'

And when supper was eventually on the table it seemed even more like it. Kate felt she wanted very little indeed and for once Mrs Wildgoose did not urge her to eat, though she did insist on an early bed 'and all packing left till tomorrow'.

'And I think we can flatter ourselves,' she said to Mr Wildgoose when presently, with hardly a protest, Kate had gone upstairs, 'that we're sending home a heavier and pinker

faced child than the one that arrived here six weeks ago.' To which Mr Wildgoose, surreptitiously feeding Jaeger under the table with cheese rind, nodded emphatic agreement.

As for Kate, she had fully intended lying awake in her little white room 'regretting' – as characters in books seemed invariably to do on such occasions. Instead, she felt so tired with the day's experiences that she fell asleep almost as soon as she got into bed, and in spite of all that had happened, and the rich, indigestible tea, slept soundly all night. And the first things she saw when she opened her eyes were the twin dolls sitting side by side on the dressing-table – the dark one looking more than ever like Peg!

*

It was a wet morning but Kate was almost glad, for it seemed less sad to leave The Dew Drop Inn in rain than in sun. But in any case there was not much time for regrets or repinings of any kind, for the packing of the two suitcases, and the best way of dealing with the goldfish and its bowl took longer than expected. Then Willie Sims had come in on his way to breakfast to say good-bye, and before they were anything like ready Mr Washer was at the door with his snorting taxi. Somehow everything was bundled into it, but there was only time for the briefest of good-byes – in fact Jaeger was getting so many kisses that Mr Wildgoose cried, 'Hey! Stop! or there won't be time for even *one* for me!'

There must be time . . . there *must*! . . . Mr Wildgoose who had been so very, very kind! . . . Kate gave Jaeger a final pat and as she straightened herself up, Mr Wildgoose took both her hands in his. 'Not "good-bye",' he said, shaking them up and down, 'but "au revoir". Come again some day, my dear. We've enjoyed having a little girl about the house,' and bending down he kissed her on the forehead. And Kate, forgiving even 'little girl', pulled her hands out of his, seized the lapels of his coat and standing on tip-toe kissed him fervently – somewhere near his ear.

'Thank you, Mr Wildgoose. Thank you *ever* so for *everything* – it's been *lovely*!' she cried, while Mrs Wildgoose called anxiously 'to hurry, *do*,' and Mr Washer hooted and shouted angrily 'you'll miss the train for sure!'

There was only time to give Elsie a very hurried kiss indeed and then tumble into the taxi.

Mr Washer drove at a furious pace, every nut, screw, and bolt in his unhappy vehicle rattling madly. But in any case the fields and hedges sped by in a blurred mist for Kate for she was trying desperately not to cry. She sat silent, her head turned away from Mrs Wildgoose, pressing her hand against her upper lip – a remedy which is sometimes successful; and when they reached the station – the train not yet signalled – while George was unloading and carrying the suitcases to the platform, and Mrs Wildgoose the goldfish-bowl, its top now neatly covered with fine white curtain net, she managed to find her handkerchief and have a good sniff and a dab at her eyes with no one but Mr Washer to see.

'It's been a happy holiday, Kate, hasn't it?' said Mrs Wildgoose when, the train now signalled, they stood waiting in the tongue-tied miserable silence which so often attends the last moments of departure on railway stations.

'Oh, it has, Mrs Wildgoose, it *has*!' And suddenly Kate flung her arms round Mrs Wildgoose and kissed her passionately. 'I'll never forget it – never, *never*!'

And presently as she turned away from the carriage window, having waved until Mrs Wildgoose and George and even the station were tiny specks in the distance and the train began to gather speed, that was what the chugg-chugging of the wheels seemed to be saying: 'I'll-never-forget-it-never; I'll-never-forget-it-never!' And in spite of the tears she had managed so long to suppress now rolling dismally down her face, Kate was filled with a strange happiness; she knew she never would forget – never.

A PUFFIN BOOK
Extra!
Extra!
READ ALL ABOUT IT!

EVE GARNETT
HOLIDAY AT THE DEW DROP INN
A ONE END STREET STORY
PUFFIN BOOK

1900 *Born 9 January in Worcestershire*

1906 *Starts school in Devon*

1920 *Studies art at the Chelsea School of Art in London and later at the Royal Academy*

1927 *Illustrates Evelyn Sharp's* The London Child, *a study of working-class life in the city. This gives her the idea for the Ruggles family*

1937 The Family from One End Street *is published and wins the prestigious Carnegie Medal for best children's book*

1956 The Further Adventures of the Family from One End Street *is published*

1962 Holiday at the Dew Drop Inn, *another sequel featuring the Ruggles family, is published*

1991 *Dies 5 April in Sussex*

WHERE DID THE STORY COME FROM?

Eve Garnett came from a middle-class family and, when asked to illustrate a book called The London Child, *was shocked to see the terrible living conditions of London's poor. Determined to bring attention to this, and also to give ordinary children from poorer areas of London stories that reflected their lives, Eve wrote and illustrated* The Family from One End Street *about everyday life in the big, happy Ruggles family from the small town of Otwell. The story was published in 1937 and has been in print ever since. She wrote two sequels –* Further Adventures of The Family from One End Street *and* Holiday at the Dew Drop Inn.

A *In one hand she carried a large toast-rack full of crisp, newly made toast, and in the other a saucer with an egg-cup in which sat the biggest, pinky-brown hen's egg Kate had ever seen.*

B *I've got the most* marvellous *macintosh, and a pair of absolutely new gum-boots in my suitcase . . .*

C *. . . had golden hair piled high on her head; long golden ear-rings swung from her ears; her cheeks were a beautiful rose pink, and her nails even pinker – and highly polished.*

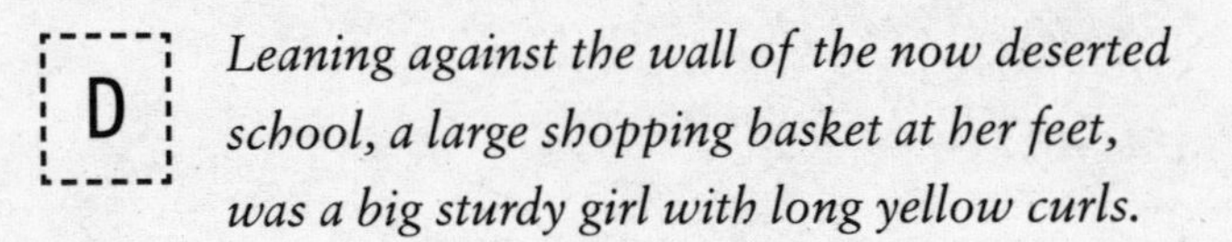
D *Leaning against the wall of the now deserted school, a large shopping basket at her feet, was a big sturdy girl with long yellow curls.*

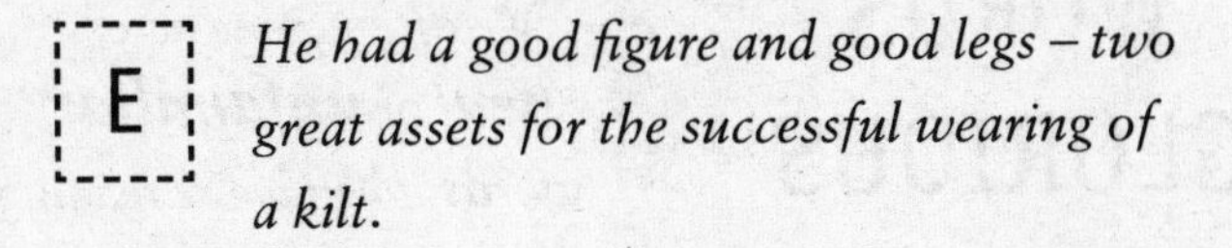
E *He had a good figure and good legs – two great assets for the successful wearing of a kilt.*

ANSWERS: A) *Elsie* B) *Kate* C) *Mrs Edwards* D) *Angela Smallpiece* E) *Lord Glenheather*

We often come across ***new*** *or* ***unfamiliar words*** *when we're reading. Here are a few unusual words you'll find in this Puffin book. Did you spot any others?*

ablutions *getting washed – bathing, showering, etc*

abstracted *not giving attention to what is happening around you because you are thinking about something else*

almanak *an annual notebook containing important dates and useful information*

bole *the trunk of a tree*

lorgnettes *a very old-fashioned pair of glasses with a long handle that you hold in front of your eyes*

kine *the old-fashioned word for cows*

perfunctory *done quickly, without taking any care or interest*

Thinking caps on –
let's see how much you can remember! Answers are at the bottom of the opposite page. (No peeking!)

1 ***After Lily Rose, which member of the Ruggles family goes down with the measles?***

a) *Peg*

b) *Kate*

c) *Jim*

d) *John*

2 ***What is the name of Peg's bear?***

a) *Buttons*

b) *Buttonbear*

c) *Buttonboo*

d) *Buttonhook*

3

After the garden at Dew Drop Inn, where is Peg and Jo's favourite place to play?

a) *The Post Office*

b) *The Buttercup Field*

c) *The Big Barn*

d) *Pond Passage*

4

What did Johnny Sears dare Jo to do?

a) *Ride a cow*

b) *Steal a turkey's egg*

c) *Dig up Mr Milton's potatoes*

d) *Swim across the stream*

5

What happens to Kate when she returns to One End Street?

a) *She goes straight back to school*

b) *She falls and breaks her arm*

c) *She is sent to hospital with the measles*

d) *She is given a piglet*

ANSWERS: 1) *a* 2) *d* 3) *b* 4) *a* 5) *c*

IN THIS YEAR

1962 Fact Pack

What else was happening in the world when this Puffin book was published?

The first James Bond film, Dr No, *is released in London, starring Sean Connery as the 007 agent.*

The first computer video game, Spacewar!, *is invented.*

Astronaut John H. Glenn Jr. is blasted off from Cape Canaveral in Friendship 7 and becomes the first American to orbit Earth. After three circuits around the globe, his space vehicle safely splashes down in the Atlantic Ocean.

The Beatles release their first single, Love Me Do.

In December 1962 Britain is in the grip of 'the big freeze'. Rivers and lakes freeze over and people are seen skating in front of Buckingham Palace in London and on the River Thames.

MAKE AND DO

Grow your own cress and mustard!

YOU WILL NEED:

- *A packet of mustard and/or cress seeds*
- *An old yoghurt pot*
- *Kitchen roll*
- *Cotton wool*

1 *Wash the yoghurt pot and peel off the outside wrapper.*

2 *Scrunch up some kitchen roll and wet it. Push this into the pot and add a thin layer of damp cotton wool, leaving a gap of about two cm from the top of the pot.*

3 *Sprinkle the seeds on top of the cotton wool and press them down lightly.*

4 *Leave the pot in a warm, light place.*

5 *Check the pot daily, adding a little water if the cotton wool becomes dry.*

6 *After a few days, the mustard and cress should begin to sprout.*

PUFFIN WRITING TIPS

Listen to your favourite piece of music and then write about what you imagine as it plays.

Read every draft out loud because it's the only way you'll find trouble spots – if you keep tripping up think about how you could rewrite those parts.

This book didn't start on a computer (because they didn't even exist!) – try writing with good old-fashioned pen and paper.

Look at your old family photos – as well as embarrassing haircuts, you might find out something you never knew!

A PUFFIN BOOK

HOW MANY HAVE YOU READ?

Animal tales

- ❑ *The Trumpet of the Swan*
- ❑ *Gobbolino*
- ❑ *Tarka the Otter*
- ❑ *Watership Down*
- ❑ *A Dog So Small*

War stories

- ❑ *Goodnight Mister Tom*
- ❑ *Back Home*
- ❑ *Carrie's War*

Magical adventures

- ❑ *The Neverending Story*
- ❑ *Mrs Frisby and the Rats of NIMH*
- ❑ *A Wrinkle in Time*

Unusual friends

- ❑ *Stig of the Dump*
- ❑ *Stuart Little*
- ❑ *The Borrowers*
- ❑ *Charlotte's Web*
- ❑ *The Cay*

Real life

- ❑ *Roll of Thunder, Hear My Cry*
- ❑ *The Family from One End Street*
- ❑ *Annie*
- ❑ *Smith*

ALF PRØYSEN
MRS PEPPERPOT Stories
MARY NORTON
The Complete BORROWERS
A PUFFIN BOOK
SUSAN COOPER
The BOGGART Fights Back
DICK KING-SMITH
THE CROWSTARVER
MADELEINE L'ENGLE
A WRINKLE IN TIME
BARBARA SLEIGH
The Kingdom of Carbonel
SUSAN COOPER
The BOGGART
ALF PRØYSEN
MRS PEPPERPOT Strikes Again
BEVERLEY NAIDOO
The OTHER SIDE OF TRUTH
HUGH LOFTING
THE STORY OF DOCTOR DOLITTLE
JOAN AIKEN
THE SHADOW GUESTS
SYLVIA WAUGH
The Mennyms
GENE KEMP
THE PUFFIN BOOK OF GHOSTS & GHOULS
SUSAN COOPER
The BOGGART and the Monster